Elizabeth Clifford Neff

A chronicle

Together with a little romance regarding Rudolf and Jacob Näf

Elizabeth Clifford Neff

A chronicle
Together with a little romance regarding Rudolf and Jacob Näf

ISBN/EAN: 9783337196950

Printed in Europe, USA, Canada, Australia, Japan

Cover: Foto ©Andreas Hilbeck / pixelio.de

More available books at **www.hansebooks.com**

A Chronicle, together with a Little Romance regarding Rudolf and Jacob Näf, of Frankford, Pennsylvania, and their Descendants, including an Account of the Neffs in Switzerland and America.

By Elizabeth Clifford Neff, 25311,

Gambier, Knox County, Ohio,

U. S. A.

Press of Robert Clarke & Company,

1888.

Cincinnati, Ohio.

"I have gathered a posie of other men's flowers,
" and nothing but the thread that binds them is mine
" own."—*Montaigne*.

"There is not so poor a book in the world that
" would not be a prodigious effort were it wrought
" out entirely by a single mind, without the aid of
" prior investigators."—*Johnson*.

(3)

Dedication.

To my parents,

PETER AND SARAH A. (BIGGS) NEFF,

The representatives, as united, of the descendants of Peter and Rebecca Neff, these pages are lovingly presented, knowing that unto none other so lenient and appreciative could they be given.

To the former I am indebted for the form, shape, and fulfillment of my work, as the necessary amount of means to promote my undertaking, was always willingly and cheerfully contributed.

To the latter a conviction of, and faith in my ability, far surpassing my deservings, which, expressed in tender and encouraging words and acts, has stimulated me to the results presented in this little book.

The efforts of the critic may have a tendency to dismay me, but my courage will be restored, if I have done my work in a measure to merit the approval of those interested in the story.

Clifford Place.

(5)

Contents.

CHAPTER I.

CHAPTER II.

CHAPTER III.

7

9

CHAPTER XI.

CHAPTER XII.

CHAPTER XVII.

CHAPTER XVIII.

Lucur Näff. Ano. 1750.

"NÄF.*

"Adam Näf, of Wallenweid, near Cappel (according
" to the certificate of citizenship given by the magis-
" trates of Husen), had, with great bravery, helped to
" rescue the banner of Zurich in the fight near Cappel,
" 1531. Therefor, he received an estate from the
" Council, and, 1533, Monday, after the anniversary,
" received as a gift the right of citizenship—('We de-
" cree, on account of his integrity, since he has helped
" to rescue the Banner and Standard of my Lord in
" the battle of Cappel, and seized it, having felled an
" enemy to the ground with a two-handed sword.')
" He is the first of the race of Näf eligible for a mem-
" ber of the Council, the greater part of whom re-
" main settled in his old home, Cappel, and only re-
" vive his gift of citizenship from time to time (1575,
" 1627, 1657, 1667, 1677).

(Here is given the coat of arms, a copy of which is
opposite.)

---

*" Taken from the 'Family Tree, of the families of Näf, of
" Zurich and Cappel, showing the succeeding generations, by
" Emil Näf, architect, Zurich (11 Y), New Year, 1881.'"

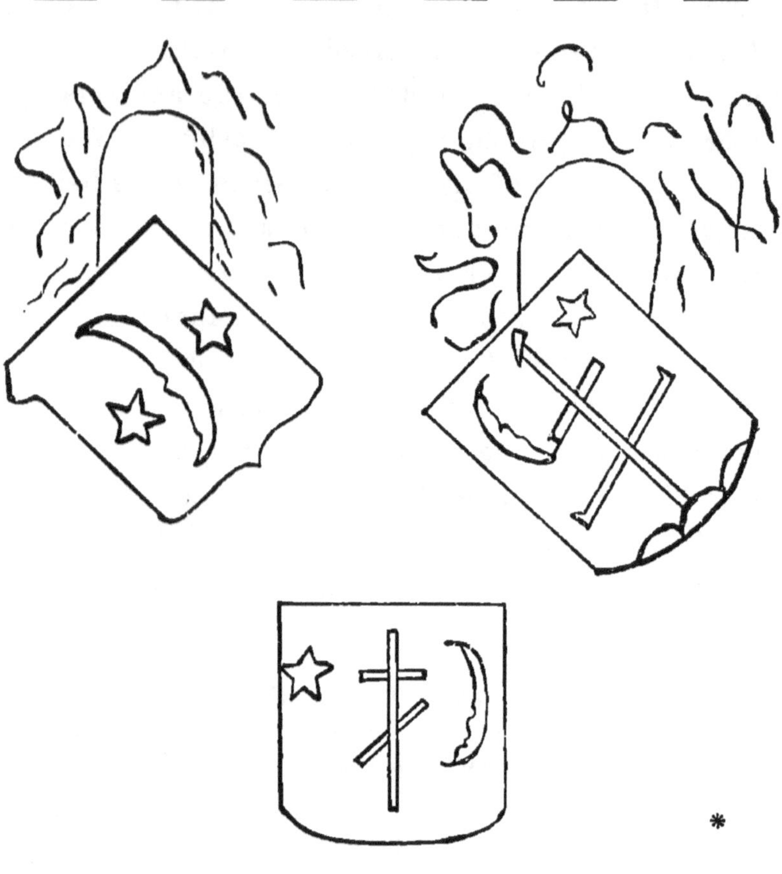

*

---

* These cuts of the coat of arms are from rough drawings sent the compiler from Canton Zurich, showing the variations of design from the same family, which always retain the star and cresent in some form.

CHAPTER I.

For the birth of the name of Neff one must turn to Switzerland, that most charming of all divisions of Europe, within whose confines the climates of nearly every part of the known world are lent, "from lands " of snow to lands of sun," and whose physical peculiarities, so well known, have produced as results a strong, rugged, yet thoroughly refined, people.

To one part of this picturesque land the attention of the reader is directed; it is the canton, "not inaptly " called an epitome of all Switzerland," and which should be properly termed the parent of Protestantism—Zurich.

Around this canton cling many memories dear to the Protestant of America. For was it not in the Cathedral of Zurich, "to which office he was installed " December, 1518," that Zwingli preached, and openly opposed the teachings of the Roman Catholic Church?

Far away in 1531 near the village "that is so pleas- " antly situated at the foot of the Albis range, and at " the entrance of the Alpine world," the ancestor, Adam Näf, distinguished the name and placed the

15   family

family historically prominent in the struggle of Protestantism in Southern Europe.

On the 11th of October, more than 353 years ago, Adam Näf, at Cappel, rescued the standard of Zurich from desecration. On the 11th of October, 1881, at Cappel, the 350th anniversary of this heroic deed was celebrated. Gathered together on that day were the neighboring families of Näf, in Switzerland, to honor and celebrate this good and great man's act.   .

It is to be remarked here as significant, that in this month of October, of this year 1881, the compiler of this chronicle first definitely determined upon a collection of facts regarding the Neff family. May not the spirits of some of these near or distant relatives here gathered have influenced by some subtle and unknown agency the mind of the compiler?

To the courtesy of a friend and correspondent in Canton Zurich, the compiler is indebted for the following description, of the festival of the Swiss Näfs in 1881 :*

---

*Rev. Arnold Näf, Ruschlikon, Canton Zurich, Switzerland.

Gedenkblatt

"   Gedenkblatt

"   An die

"   Näfen-Feier

"   gehalten in Kappel

"   den 11 Oktober 1881

" Am 350 jæhrigen Gedæchtnisstage der Kappeler

"   Schlacht

"   Den Stammgenossen gewidmet

"   von

"   Arnold Näf—Schnorf

"   Pfarrer

                    —Translation—

"   Remembrance Pamphlet

"   of the

" Näf celebration held in Cappel on the 11th of October

"   1881

" On the 350th Anniversary of the Battle of Cappel

"   Dedicated to the members of the family by

"   Arnold Näf—Schnorf

"   Clergyman.

          17   It

"It was a mild autumnal day of the year 1881.
" From different sides we saw on the 11th of October
" members of the Näf family journeying to Cappel,
" the village that is so pleasantly situated at the foot
" of the Albis range and at the entrance of the Alpine
" world.

" Joined with their family relations who live there,
" they wished to hold a family festival in grateful
" memory of their ancestor, Adam Näf, who, 350 years
" before, in the battle near Cappel, rescued the stand-
" ard of Zurich.

" In the early morning streaks of mist hung over
" the landscape, but little by little the country bright-
" ened up, and when the festal pilgrims entered Cap-
" pel they were greeted by clear sunshine. In the
" Hotel Muehle (Mill), where at that time one of the
" Näfs was landlord, the stranger guests found the
" most cordial welcome, not only on the part of the
" landlord, but also from the already assembled mem-
" bers of the family, who are yet domiciled in Cappel.

" The large room of the house had been ingeniously
" adorned with ivy and all sorts of national emblems
" by well wishing hands, and on the south wall
" sparkled the ancestor's ancient sword and escutcheon,
" imbordered with wreaths.* At ten o'clock A. M. the
" number of partakers had grown to nearly seventy. In
" joyful association they exchanged greetings, learned

---

*For representations of the coat of arms of the Näf family
descended from Adam Näf, see plate and cuts at the beginning of this chapter.

                                                                to

" to know each other, and forthwith grew together
" into a family, and took refreshment as they needed it.

" Towards eleven o'clock all the participants went
" up the main street to Zwinglisten [Zwingli monu-
" ment], whither the serious part of the festival had
" been removed. Around the monument the neigh-
" bors had wound wreaths and had erected a simple
" platform before it. On the left and right of this
" platform were placed the boys and girls, who had
" been dressed in the ancient Swiss costume and the
" colors of Zurich.

" Around about these the other festival folks placed
" themselves. On the opposite elevated side of Albis
" street a considerable multitude of people from the
" neighborhood assembled themselves. The whole
" presented all the more a picturesque and festival
" sight, as the scene was sweetly lighted by the au-
" tumnal sun.

" Then a member of the Näf family ascended the
" platform to deliver an address, the tenor of which
" was as follows :

" *Honored ones, dear relatives and friends !*
" To this memorable place I bid you all at the out-
" set, in the name and by order of the committee
" that has invited you to to-day's celebration, a hearty
" welcome.

" Last New Year an honored friend [from foot note,
" the architect, Mr. Emil Näf, Hatt] surprised and re-
" joiced us with a newly prepared ancestral tree of our

                                                    race

"race, from Adam's time down, for which hearty
"thanks ought to be here returned to him. The
"thought soon became public that it would be nice if
"all the persons who there stand so peaceably together
"on the paper should also come together in nature
"once, so far as they are yet living, in order to look one
"another in the eye, and fellow like to press the hand.

"This idea found, wherever one expressed and dis-
"cussed it, every-where general approbation. There-
"fore it was not difficult to come to the resolution to
"lay hands to the work and to invite to a little festi-
"val all, young and old, who are reckoned in our
"family.

"We were at first undecided, whether we ought to
"call the reunion together at Zurich or our native
"town, Cappel. But soon the leaning towards the
"original home overruled, and with jubilant hearts
"we joined in the watchword : Let the native and
"homely Cappel be our place of meeting and festiv-
"ity! There, where Zwingli stood so faithful to
"his work, and sealed it with his heart's blood—there,
"where our blessed ancestor heroically swung the bat-
"tle sword and rescued the banner of Zurich—there,
"and in no other place, shall our meeting again be
"celebrated!

"Concerning the time of our coming together we
"soon came to an agreement. To-day's 350th an-
"niversary of the battle of Cappel, of Zwingli's death,
"and of the glorious deed of our ancestor, appeared
"to us without any thing farther as the time as if given

                                    for

" for our purpose. We accordingly let our invitations fly
" joyfully out into the world in every direction, where
" people dwell in whose veins the blood of the Näfs
" flows.

" Our hope did not delude us. You received our
" invitation kindly, and to-day, the 11th of October,
" have completely burst upon Cappel.

" Not only from the neighboring Näf houses, but
" from greater distances many of you have hastened
" hither.

" Thanks for this, and to all a hearty welcome to
" this consecrated spot of earth.

" May the hours of our association be such that
" they shall remain a happy recollection to us to the
" end of our life. May this be our reward, that old
" ties of friendship, of love, and fellowship be re-
" newed among us, and new ones be knit, and that
" our hearts may glow more powerfully for the high-
" est blessings of life, for which there was once a
" struggle in this place! and when we return home
" in the evening, each one to his sphere of life, may
" it be with the feeling in the heart and the ac-
" knowledgment on the tongue: It was a beautiful,
" good day; thank God that I was permitted to live
" to see and celebrate it!

" The unostentatious festival, that unites us to-day,
" belongs undoubtedly to the most peculiarly pleasing
" that can take place. It is of a sad, domestic sort,
" passes quietly away and in a narrow frame, and yet
" our view is by it involuntarily widened, fatherland

 and

" and church stir our hearts, the forms of heroes of
" former days move before our eyes. The historical
" ground, upon which we stand, the delightful coun-
" try that lies in sunshine before us, lend our festival
" a superior ratification.

" Even nature speaks here powerfully to the soul.

" In few places does a more charming, sublime
" panorama present itself than from here towards the
" south, where Rigi dips its foot in the dark waves
" of Lake Zug, Pilatus stretches aloft its rough, won-
" derful rock peaks, and in the back ground the snow
" mountains with their glaciers and piles of last year's
" snow tower towards heaven. Still more charmingly
" than here by Zwingli's monument an outlook presents
" itself to the friend of nature, yonder on the heights
" towards Ebertsweil, than which he can scarcely
" have found one more wonderful far and near.

" Yet much more cordially does this rural neighbor-
" hood address us for this reason, because we call it
" more strictly our home. With it the career of most
" of us is most closely linked.

" Many of you have yet at this hour here your
" sphere of action, your family, the place in which
" you daily work with and care for your dear ones,
" are rejoiced and bear the burdens that are laid upon
" you, till you go to your eternal home. Many of us
" were born here. Down yonder in the houses, that
" look up from between the trees at us, stood our
" cradles. Over these meads we wandered in the
" happy time of youth, plucked flowers on them, and

                                        wound

" wound them into wreaths. Through those forests
" we strode and meditated on harmless adventures,
" till riper age and the seriousness of life called us to
" go other ways. It seems to me as if every tree and
" every path in this neighborhood would tell me
" many things of that time of youth, free from care,
" that has long since vanished; and this morning
" when I once again from a distance saw the church
" spire of my native place wink over at me, my heart
" longed to break forth in the Jubilee-Home, over ev-
" ery thing in the world—for thee only do our hearts
" beat, thou alone art our world. O, let us greet thee
" anew and embrace thee with thankful love, thou
" dear, trusted home! Let those, who here stay year in
" and year out in joy and in sorrow, greet thee! Let
" us, who were born here, but later have found our
" little place far from thee, greet thee! Let those
" also, who see thee to-day for the first time, greet
" thee! Receive us all kindly and peaceably, let us
" be right glad of thee, awake in our hearts new love
" to thee! But when we remember the historical
" consequence, that belongs to this vicinity, we can
" not refrain from deeper and more earnest expres-
" sions.

" Yonder stood and yet stands in its ruins the Cis-
" tercian Convent, founded in the year 1185 by the
" barons of Eschenbach. Many storms passed over it
" in the course of the century. It was long a lamp
" of knowledge, faith, and Christian life for a wide
" circuit. When other cloisters had long since fallen

                                                                        in

" in with every possible ruin, men yet lived behind its
" walls, who had preserved hearts open for the truth
" and every thing good, and fostered an influential
" school. It early opened its doors to the Reforma-
" tion ; its last venerable abbot, Wolfgang Joner,
" fought in the battle for the cause of the gospel, fell
" alongside of Zwingli, and was buried with hundreds
" in the ' old cellar in the barn ' [at Scheuren]. That
" brings me to the memorable, war-like event, of which
" Cappel was the scene, 350 years ago. At least, in
" brief I will and must join to that event, in order to
" be able to place the deed of our family sire, Adam
" Näf, in the right connection and in the proper
" light.

" From 1519 on, Ulrich Zwingli, in Zurich, from
" the pulpit of the great Cathedral, worked for the
" renovation of the Christian belief and life on the
" ground of the simple, wholesome gospel of Jesus
" Christ. His reformation ideas found approbation
" first in Zurich, then also in Berne, Basil, St. Gallen,
" and elsewhere. The interior cantons, on the con-
" trary, the five old places, remained conservative, and
" showed themselves resolved, in respect to the main
" points, to abide by the teachings and customs of
" the hitherto church. Mutual collisions arose, which
" increased from year to year. Political intentions
" and personal interests, that mixed in, made the sepa-
" ration so much the greater and more dangerous.

" In the year 1527 the reformed classes made up the
" *Christian citizenship*, an alliance for the promotion of

24the

" the reformation ideas. The catholic places replied
" by going into an alliance, at Waldsbut, in April,
" 1529, with Austria, the old hereditary enemy of the
" members of the alliance, that had been repulsed on
" the Morgarten near Sempach and Näfels, at so dear
" a price. From this resulted the first Cappel war.
" What would have been better fought out by the
" weapons of the spirit, of faith, and of love, they
" must, alas, decide by the sword.

" On the 9th of June, 1529, the standard of Zu-
" rich, with 4,000 men, moved toward Cappel. On
" the following 10th of June, the declaration of en-
" mity was sent over to the (5) five cantons, that had
" collected on the Baarerboden, and on the same day
" the boundary was crossed and the little territory of
" Zug was invaded by soldiery. The common people
" in both camps were, however, not so hostile as many
" of their leaders. Mutual visits were made. Well
" known is the charming tradition of a repast of
" milk soup on a land-mark on heaps of stone or
" turf.

" The noble Landamman [a Swiss magistrate], Hans
" Aebli, of Clarus whose heart was long since almost
" wrung, over confederates being willing to go to war
" against each other, observed such an inclination
" towards a friendly intercourse on both sides.

" Like a second Niklaus of the Flüe, in the last
" agreed upon hour, he placed himself between the
" combative camps. His pathetic plea for peace
" found a hearing. Negotiations were brought about

                                    and

" and led to the wished for result. Without a drop
" of blood having flown the first public peace was
" brought about on the 25th of June, 1529. The
" same required, among other things, that the five
" cantons should give up the document relating to the
" confederation with Austria. After long delay it
" was given up. In the hall of the convent in this
" place Landamman Aebli tore it into shreds, that its
" contents should not be known and the flame of pas-
" sion kindled anew. But the troops of both parties
" returned home exulting, glad of the peace, to their
" cottages. But the gaping wound was only super-
" ficially closed. The peace was not to be of long
" duration. Zwingli, who looked deeper, had prophet-
" ically foretold it, when he said to Aebli, 'Alas! dear
" good father, this peace is our destruction.' The old
" frictions continued and new ones were added; on
" both sides the souls constantly became more in-
" censed. As early as the year 1531 the second Cap-
" pel war followed, after several acts of hostility on
" both sides had occurred and the reformed had de-
" creed against the interior cantons an embargo on
" the exportation of grain. This time it was the
" catholic clans who got the start of the careless re-
" formed with the declaration of war. On the 9th of
" October their messengers assembled at Brunnen and
" resolved to resort to arms. On the 9th and 10th of
" October they drew their war power together near
" Zug on the Baarerboden.
    " In order to offer resistance, the people from the
                                        neighborhood

" neighborhood first of all assembled near Cappel.
" Many messengers hastened to Zurich to make the
" danger known there. On the 10th of October,
" in the evening, Zurich sent a vanguard of several
" hundred, and with a few guns, by way of the Alvis,
" under the lead of Sir George Göldli, of Tiefenau, and
" Peter Füssli, captain of rifles. At the same time
" the people of Kilchberg, Thalweil, and Horgen
" were warned to set out for Cappel. Upon new
" alarm reports Zurich, finally, in the evening at
" seven o'clock, let the common storm be promul-
" gated, in order to be able soon to follow with the
" main standard. But it was too late, for as early as
" the next day, Wednesday, the 11th of October, on
" the day of the inoffensive infant, a bloody battle
" took place at Cappel. I must surely, for want of
" time, forbear to paint in detail the particulars of
" this fight, yet I must mention the main points, be-
" cause that much will be necessary to bring the
" deed of Adam Näf plainly before our eyes. The
" army of the five cantons, on the 11th of October,
" on the Baarerboden, held its divine service, prayed
" five Paternosters and five Ave Marias, and sent a
" messenger with the challenge to Cappel. Then it
" set forth, and towards noon appeared beyond the
" convent in Schönenbühl [Schönen Hill] and on
" Mount Islis. Göldli, with the vanguard and the
" forces from the neighborhood, took a position at
" Scheuren; that is, near the now existing Näf houses.
" Many urged him to retreat to the wall situated at
27   Münchbühl

" Münchbühl [Munch Hill]; others advised against
" it, and Göldli was not willing to give his consent.
" Forthwith a fight developed between the vanguard
" of the five cantons and Göldli's troops. The
" former advanced by way of Langfeld towards the
" latter, but were kept in check by the Zurich guns,
" and were not able, from the difficulties of the
" ground, to come nearer. They soon desisted from
" further advance and withdrew to their own by way
" of Lindenfeld. In the afternoon the army of the
" five cantons changed its position. From the south
" side of the convent it moved by way of the Biden-
" los meadow to the chapel of St. Marks, past the
" present churchyard, by way of Hofacker and Allen-
" winden to Ebertsweiler summit. During this disloca-
" tion many Zurichers wished to fall upon the enemy,
" as they imagined, ' now they are ours;' but Göldli
" and others hindered it. The Catholics had scarcely
" reached the summit when the Zurichers, with the
" main standard, came up, between three and four
" o'clock, led by Rudolf Lavater, governor of Kyburg,
" originally Glaser, and William Töning, captain of
" rifles, landlord of the Red House, accompanied by
" Ulrich Zwingli as chaplain. The troops were tired
" and numbered scarcely 700 men. When at the
" Albis some advised to await the arrival of the troops
" marching behind. Lavater and Zwingli exhorted
" them to hasten forward in order to assist their dis-
" tressed brothers.
" The Zurichers, at most 2,000 men, had to oppose

28themselves

" themselves to 8,000 enemies, it is said. Immedi-
" ately after the arrival the Zurichers arranged their
" battle lines. The 'upper troop' or right wing
" took position at Scheuren, beyond the Näf houses;
" the 'hinder troop' or left wing behind the Zwingli
" monument, north-east from the same. The latter
" wing constituted the 'power band,' with the main
" standard. It was decided by the leaders in the
" camp of the five cantons to defer the attack till the
" following day. But John Jauch, of Uri, ventured
" into the Scheuren wood, a little beach grove, be-
" tween Ebertsweiler summit and the main force of
" the Zurichers, that had been left unoccupied. He
" looked on just as a part of the Zurichers withdrew
" towards Münch Hill, and disorder on their account
" reigned. The moment seemed to him a favorable
" one for an attack. With a few hundred he rushed
" forth independently from the beech grove towards
" the enemy. The leader of his party quickly per-
" ceived it to be advantageous not to leave Jauch in
" the lurch, but to take up, with all his force, the
" battle independently begun by him. And so they
" advanced in two divisions towards the Zurichers
" from the beech grove out against the left wing, be-
" hind the Zwingli monument, and through the Cap-
" pel meadow, against the right wing at Scheuren.
" Vehemently surged the fight; it was fought with
" heroic courage; the Catholics saw themselves repeat-
" edly pressed back. But their superiority was too
" great. In an hour's time, towards five o'clock, the

                                                    dice

" dice had fallen and the battle was decided fatally to
" the Zurichers. The wing at Scheuren was pressed
" back, and the enemy now succeeded in falling upon
" the side of the wing behind the Zwingli monument.
" Yonder, by the moss-covered tomb and the Zwingli
" tree was the most bloody struggle. Yonder the
" standard-bearer, John Schweizer, held aloft the ban-
" ner of Zurich, and, like a hero, inflamed the fighters
" to its defense. Yonder, in the midst of the danger,
" stood the leaders, Lavater and Töning, the latter of
" whom fell. Yonder, in the foremost ranks, Zwingli
" exhorted the fighters and comforted the dying, till
" he himself, wounded on head and thigh, sank down,
" crying out, ' What is this for a calamity? you are
" able to kill the body, but not the soul.' The motion
" of the fight became constantly more violent; but
" the standard-bearer would not yield. The enemy
" pressed constantly more powerfully on the troop of
" Zurichers; these fell by hundreds around the stand-
" ard. Now flight became the order of the day with
" the rear guard, especially after Zuger had mingled
" himself with the Zurichers and called to them, that
" they should fly and save themselves. After long re-
" sistance the standard-bearer, Master John Schweizer,
" of the forges, was also carried away. He reached
" the mill stream. When he attempted to cross he
" fell in, and, weighed down by his arms, he perished.
" Standard-bearer Kleinbaus Kambli rescued the
" banner from the hands of the dying one, and
" hastened farther with it. Some of the enemy over-

                                          took

" took him; one of these had already seized the ban-
" ner; Kambli cried: 'Is there no honorable Zurich-
" ers there to save his army's banner?' This Adam
" Näf, from Vollenweid, heard. This was the decisive
" moment, when this dear man approached as rescuer
" of the standard. As arquebusier, under John Hu-
" ber, of Teufenbach, he had already fought manfully
" in the battle. Now he courageously swung his
" sword that he carried with him, and struck from its
" body the head of the enemy that had seized the
" banner. Jungbaus Thumysen, who afterwards fell
" near the church in Hausen, aided him in the fight
" with the halberd. Kleinbaus Kambli was able to
" hurry farther with the banner. On the other side
" Ulrich Denzler, of Nänikon, took it and brought it
" uninjured to the Albis. Kambli also recovered him-
" self, and was able during the night to mount the
" hill. On the field of battle and in the flight the
" Zurichers left 512 of their number behind, among
" them 25 clergymen, 26 members of the council, and
" 65 other citizens of the town. Two large graves,
" one at the old cellar at Scheuren, and another on
" the right of the road to Zurich, before you come to
" the mill creek, were afterwards their resting place.
" The Catholics took their killed, the number of whom
" has remained unknown, with them, and placed them
" in the church-yard at Baar. The approach of night
" made an end of the pursuit of the fleeing Zurichers
" at the foot of the Albis. The five cantons turned
" back to the field of battle, thanked God, and unfor-

                                              tunately

" tunately cooled the passion of their enraged souls
" yet on the dead and wounded.

" Zwingli, lying in the struggle of death, was also
" discovered among these. After he refused to deny
" his faith Captain Bockinger, from Unterwalden,
" gave him the death thrust. In the morning, despite
" the dissuasions of many leaders, his body was quar-
" tered and burned by the executioner from Lucerne.
" But Chaplain John Schönbrunnar, of Zug, who had
" formerly been canon of the Cathedral of Our Lady,
" in Zurich, spoke this magnanimous word concern-
" ing the dying Zwingli: 'Of whatever faith you were,
" you were still a good ally.' Zwingli's body they have
" killed and burned, but his soul lives, and his work
" for God has not been destroyed. The word of truth,
" that his mouth announced, resounded yet again to-
" day in our hearts. His blood, that they have poured
" out, became holy seed, from which ripened, and
" shall further ripen, fruits which remain forever.
" After this battle followed many disturbances and
" events unfavorable to the Reformation, like the bat-
" tle on the Gubel.

" Finally negotiations for peace were brought about.
" A month later on, the 15th and 16th of November,
" the second public peace was arranged in a meadow
" near Deinikon, between Cappel and Baar, by ambas-
" sadors from both sides, and on the 20th of Novem-
" ber, it was ratified in Zug. That it was a more un-
" favorable one for the reformed than the first one is
" evident. Delays of all sorts, that had occurred

                                   simultaneously

" simultaneously between the city and province of
" Zurich, found their release through the Cappel letter
" agreed upon on the 1st of December. Subsequently,
" at Zurich, an investigation was instituted against
" Lavater, the leader of the main force, and against
" Göldli, the commander of the vanguard, because
" they were accused of having brought on the sad result
" of the battle by inconsiderate, yea treasonable actions.

" Both went forth from the investigation as guilt-
" less, Lavater retained the office of Judge of Kyburg,
" and afterwards rose to great honor as he filled the
" office of Burgomaster for 18 terms from 1544. He
" died in 1557. Göldli, on the contrary, found it nec-
" essary to leave; he changed his settlement to Con-
" stance, where he died in 1536.

" His brother Caspar, who had already years before
" taken up his abode at Lucerne, fought at Cappel in
" the ranks of the five cantons.

" After the war the council of Zurich honored sev-
" eral men, who had distinguished themselves in bat-
" tle, by especial rewards and high attestations of
" honor.

" Kleinbaus Kambli, the bearer of the banner, and
" one of the rescuers of the same, received the man-
" agement of the governorship of Egislau [1532–
" 44]. To Ulrich Denzler, of Nänikon, was presented
" the citizenship of Zurich, and the so-called ' little
" banner estate,' was given out to him. The council,
" in the spring of 1533, likewise honored and rewarded
" our worthy ancestor, Adam Näf, of Vollenweid, by

                                        bestowing

" bestowing upon him and his descendents the citizen-
" ship of the town of Zurich, further with the surren-
" der in fee of the herdsman's house at Scheuren, on
" extremely advantageous conditions.

" We have assembled here to-day in order to lay
" upon the grave of this, our noble ancestor, Adam
" Näf, a wreath of honored and thankful remem-
" brance. We honor and praise his bravery, his
" courage, his presence of mind, with which he dis-
" tinguished himself during and after the battle. We
" honor and praise his love for the fatherland and for
" his narrower home, which inflamed him to expose
" his heart to the enemy.

" We honor and praise his hearty assent to the
" good cause of the gospel, which drove him into the
" ranks of those who fought around Zwingli. We
" honor and praise his love to wife and child, which
" pressed the sword into his hand to fight that his
" homely hearth might not be invaded.

" He was a brave old ally, a whole man, to whom
" God and the fatherland and family lay near to the
" heart, and it fills us with noble pride to be able to
" call him our sire.

" At this celebration of the memory of him we bow
" to show ourselves worthy of him, to stand as he,
" true to the banner of our country, to Zwingli's
" church, to the pure gospel and word of God, to wife
" and child.

" On this soil, which drunk the blood of the noblest,
" we pledge our word to fight for every thing that is
                                good

" good, and that pleases God : to exhibit a heart glow-
" ing for whatever benefits home, church, and our
" family.

" May scions never be wanting even to the latest
" descendants of our race, who may do honor to our
" ancestor, and worthily plant his name wider. Three
" and a half centuries now has the dear God, blessing
" and guarding, ruled over our family. From the
" depths of our hearts we to-day with one accord pre-
" sent to him for this the offering of thanks.

" But may he be with us still farther, and carry us
" on and on, on the wings of his power and love, and
" permit the Näf trunk to bear to the latest time twigs
" and branches, healthy and green with life.

" The circumstance that it was held in the open air,
" on the consecrated spot itself, where, 350 years be-
" fore, the battle heavy with consequences took place,
" lent to this simple festival a peculiar charm, and sig-
" nificance.

" At the thought of what took place here once,
" many an eye was moistened. After they had given
" themselves up to various earnest observations in the
" way of conversation, for a while longer they took
" leave of the Zwingli monument in order to make
" the Näf houses a visit, of which Adam's family
" mansion was adorned with wreaths. A few decades
" ago still only Näfs lived here. Modern time has
" now asserted its right even here, as a part of the
" houses have passed into strange hands. From the
" Näf houses a pleasant foot path leads through green

                                    meadows

" meadows to the near convent. This way this festi-
" val caravan now took in order to reach the church
" of the former convent, the no longer public church.
" As a precious monument to Gothic art it stands there
" in the midst of green meadows in face of the majestic
" mountains.

" With hearts lifted up the feast fellows wandered
" through its holy spaces, the lofty middle nave, the
" two side naves, the great choir. The existing
" grave-stones spoke of times long past, of the found-
" ers and supporters of the convent. The paintings
" on glass yet remaining restored by Röttinger,
" awakened a suspicion of the splendor that had once
" spread over this house of God, of the holy art that
" had once found here a consecrated place. The dates,
" 1527 and '28, on the pulpit and baptismal font, re-
" called those days when the gospel came to light
" again here, in order to awake a new spring time for
" souls. And that it might not end with the mere
" thoughtful looking at the silent, venerable spaces,
" but might elevate the hearts, some choral songs
" were harmoniously sung.

" With this closed the earnest part of the celebration.

" The proper hour was now at hand to return to
" the ' Mill,' in order at a festive meal to yield them-
" selves to generous joy and come yet nearer to each
" other.

" All the guests were well entertained by their rela-
" tive, the landlord. Whatever strengthens mankind
" and rejoices his heart was richly provided.

                                        Soon

" Soon one mouth after another opened itself in
" order to regale the assembled ones with mental de-
" lights in prose and poetry, and to give expression
" to the enthusiastic and earnest holiday thoughts
" that moved the hearts of all. Two strange guests,
" who had in a friendly manner accepted the invita-
" tion to the feast, also spoke to the company; the
" clergyman of the place of festivity, and a curate
" from Lake Zurich, who without knowing of the
" pictured celebration was making a visit to the field
" of battle.

" The deed of the ancestor was praised in song.
" We heard his battle sword speak in poetical repre-
" sentation. The family tree was ingeniously and hu-
" morously arranged and grouped. The glasses re-
" sounded to the welfare of the young generation. A
" second toast was given to the absent ones.

" The festival mood was kept up by declamation;
" in the midst of all, letters and telegrams of greet-
" ing from Zurich, Yocrdon, and Pesth were read. In
" the course of the beautiful sunshiny afternoon, a
" part of the festival guests took a walk to the
" Ebertsweiler summit, past the little forest that had
" been so fatal for the battle. All saw themselves richly
" rewarded and refreshed by the outlook to the plain
" of the Baarerbodens [ground about Baar], the Rigi,
" and Pilatus, and the snow peaks of the wreath of
" Alps. On their return they found the young world
" engaged in song and dance. Once again the entire
" company assembled. But swiftly flew the hours

 and

" and only too early fell the night on the native fields
" and warned the far dwelling ones to return home.

" Surely all went home with thankful feeling in
" the heart; those were hours of joy and pleasure
" that we have spent in celebration. We were united
" by a family festival of the most beautiful kind; at
" the same time we felt our breasts strike higher for
" fatherland and church, for that which remains above
" all change.

" What on that day was found out may work on
" in the souls of all and ripen to precious fruits!
" After 50 years, when the most of us are no longer
" here, be it permitted a new generation, happy, fresh,
" and free to celebrate the 400th Jubilee of our family
" and of the battle of Cappel!

" Under the protection and blessing of the Most
" High, may the race of Näfs grow and flourish on
" and on !

Amen."

To those of the name of Neff this locality should
be always cherished, for upon Adam Näf and his descendants was bestowed the *citizenship* of the town
of Zurich. But its charm does not end with this sig-
nal character. "Down yonder beyond Cappel in the
" houses that look up from between the trees " stood
the cradles of others of our name, upon whose lives
the world has paid its tribute of honor. From this
rugged country came Barbara Neff, whose faith in the
reformed religion was as firm and solid as the hills of
her native Zurich. She could not be shaken, and for

                                                    her

her cause, she together with many of her heroic coun-
trymen, suffered death between 1638 and 1643.*

Almost within the influence of the Cistercian Convent Felix Neff was born. He who an earnest Protestant and zealous worker became, when twenty-one
years of age, a pastor of the High Alps, going from
hamlet to hamlet on the mountains of Switzerland,
bearing the good news of the gospel, every-where his
presence being hailed with delight, turning many souls
from the darkness into the light.

His energy and earnestness being greater than his
physical strength, the latter gave way at the age of
thirty-one, he dying on the 12th of April, 1829.†

From this sublime locality, where one can look
" towards the south where Rigi dips its foot in the
" dark waves of Lake Zug, and Pilatus stretches aloft
" its rough, wonderful rock peaks," came Timoleon
Carl von Neff, an artist of eminence, who wandered
from these artistic scenes to die in Russia.‡ How
strange it is that the spot of all others that should rejoice the heart of the artist, and which should produce
the largest number of such people, is of all others so
devoid of artists; but if one does find embosomed

---

*It is singular that portions of the family hold such a tradition
regarding the martyrdom of Barbara before the record confirmed
it.—See Rupp's History of Lancaster Co., Penn., page 72.

†Life of Felix Neff, pastor of the High Alps.—American Sun-
day-School Union print.

‡Timoleon Carl von Neff, painter of the picture of St. Isaac, of
Dalmatia, in the Cathedral of St. Petersburg. Died in St. Petersburg in 1879.

                                          within

within his soul there such talent, as did Timoleon,
they wander to other countries less picturesque.

Out of this land filled with grand memories and
grander scenes, Paul Neff went forth to make his
name famous as a publisher at Stuttgart, and who now
points with pride to his ancestral home in Switzerland.*

In the midst of all the grand and majestic scenery
of the place rise the mounds to mark the graves of
four brothers who fell in one battle, an undoubted at-
testation of the valor of the name.†

In this locality, where the Neff family are so prevalent, it is gratifying to learn, as a historical fact,
that its people are among the most prosperous and
best educated workingmen in Europe.

And it is comforting to people whose parentage
claims home *there*, that its people were so progressive
and advanced as to make it one of the earliest seats
of the cotton manufacture in Europe, and that its
looms and spindles have for years produced a product
in demand throughout civilization.

Its corn and pasture lands, its vineyards and
orchards, are evidences of the quiet peaceful industry
of a people whose representatives scattered out upon
the earth are making their lives a reflection of their
fatherland. With all these facts before one it will be
no wonder if the mind turns eagerly to any chronicle

---

* Paul Neff, publisher, Stuttgart, Germany.

† The above fact is attested by Paul Neff, of Stuttgart.

or

or romance regarding the name of Neff. Do not believe that all that is to follow will be sunshine.

The heroes are human as are all others who enter into this history, and may err, and as " into each life " some rain must fall, some days be dark and dreary," so we may find it to have been for them and their descendants. What in the lives of any of those whose history may enter into the chapters of this volume is good and Christ-like, take that home to yourself—and wherein they have done ill forgive, and may their failure be but as a light-house, to turn you away from the same reef.

CHAPTER II.

Thus circumstanced and surrounded this canton
Zurich, should, and did play a particular and weighty
part in the conflicts raging in Switzerland in the
struggle against the Roman Catholic power—its people individually as well as collectively, even down to
latter days, feeling the influences thus brought to
bear upon all. Turning our thoughts particularly to
this canton, it will be found that these influences have
shaped even the course of the lives of those who become of deep interest as the story of this volume
rolls on.

In the reformed religion, Zurich must be accorded
leadership, for in her train followed "Berne, Basel,
" Schauffhausen, a great part of Glarus, and the ex-
" terior communities of Appenzell," and on account of
their devotion bore the proud title of " Calvanistic or
" reformed cantons."

Standing thus opposed to the power and teachings
of Rome with her allies, the " five cantons " leagued
together to defend the old faith, it is not surprising
that persecution should have been present here.

The conditions were no different here than in other

countries

countries where the iron hand of popery had made red the land.

The persecution, however, appeared in Switzerland in a milder form.

It was a kind of persecution [and it is indulged in even to-day in a modified form], that although lacking the rigor and severity of the religious movements elsewhere, and unknown to the world, yet had the effect to drive the men of Zurich, and the other Protestant cantons, hither and thither over the earth.

Not, however, without sacrificing some victims to the faith*—some who now calmly and sweetly rest in beloved Switzerland, awaiting the day when as jewels they shall shine in His crown of glory.

We know of a surety that at the period of the persecutions in Switzerland, and in the early days of the knowledge that freedom to worship God according to the dictates of conscience was enjoyed in America, many noble, patriotic, energetic Swiss left their fatherland and ties, and planted their own church in catholic America.

The object of this narrative is not to dwell upon the people as a whole, but upon two persons who, living in Switzerland, and experiencing the feelings, and sharing the trials above indicated, left their native home Zurich, never to return to its beloved although trying associations.

No part of Switzerland differs in regard to wealth,

---

* History of Lancaster County, Penn., by J. D. Rupp, 1844.

                    the

the dense population, the absence of a titled or noble class holding an excess of wealth, levels its population to a plane of simple competence and content.

Fancy, if possible, some rural spot in this canton Zurich, where wealth and large land holdings are absent, and you possess the nativity of the Neff ancestry.

Not to the class of early immigrants, who came to this country empty handed, with no other object in view than the love of exploit, or desire for sudden and unearned possession of wealth, that they fancied a new country offered, do the subjects of this sketch belong, but to that class who desiring the accumulation of wealth, yet knew that even in a new country work must precede success.

The subjects of this sketch as has been intimated, were also actuated by religious motives, to join their brethren in this country who having preceded them many years, owing to definite and direct persecution, had found enjoyment in the freedom obtained in America. They were possessed of sufficient means to enable them to reach this country comfortably, and after their arrival by economy and Swiss, or German thrift, they were soon enabled to acquire for themselves wealth.

The two persons who thus together start off from their native land, to realize their hopes in America, were brothers; the one Rudolf Näf, the other Jacob Näf.

The port from which they sailed was Rotterdam.

                                    The

The journey from Zurich to Rotterdam, in Holland, must have been long, tiresome, and tedious in those days. The brothers probably left Zurich in the spring, as they reached Philadelphia, Penn., U. S. A., on the 11th of September, 1749. The ship they sailed in was named "Priscilla; William Meier, captain; " from Rotterdam; last from Cowes; 299 passengers."*

An interesting fact, to be stated here, showing the education and ability of Rudolf and Jacob, compared with other immigrants, is that they signed their own names, instead of having the clerk do so for them, and spelled the name as follows: Rudolf Näf, Jacob Näf. A fact that strikes one as a little singular is, that wherever their names have been found written together, Rudolf's comes first, although he was the younger. The following certificate explains this *fac simile:*

"*Secretary of the Commonwealth, Pennsylvania, ss:*
"HARRISBURG, *June 4th*, A. D. 1885.

"I do hereby certify, that " the annexed is a true pho- " tographic copy of the orig- " inal signatures of Rudolf " Näf, and Jacob Näf, with " others, who arrived at Phila- " delphia in the Priscilla, Capt. " William Meier, from Rotter- " dam, and last from Cowes, in England, and took the

*Rupp's collection of thirty thousand names of Immigrants in Pennsylvania, pages 196 and 197.

                                usual

" usual oaths to the Government, on the 11th Septem-
" ber, 1749, as the same remain on file in this office :

" In testimony whereof, I have hereunto set my
" hand, and caused the seal of the Secretary's office to
" be affixed, the day and year above written.
"   Jno. C. Shoemaker,
"   *Deputy-Secretary of the Commonwealth.*"

The two brothers, Rudolf and Jacob, having left
their home, the picturesque and inspiring Switzerland,
came to America, bringing all the activity of moun-
taineers, coupled with the determination to brave all
dangers, and, in this new and prosperous country,
make for themselves a future worthy their ambitious
hopes. Their parents had been carefully educated,
and it was their object and desire to give to their
children such advantages as would enable them to
keep abreast their times, to reach out farther, and, in
short, accomplish more than they had done.

The disease which caused the death of the father,
in a few days prostrated the mother, and her strength
failing, she, too, secure in the salvation, made possible
through her loving Saviour, passed to her rest.

At the time of the death of the parents, Jacob was

                                                    in

in his twentieth, and Rudolf in his eighteenth year.
There were several other children, sons and daughters,
who were older, all of whom were married, and settled
in homes on the mountains of Switzerland; each finding a world of interest and activity in their own home-
life, which satisfied them, without venturing to a new
country. In the death of their parents, Rudolf and
Jacob acquiesced, yielding as to a decree of Providence, to which they should submit.

They did this from a knowledge acquired in their
home training, that "He doeth all things well," yet
not at that time realizing in its fullness the relationship to Him, who later became their guide and
support.

The religion of the parents was not of form and
outward observance, but in "the hidden man of the
"heart," yet they openly professed Christ, and were
zealous Protestants.

At the time our narrative begins the parents had
been dead about four years, and the relatives, kind
and generous, as a rural and hard working class are
in such a country as Switzerland, had assisted the
boys, until they found themselves well equipped for
the struggle necessary in early Pennsylvania.

They located at Frankford, near Philadelphia, Penn.,
and with hearts full of each other, and a feeling of
love for the new country, which they ever after cherished as home, they quietly settled down to work,
having learned by a careful education, an education

                                        derived

derived from earnest parents, that honest toil is always honorable.

That the brothers located in this portion of Pennsylvania may be explained by the fact, that as Frankford was then somewhat remote, and greater dangers awaited the early settler, the colonies offered unusual inducements in their grants of land, as observe the following:

"Though," says Peter Kalm [*Peter Kalm, a Swedish natural philosopher and traveler, was born at Ostro, Bothnia, in 1715, traveled from 1748 to 1751 in North America, and at a later period in Russia; he became Professor of Botany at the University of Abo, and died 1779*] "the Province of New York has been inhab-
" ited by Europeans much longer than Pennsylvania,
" yet it is not by far so populous as that colony.

" This can not be ascribed to any particular discour-
" agement arising from the nature of the soil, for that
" is pretty good; but I am told of a very different
" reason, which I will mention here. In the reign of
" Queen Anne, about the year 1709, many Germans
" came hither, who got a tract of land from the En-
" glish government, which they might settle. After
" they had lived there some time, and had built houses
" and made corn-fields and meadows, their liberties and
" privileges were infringed, and under several pretenses
" they were repeatedly deprived of part of their land.

" This at last aroused the Germans. They returned
" violence for violence, and beat those who thus rob-
" bed them of their possessions. But these proceed-

ings

" ings were looked upon in a very bad light by the
" government. The most active people among the
" Germans being taken up they were roughly treated
" and punished with the utmost rigor of the law.

" This, however, so far exasperated the rest, that
" the greater part of them left their homes and fields
" and went to settle in Pennsylvania.

" There they were exceedingly well received, got
" a considerable tract of land, and were indulged in
" great privileges, which were given them forever,
" The Germans, not satisfied with being themselves
" removed from New York, wrote to their relatives
" and friends, and advised them if ever they intended
" to come to America not to go to New York where
" the government had shown itself so unequitable.

" This advice had such influence that the Germans
" who afterwards went in great numbers to North
" America constantly avoided New York, and always
" went to Pennsylvania. It sometimes happened that
" they were forced to go on board of such ships as
" were bound for New York, but they were scarce
" got on shore when they hastened on to Pennsyl-
" vania, in sight of all the inhabitants of New York."*

Hence Rudolf and Jacob, with the keen insight
that prompted them through life, came to Frankford,
to avail themselves of colonial offers.

Their first effort was to secure comfortable home
quarters, which they found with a kind old Quaker

---

*Peter Kalm's Travels in America in 1747 and 1748, Vol. I.,
pages 270–271.

                                    lady

lady [you know the Friends have always been numerous in and about Philadelphia, with their sweet,
kind, loving faces, their quiet dress, and the all-entranc-
ing " thee " and " thou "].

It was the engaging and promising countenance of
Rudolf, as dear old Mrs. Morse used to say, that made
her open her doors to those two young men, Rudolf
and Jacob.

CHAPTER III.

You would doubtless here like to know something of dear old Mrs. Morse, her home, and her surroundings.

An endeavor will be made, as clearly as possible, by means of pen and paper, through the medium of words. Such a picture will necessarily have many incomplete points, but the reader must from his own imagination perfect the portraiture.

Of English descent, she has inherited many of the peculiarities of that people, tempered, however, by the generous impulses prevalent among the people of a new country. As to figure and carriage she is above medium height, well-proportioned, and of a dignified yet kindly bearing. Her face is of that sweet, peaceful kind, restful, hopeful, and trustful [too few of such faces do we find in our hurried life], but in which there is a hint of sadness, occasioned by a grief of five years duration; a grief over the desolation of her house in the death of a devoted husband. You look in her restful moments upon a bright blue eye, indicative of benignity, and at the same time of resolution. Her hair is auburn, yet a few indications

of

of age creep to us in the occasional gray hairs that
are seen.

At the time that Rudolf and Jacob are first touched
by her influence, her household consisted of a son,
Joseph, and a daughter, Hannah. With the means
left her, she has given her son and daughter all the
advantages of education possible in so new a country.

Joseph has inherited much of the appearance and
disposition of his mother, and has by will and energy
now become a comfort and support to his mother.

Hannah has partaken her father's bright black eyes,
quick perception, and rather hasty disposition. She
is a woman having all the elements of sterling worth
and telling influence to be observed, not only in her
own life, but which will be felt by those with whom
she shall come in contact; all of which is controlled
and directed by a Christian character, that had taken
the form of membership in the " Society of Friends,"
to which society her mother had always been devotedly and conscientiously attached.

Fancy the hurry of the work of Monday and Tues-
day over, and Mrs. Morse settled down for the rest
of the week, only attending carefully to the wants
of her little family, in the way of sewing and preparing the daily three meals, and you are able to appreciate the contented condition in which Rudolf
and Jacob found her on a Wednesday morning in
September, 1749. It is necessary to the story to say
that at the corner of two streets, in Frankford, stood
the brown frame house in which Mrs. Morse and her

son and daughter lived, for it was at the door of this house that Rudolf and Jacob Näf first knocked.

Their knowledge of the English language had all been gathered on their journey to this country. You may imagine they could make themselves but little understood, having always spoken the dialect of their native canton in Switzerland, which partook largely of the German, yet was not pure German. It was consequently doubly difficult for them in their present situation. Mrs. Morse's perceptions, sharpened by Christian hospitality, understood their desire, where words failed them, and, after talking a short time with them, she agreed to take them into her house.

Provision was made to board them—each to pay her seven shillings and six-pence a week—these terms to include washing, board, and their room with light [fire was never thought of as necessary for young men to have in their room], but light was seldom used. As an earnest of their good intentions, they each advanced Mrs. Morse one week's payment.

Cheap living, you may say, but you must remember times have changed since then, for it was harder at that time to earn seven shillings six-pence, than it is now to make twice as much. After partaking of a little luncheon prepared for them by their kind hostess, they pause for a moment and view their situation.

Strangers in a new country, wholly without friends, it is not found that they sat down to regret and think

of

of their lot, but immediately start out in search of work.

They had not gone far from Mrs. Morse's house, ere they came upon a party of men at work digging a cellar for a new house; the appearance of the brothers, and their broken language, was the subject of much jest and merriment among the men—after waiting about, and trying to be understood, the brothers at last succeeded, and were given work excavating and preparing the cellar, of what was to be a large double brick house, so arranged, that two families could occupy it. It did not take them long to prove to the men and their employer, that they were no triflers, but honest young men, who would build themselves up in this new country, and give strength to its history.

Thus, from day to day, working faithfully at whatever they could obtain to do, they earned sufficient, not only to pay for their living, clothing, etc., but carefully to husband a little for days in the future.

It is not possible to stop long, nor note in detail the home life of these young men with Mrs. Morse. They received every comfort and kind care that a loving mother could bestow. Their evenings were spent, usually, around the fire-side. The day's work done, Joseph would return from his shop, and complete the fire-side circle composed of Mrs. Morse, Hannah, Rudolf, and Jacob. He would tell the little family thus assembled, of trade and business, relate to them the news that passed to and fro during the day at the shop, the discussions that occurred between the great

minds

minds of the village—the talk of neighbors and a stray newspaper being the only means of obtaining current news at this early day.

Thus, evening after evening, Rudolf and Jacob were being unconsciously educated in our language, our customs, our laws, and our methods. In the homely and simple ways of neighborhood gossip, the brothers were building elements of character, suitable to the coming republican institutions.

If the evening's talk related to the unfriendly efforts of England to lay her iron grasp upon the best interests of the colonies, or the conversation had reference to the unequal contest that would ensue if England and the colonies should face darker days, it all had the effect to warm the hearts of Rudolf and Jacob toward the colonies, and to increase the growth of genuine patriotism, which crowned their lives and honored their deaths.

These evening talks embraced almost all good subjects, and the effect of them upon the minds of these two foreigners, is but an epitome of the genuine sentiment that pervaded the early settlements, and molded the new comers into the race of strong and healthy patriots, that two generations ago peopled our land, and tends to prove how God worked with his people in America, and enabled them to attain what they sought after, and which kept building them more firmly into a patriotic people, and the country into a God-fearing and God-serving land. When the news

gathered

gathered had been related and discussed, Joseph would resume some reading, continued from a previous evening. Thus the evenings passed in these wholesome and delightful ways, the brothers thoughtful, attentively considering all that passed, and without much outward observation, appropriating all they heard in some way to their good.

Meanwhile, the mother and daughter were not idle, the former at her spinning-wheel, the latter at some bit of homely sewing that a young lady of the nineteenth century would consider far beneath her notice, though none the less essential to family happiness and concord, reserving her almost wasted energies as she does, for some " æsthetic craze," though her soul can not begin to boast of half the æstheticism, Hannah, in her humble and thankful discharge of every known duty, displayed.

Their sabbaths were spent peacefully and quietly ; Jacob often going to the "Friends" meeting with Mrs. Morse, which at this time " was the only place " of worship in Frankford, and called the ' Old " Friends' Meeting House,' the second in the state," and anon to the Dutch Reformed Church in Germantown. Rudolf realized a home feeling with the members of the latter persuasion, but was most constantly found in a place at the " Old Friends' Meeting " House," which, strange as it may seem to you, was always rather near to Hannah.

From the evenings described, and the home influ-

ences

ences brought to bear upon these young men, together
with their religious observances indicated; a sufficient
guide, it is hoped, has been given to the reader to supply, by his own imagination, the deficiencies which
would otherwise exist in this history.

CHAPTER IV.

The family circle, as has been described, continued unbroken, for some two years, during which time Rudolf and Jacob had enjoyed the kind and Christian hospitality and counsel of dear old Mrs. Morse.

In the spring of 1751 Joseph Morse married, and immediately began life in a house of his own in Philadelphia, the mother and daughter continuing in the little brown cottage, protected, as they were, by the companionship of Rudolf and his brother Jacob.

Into this little brown cottage crept unawares the visitor, whose coming is hardly announced by stir of drum or herald of trumpeter, who, nevertheless, does enter, despite bolts, bars, or locks, and having once found entrance, will not be driven thence by any known force, but chooses for his arrows whom he will; thus intruding, the unbidden visitor chose for his subjects Rudolf and Hannah, who little dreamed, as the hours rolled round into days, and from days to weeks and months, that a stronger tie was binding them than that of friendship.

Rudolf was the first to discover, and having once realized, that there was but one who could for him "make the home," did not long conceal his knowledge,

 but

but soon communicated to Hannah his new found
hopes and wishes. A willing and interested counselor
she found in her mother, who had grown to love the
two young men as her own children.

No wonder then that Hannah did not hesitate, but
entered with bright anticipations upon the future.
Dear old Mrs. Morse had changed in the past few
years, and was at this time beginning to show indications of declining health and strength.

Not much time was consumed in getting ready; a
few homely garments, made by the bride for herself,
was all that was deemed necessary, and on the 6th of
January, 1752, Rudolf and Hannah were married.

According to the marriage custom of the "Friends,"
where a member marries "out of meeting," no record
is kept of such marriage ; for, unless the member re-
pents, they are removed from all connection with the
society.

If Hannah had not so much to prepare, Rudolf had
more, for, entirely unknown to Hannah, he had purchased the large double brick house in Frankford, in
the cellar of which, six years before, he, with his
brother Jacob, had begun his labors in this country.
You will wonder how Rudolf was able to acquire so
much in so short a time. He did not work at his
trade, which was that of a wheelwright, but at whatever he could find to do, and it did not take him long
to secure plenty. Observe, too, that while he had
received in his native country a good and sufficient
education for his time and station, yet when the activ-

ity

ity and condition of the country and his own necessities required it, he could, and did turn, a willing hand to the homely, but honest, labors, that, magic like, as in the fable of old, were transformed into gold by his touch. He would, as opportunity occurred, buy land and sell it at a profit; so, by making something each time to lay aside, soon accumulated wealth. You must not forget that the grant of property to the early settlers in this locality, added to his own accumulations, brought him to the position of prosperity in which he is now observed.

To these circumstances must be also added his stability of character, which increased his influence and opportunities, and he is found revered and respected by all who knew him. His age at this time, you must remember, was but 25; yet his few years of experience had made him appear much older; his companions, friendships, and all his associations had been with those older than himself. No wonder then that his beloved wife, Hannah, is found to be six years his senior. She is consequently now in her 31st year.

Ponder this, ye young girls who rush headlong into the responsibilities of married life as a wife and mother, ere you have first learned the art of governing yourselves. Hannah's "*opportunities*," as you are pleased to call them, had been many, and of the best, but the heart had never responded until now, and in those days they married for love, and for life, not for position, wealth, and separation, if incompatability of temperament appeared; all these were weighed in the

 balance

balance before the vows were spoken, that should be sacred, "till death us do part."

To this new house and home Rudolf took Hannah, with her mother and his brother Jacob; the half of the house, intended for another family, he rented, and the little old brown cottage at the corner of a street, dear to both of them, and Hannah's legacy, when her mother died, was sold, and its place supplied with a more pretentious building. The site always suggested recollections to Rudolf and Hannah, for was it not his first home in this new country?

Dear old Mrs. Morse lived but a few weeks after they moved to the new house, when, rejoicing in a complete faith, she passed outward to her final reward.

It is an old and homely adage, yet how true, that " it takes living with people to find out what they " are ;" yes, and married people have to remember that the first and most useful lesson for them to learn is expressed in the motto, "Bear and forbear."

Something is known of Hannah's disposition, and it may be fancied that, had not the love of God controlled her, her temper would have often caused her pain, for as it was, she often did or said what she at once regretted, but was always ready and free to acknowledge her faults. In succeeding years, observe how her strength of character, and, if you choose to call it, peculiarities of disposition, present themselves from time to time in her descendants.

To turn for a moment to Rudolf's disposition, it should be said that it was marked with strong and

noble

noble peculiarities, which are never lost in succeeding
generations, coupled with a gentle yet positive manner, making his mark in the world by patience, and
quiet endeavor, not venturing largely, but adhering
steadily to a purpose.

There was a something in his character, as well as
that of Jacob, that marks all of their descendents,
not that it can be defined, yet to know the families, is
to see and know that there are strong and pronounced
peculiarities. Hannah, quick, ambitious, and aggres-
sive, would have ventured much if left to herself.

They mutually aided and balanced each other. In
appearance, Rudolf was quite tall, and rather slender,
moving slowly and deliberately.*

In closing this chapter, Rudolf and Hannah are
left in their new home happy with each other, and at
peace with the world around them, sharing the pleasures of this new hearth with the beloved brother
Jacob.

---

*What matter of regret it is that in those early days there
were not some of the modern appliances for taking pictures, that
could gladden the eyes, as well as the hearts, of the descendants.
As it was, Rudolf and Hannah never would consent to have
their portraits painted, and so no other likeness of them can be
had than that gathered from their characters and dispositions.

CHAPTER V.

" Where did you come from, baby dear ?
" Out of the every-where into the here.

" Where did you get your eyes so blue ?
" Out of the sky as I came through.

" What makes the light in them sparkle and spin ?
" Some of the starry spikes left in.

" Where did you get that little tear ?
" I found it waiting when I got here.

" What makes your forehead so smooth and high ?
" A soft hand stroked it as I went by.

" What makes your cheek like a warm white rose ?
" Something better than any one knows.

" Whence the three-cornered smiles of bliss ?
" Three angels at once gave me a kiss.

" Where did you get that pearly ear ?
" God spoke and it came out to hear.

" Where did you get those arms and hands ?
" Love made itself into crooks and bands.

" Feet, whence did you come, you darling things ?
" From the same box as the cherub's wings.

" How did they all just come to be you ?
" God thought about me and so I grew.

" But how did you come to us, you dear ?
" God thought of you and so I am here."

—GEORGE MACDONALD.

Elizabeth

Elizabeth Näf; born 8th November, 1752.

This little stranger, ushered into this strange world, opened up to Rudolf and Hannah, whole volumes of knowledge and love. Their object and aim now in life are to teach these little feet, hands, and heart, the ways of truth and right; they know that the earlier the guiding hand is extended, the easier will the child follow in after years.

In business relations Rudolf is found stepping steadily forward, with his whole life as true to honorable living as the magnet to the pole. What wonder, then, that his name is daily growing in esteem, while his worth and influence are felt far and near. To this happy home circle of three, on the 2nd of February, 1754, came another little wanderer, Barbara, named in reverence for the historical ancestor, who suffered martyrdom; and as the cares and anxieties increased, so did the blessings. Hannah found by this time that some way must be arranged that other hands might come in and help in the care of the children, or rather so help in household work, that Hannah, as a true mother should do, could devote herself entirely to their care and education. On the 3rd February, 1756, Jacob married Anna Buser, who was of German origin, and they bought a farm on the Oxford road, and settled down as energetic farmers.

Again the family circle was added to by the birth of another soul into this world of sin and trouble. This, too, was a daughter, Hannah Näf, born May 6,

1759;

1759; none the less welcome because a daughter, yet how earnestly hoped Rudolf for a son, to bear the name he so cherished, may be believed by the earnestness with which, in subsequent years, he to his grandchildren would say that he prayed " that God would " never permit the name of Näf to die out."

On the 26th day of January, 1762, Mary Näf first saw the light of day, at their home in Frankford. True had these older children been sons, they would have been called upon to defend and fight for our freedom in the years that were to follow. So when the years of turmoil are reached for this land of ours, in narrating this family history, do not think that these truely noble Swiss, and their descendants, will be wanting in courage or patriotism, for not being in the foremost ranks.

Rudolf, you will see, will be too old for active service, and his sons below the accepted age. And here turn for a moment from home life to the outside world, as it affects and is affected by Rudolf and Jacob Näf. The two brothers have been in this country about fourteen years, and have established homes and secured competence. With a home life and family of their own, and having truly adopted this as their country and dwelling place, they determined to take the step that will make them citizens indeed, and subjects of the English, who at this time claimed and received the obedience of the colonies. Therefore, "At a Supreme Court, held at Phila-" delphia, before William Allen and William Cole-

man,

" man, Esqs., judges of said court, the eleventh day
" of April, in the year of our Lord one thousand
" seven hundred and sixty three, between the hours
" of nine and twelve, in the forenoon of the same day,
" the following persons being foreigners,* did appear
" and were duly qualified and made subjects of Great
" Britain, under the following act, to wit:

"   Persons Naturalized in Penn.
"   Pennsilvania,
"   Secretary's Office.

" In pursuance of an act of parliament, made in the
" thirteenth year of the reign of his present Majesty,
" King George the Second, Entitled An Act for nat-
" uralizing such foreign Protestants and others therein
" mentioned as are settled or shall settle in any of His
" Majesty's colonies in America.†

" The following persons being foreigners, and hav-
" ing inhabited and resided the space of seven (7)years
" and upwards in His Majesty's Colonies in America,
" and not having been absent out of some of the said
" colonies for a longer space than two (2) months at
" any one time during the said seven (7) years, and
" having produced to the said court certificates of
" their having taken the sacrament of the Lord's Sup-
" per in some Protestant or Reformed Congregation in
" this Province within three (3) months before the
" said court took and subscribed the oaths, and did

---

* Pennsylvania Archives, II series, vol. 2, page. 442.
† Pennsylvania Archives, II series, vol. 2, page 347.

                                    make

" make and repeat the Declaration prescribed by the
" said Act to entitle them to the benefit thereof, and
" thereby become natural-born subjects of Great Brit-
" ain, as the same is certified into this office by the
" judges of the said court, viz: William Allen and
" William Coleman, Esqs., judges of the said court.*

" Jurors' Names.	Philadelphia County, Township.	Sacrament, taken when.
" Rudolph Neff.	Northern Liberties.	April 8, 1763.
" Jacob Neff.	Oxford,	April, 8, 1763." *

Thus is observed the close and loving intercourse between the brothers, continuing even in this act.

The reader will notice, as before, that though the younger, Rudolf took the lead. A still more important fact is here to be noted, and one that the descendants have perpetuated, which is the changing of the spelling of the name—as originally signed by the brothers, it will be remembered it was Näf; and, though in its pronunciation it is like the Neff of later years, yet it denotes a change, and subsequent chapters may prove, that the brothers, Rudolf and Jacob Näf, were of a different family in Switzerland, from that of others bearing the name of Neff in this country, who, in subsequent years, become Neff, having spelled their name variously as Nelf, Nclff, Nouf, Nuff, Noef, etc.†

---

*Pennsylvania Archives, II series, vol. 2, pages 442 and 444, and certified copy from the Secretary of the Commonwealth of Penn., in the hands of the compiler.

†Rupp's collections of 30,000 names of immigrants in Pennsylvania.

                    Observe,

Observe, also, that Rudolf is no longer Rudolf, but Rudolph. From this being the first record of the change in the name from Näf to Neff, it may be assumed that Rudolph and Jacob only now fully adopted it. The brothers will not, for this change, lose their identity; for character, worth, and perseverance prove the man, and not the name only. To return to the home circle of Rudolph and Hannah, it should be asked if sons have been spoken of? Yes, sons—Pause!

For on the 15th day of February, 1764, a worthy son, of a most noble father and vigorous, active, and intelligent mother—Peter Neff—came to rejoice the hearts of these parents—a future honor to his father's name, and who, from the first moment it was possible, became his constant companion. Not long after Peter's birth, Johannes was born, on the 22d September, 1766, a bright light to his parents that was soon extinguished, as he died on the 6th July of the following year, 1767. Once more the home circle is added to in the birth of Samuel, on the 27th June, 1768, and who, as the youngest, was the great object of interest and solicitude of his mother. His physical development was remarkably handsome, accompanied with an agreeable, bright manner.

The year 1770 is of particular importance, as regards Rudolph in his relation to church and people.

A few facts centering about this time and circumstance have a peculiar interest, and will, it is hoped, be valued by the reader.

Before closing this chapter, and resuming the his-

tory

tory of the descendants of Rudolph through the line
of Peter, his son—in chapter 8th—the number of the
descendants in 1784 are found to be as follows:

Rudolph Neff,   Hannah Neff,
In his 57th year.   In her 63rd year.

Their children:

Elizabeth Neff,*
Barbara Neff,†
Hannah Neff,‡
Mary Neff,§
Peter Neff,
Johannes Neff—Deceased.
Samuel Neff.

* Married Adam Baker.
† Married Adam Stricker.
‡ Married Phillip Buckius.
§ Married John H. Worrell.

CHAPTER VI.

Soon after Rudolph's marriage with Hannah, he became a thoroughly converted man, though his life before had never been evil. The form of religion that he adopted, was that of the Dutch Reformed Church, the faith of which was the same that had caused the brothers' ancestors to suffer persecution, and which continued its milder influence even on the young men, suggesting their departure from their native home. Jacob also united with the same church, and they all held their membership in the church of that persuasion in Germantown.

To this town and church, " The Market Square " Church," it was customary for their children to go to be catechised, as there was no church in Frankford, until 1770, when, owing largely to the influence and energy of Rudolph and Jacob, a plain little structure was erected and dedicated to Almighty God.

You can best understand the energetic spirit of Rudolph by quotations from " One Hundred Years of the " Presbyterian Church of Frankford," by Dr. Thomas Murphy, which is a little volume printed in 1872, of the centennial services in 1870. " Its founders were " most of them Swiss from the city of Basle. A few " of them were of the original German settlers of Ger-

mantown

The Frankford Church, of 1770, as enlarged
in 1810.

" mautown and all this region. They therefore com-
" menced it as a German Calvinist or German Re-
" formed Church, with all its services and all its
" records in the German language.

" The only important document we have remaining
" to us of the first period, the period of thirty-two
" years, the period during which the church con-
" tinued German Reformed, is a sort of dedicatory
" record. It is in German.

In order that its very spirit may remain,"* the following is a copy of the same in the German, also a transla-
tion ; both taken from the original document in the records of the church at Frankford. For which privilege
thanks are due to the Rev. Dr. Murphy, and to the party
who so generously copied and translated the same.

" Im Namen der hochgelobter dreifalltigkeit. Amen.

" Nachdem es dem Allmachtigen und allein weiszen
" Gott durch seine göttliche vorsehung gefallen hat.

"   Heinrich Rohrer, sen.,

"   Rudolph Neff,

"   Jacob Neff,

"   Sirach Schudy, und

"   Georg. Carster, sen.

" durch seinen heiligen Geist dahin zu leiten. Ihm zu
" seines Nahmens Verherrlichung ein Hauss zu bauen.
" So haben sich die ebengemalde mit mehrenen ihren
" guten Freundem zur besern Ausfahrung ihres guten
" Vorhabens besprochen zu welchen dann auf sobald

---

* The Presbyterian Church of Frankford, page 50.

                                        beitratten

" beitratten und ihre Hand—leistung in allen Stüden
" auf des fleiszigste zu geben versprochen:
"   Freidrich Carster,
"   Rudolph Mauer,
"   Jacob Zebcly, und
"   Jacob Meyer.
" Der Anfangs von sammtlich diesen Gleidern ward
" in Jahr, 1769, im Mouat Januar mit Kaufung eines
" Platzes zu einer Begrabnisz-Statte gemacht, darnach
" aber werde auf dem nehmlichen Begrabnisz—Platz
" durch Beistand des Allerhochsten, und mit Hulfe wil-
" ler Freunde und Gömer, deren fast jeder benahmt zu
" finden in dem Beilaags Buch No. 1, und denen wir
" und unsere Nachkomman jedenzeit den Verbindlich
" Schuldig sten dank beibehalten werden in Aprill
" Monath des 1770 sten Jahres diese Kirche zu bauen
" angefangen man darf wohl sagen, dasz die Fortsets
" zung dieses Hauses auf eine erwunschte Art unter
" göttlichen Siegen eines eintrachtigen Verstandnus-
" zes, eines friedsamen und unermudeten Eifers auch
" einer gleichmusegin Einigkeit ist beschleuniget
" worden. So dasz schon den 4th May gleichen Jahres,
" diese Stella durch eine Predigt von Herrn Fehring
" damahligen Pfarrer dem Herrm geheiliget, und so
" dam den machten 11th Navember durch ebengem-
" alde Herrn Fehring wurtlich eingesegnet wurde,
" diese Kirche ist nicht weniger vom allen Schulden
" fast gatzlich frei, wie wir hier nachst in diesem
" Kirchen Protocoll sehen und wie deszen Beitag, vor
" Pasten sammt uber die mancherlei, sowohl von Ru-
      · 72   dolph

" dolph Neff als Freidrich Carster empfangene Gel-
" der, gegoben und uber die gethane Auszahlungen
" erfahlene Quittungen und Scheine nebst denen von
" unserer Trusteece empfangenen General Scheine das
" mehrere zeigen.

" So und dermaszen dasz wir nicht haben ungehen
" kommen allen unsern Nochkomman und denen es
" zu wiszen nothigen ist, einen ausfuhrlichen Bericht
" zur Legitimation, einem jeder zum Andenken hie-
" mit zurudzulaszen. Habt fleiszig Acht unsere Noch-
" folger, seid warden und besorgt dieses Haus zu
" pflantzen und die Gemeine und Versammlung je
" langer je mehr zu vermehren und zu verweiten und
" selbst die Unterhaltung dieses Baues lasset euch in
" allen wegen angelegen sein.

" Wir wunschen darum Jerusalem Gluck machet die
" Thore weit und die Thore sehr hoch dasz der Herr
" Zebaoth, der Herr stark und machtig, der Herr, der
" König, dir Ehre ein ziehe. Num der Herr allmachti-
" ger Gott, Schopfer Himmels und der Erden, wir
" empfehlen dir dieses Hausz welches wir auf deinen
" allerheiligsten Nahmen und zur Verherrlichung de-
" nies Nahmen's erbauet haben, in deinen gnädigen
" Schutz und Schirm samt denen die darinnen wohen :
" Zerstore alle falschen Rathschläge die wie der dein
" Wort und Kirche er dacht werden. Gieb jetz, und
" alle zeit Gnaden, Segen, Frieden und Einig keit,
" dir sei lob und Dank, Ruhm, Ehr, und Preis in
" Ewigkeit. Amen."

73   " In

"In the name of the Holy Trinity, Amen."

"Whereas, it has pleased the almighty and all-wise
" God by his providence to inspire by His Holy Spirit
" the following persons,
"   Heinrich Rohrer, sen.,
"   Rudolph Neff,
"   Jacob Neff,
"   Sirach Schudy, and
"   George Carster, sen.,
" To build a house to him for the glorification of his
" name, so the above named persons have consulted
" with many of their good friends for the better car-
" rying out of their good intentions, to which the fol-
" lowing persons, viz :
"   Fredrich Carster,
"   Rudolph Mauer,
"   Jacob Zebely, and
"   Jacob Meyer,
" have acceded and have promised to give their assist-
" ance at all times most diligently.

" The beginning was made by these persons in Jan-
" uary, 1769, by the purchase of a piece of ground for
" a cemetery ; but after that this church was begun to
" be built, in April, 1770, upon the aforementioned
" burial ground, through the assistance of the Most
" High and with the help of willing friends and well-
" wishers, the name of each one of whom can be
" found in the minute book, No. 1, and to whom we
" and our descendants will preserve, at all times as in
" duty bound, the sincerest thanks.

                                        "One

" One may well say that the progress of this house
" has been carried forward, in a desirable manner,
" under God's blessing, through an harmonious under-
" standing, a peaceful and untiring zeal, and an equally
" unimpaired harmony. So that on the 4th of May,
" of the same year, this place was hallowed to the
" Lord by a sermon of Rev. Fehring, the pastor at
" that time, and then the following 11th of Novem-
" ber it was consecrated by the same pastor.

" This church is not entirely free from all debt; as
" we lately saw in the Church Minutes, these debts
" cover all items, as well as the money received of
" Rudolph Neff and Fredrich Carster, and the receipts
" for payments made, together with the general re-
" ceipts of our trustees, show still more.

" Therefore, we could not help handing over to our
" successors, who will know nothing about this, here-
" with a complete account as proof, to keep it in the
" remembrance of every one.

" Let our successors be diligent, and let them have
" a care to the keeping of the house, and for the en-
" larging and widening of the congregation, employ
" yourselves in the maintenance of the house in every
" way.

" We wish you success, Oh, Jerusalem. 'Lift up
" your heads, oh, ye gates, and be ye lifted up, ye
" everlasting doors, and the King of Glory shall come
" in.'

" Now, the Lord, Almighty Creator of Heaven and
" Earth, we commend to Thee this house which we
75have

" have built to Your All Holy name and to the glorifi-
" cation of Your name to Your gracious defense and
" protection, together with those who dwell therein;
" destroy all false doctrines with which we would
" cover Your word and Church.

" Give now and forever Grace, Blessing, Peace, and
" Harmony, and to You be Praise, Thanks, Honor,
" Esteem, and Glory forever.   Amen."

" This devout and very important document is writ-
" ten in a beautiful hand, at the beginning of what
" was intended for a Book of Records; but, alas, ex-
" cepting some accounts, it is the last record made for
" thirty-two years, whilst the church was German Re-
" formed.

" We must pause to look at the honored names with
" which this church originated :

" George Castor, Rudolph Neff, Henry Rohrer,
" Sirach Schudy. Excepting the last, their descend-
" ants are still with us. The first is grandfather of
" another George Castor, to whom the church is more
" indebted than to any other man.

" And with them were other names not to be for-
" gotten, some of whose descendants are still promi-
" nent in the church—Jacob Myer (now Myers), Ru-
" dolph Mowrer, Jacob Zebley, and Frederick Carster
" (now Castor), son of George. Their names must
" never be forgotten while this church stands. It is
" believed that all these had either come from Switz-
" erland or were of Swiss descent. We must also put
" on record the names of some others of those who,

                                                    by

" by their contributions, helped to erect the original
" edifice. Among them we find Samuel Neswinger,
" Rudolph Shutz, Leonard Froelich, Yost Myers,
" Jacob Madeira, Jacob Schmid, Jacob May, David
" Bleuh, Christopher Bender, Frederick Scheibly,
" George Wilkins, Edward Steils, . . . and a
" long array of other names, which we must omit.
" All these helped the good work.

" It may be curious to learn the dimensions and the
" cost of the original building (it being enlarged in
" 1810). The record of these is found in fragments
" of the old minutes, still remaining.

" The church edifice, as it was first erected, was
" only forty feet wide and thirty feet long. That
" made it just about one-fourth as large on the floor as
" this building in which we are assembled. Even the
" specific cost of the various articles of its construc-
" tion is preserved.

"As a curiosity, I will name it here :

	£	s.	d.
" The stone, lime, sand, hair, and hauling,	133	2	10
" Boards, planks, shingles, and other lumber,	109	6	3
" Paint, oil, glass, and painting,	27	16	8
" Mason work and plastering,	64	16	0
" Carpenter and cabinet work,	97	16	9
" Blacksmith work, and other incidentals,	28	17	5
" Whole cost of building, when finished,	461	15	11

" or, about two thousand, four hundred dollars ($2,400).

" For thirty-two years after its commencement, or
" until 1802, we know but very little, indeed, of the

                                        history

" history of the church. There were no records kept;
" or, if they were, they are lost.

"One or two incidents loom up distinctly in the
" darkness. One is peculiarly interesting.

"During the Revolutionary War, after the battle of
" Trenton, some of the prisoners captured in that en-
" gagement were brought and for a time imprisoned
" in the old building. Of this fact there is no doubt.
" We were first made acquainted with it by traditions
" lodging in the memory of the aged. But, besides
" this, the Rev. D. S. Miller, D.D., of the Episcopal
" Church, in this place, has kindly communicated the
" remarkable fact of his having examined a journal,
" found lately in Hesse Cassel, Germany, which had
" been written by a Hessian officer who was in the
" battle of Trenton, and was amongst the captured,
" and states that they were imprisoned for a time in a
" church of a little village called Frankford, above
" Philadelphia.

"Another interesting fact of that early day was that
" the old Lutheran Church, on the corner of Church
" and Adams streets, was built by a few of the older
" Germans who broke off from this church because
" the younger members insisted on having occasional
" services in the English language.

"But who were the ministers of this church during
" that first period of thirty-two years?

" Tradition gave us the first clue.

"Old people told us that they had heard of the
" preachers in this church coming from Germantown.

                                   They

" They recollected to have heard the names of Helf-
" fenstein and Hermann among these preachers. They
" told us of their fathers and mothers going to Ger-
" mantown to be catechised.

" This sent us to examine the records of the Mar-
" ket Square Church, the old German Reformed
" Church, of Germantown. We found their records to
" be mere registers of baptism, deaths, and marriages.

" But if their preachers officiated at Frankford, we
" ought to find Frankford names among those bap-
" tisms and marriages. There we found the names of
" Neffs and Mowrers and Zebleys and Myers and Froe-
" lighs. This seemed to make the probability very
" strong. But another fact reduced it almost to a
" certainty. The minister who dedicated our old
" church building was the Rev. Mr. Foehring. Then,
" as the thirty-two years of darkness are broken in
" upon by the return of our records, in 1802, we find
" a minute of a settlement made with the Rev. Wm.
" Runkle for his pastoral services. But in the Ger-
" mantown registers we find that the pastor of that
" church in 1770 was the Rev. Christian Frederick
" Foehring, and its pastor in 1802 was the Rev. Wm.
" Runkle. Now, if the pastors of that church, at the
" beginning and at the end of the period, preached
" here, and if we have the other corroborative evi-
" dence already named, the conclusion is tolerably cer-
" tain that the supplies for this church during all that
" period came from that source. This theory was after-
" wards confirmed when we discovered several works

                                        pertaining

" pertaining to the early ministers of the Dutch and
" German Reformed Churches in this country : among
" them ' The Fathers of the Reformed Church,' by the
" Rev. H. Harbaugh, and 'A Manual of the Reformed
" Church in America,' by the Rev. Edward T. Cor-
" wan. Mr. Foehring supplied this church only a
" short period—probably from one to two years.
" This church subsequently became Presbyterian.
" At first there were no pews in the church.
" For thirty-seven years there was nothing but
" benches. But in the year 1807, by great exertion,
" as the church was still very weak, the benches were
" removed, pews erected, and a new roof put upon the
" building. This year, 1807, was a very important
" one in the history of the church for the event just
" stated, and others. It was in this year that it form-
" ally dropped its connection with the German Re-
" formed body and became connected with the Pres-
" byterian. The record of this event is tolerably full.
" On the 18th of April, Mr. George Castor was ap-
" pointed to visit the Presbytery of Philadelphia and
" solicit from it a supply of ministers for the pulpit.
" In consequence of his visit and statements, by ad-
" journment, Presbytery met in this church for the
" first time on the 8th of December, 1807. This was
" a memorable meeting in our annals, and we must
" preserve the names of those who composed it ; they
" are prominent in the history of Presbyterianism.
" They were the Rev. Messrs. William Tennant,
" Green, Archibald Alexander, Janeway, Latta, and

                                                    Potts.

" Potts. Before this meeting was laid the petition of
" the German Reformed Congregation of Frankford
" composed of about thirty families. The peti-
" tion asked that the congregation be taken under
" care of Presbytery, and pledged that they should be
" governed by the rules of the Presbyterian Church.

" Presbytery being assured that these families were
" nearly all that composed the congregation and that
" they were then in no other ecclesiastical connection,
" agreed to take them under its care, and make ar-
" rangements for furnishing them supplies. This was
" in the close of the year 1807 when the ecclesiastical
" change was made. In the next year the transfer to
" the Presbyterian connection was legalized by an act
" of incorporation from the state. In this article the
" reasons given for the change of connection are these :

" 1st. There were not enough members in the old
" connection to fill the places of trust required by law.

" 2d. The shades of difference between the princi-
" ples of the German Reformed Church and those of
" the Presbyterians of the United States were unim-
" portant.

" 3d. The ministers of the gospel could be maintained
" only in connection with the Presbyterian Church.

" To this they subscribed with one mind and left us
" their names, forty-six in number. After this, one
" of the first acts of the church in its new connection
" was the purchase, in the same year (1808), of the old
" Frankford Academy at the price of two thousand
" dollars. This the church kept in operation for a

                                    great

" great many years afterwards. Frankford and the
" vicinity were indebted to it as their principal place
" of learning for a long time.

" The third period of our church's history begins
" on the 18th of June, 1809, when the Rev. John W.
" Doak was installed its pastor, and extends twenty-
" two years to the fall, 1831, when the pastorate of
" the Rev. Thomas J. Biggs closed.

" The outline of the history in that time is this:
" The pastorate of the Rev. John W. Doak lasted
" seven years, commencing June the 18th, 1809, and
" closing September 1st, 1816. Then the church for
" two years had no stated pastor. On November the
" 10th, 1818, the Rev. Thomas J. Biggs was installed
" pastor, and he remained thirteen years, until the
" fall of 1831.

" The Sabbath school of the church was commenced
" in the spring of 1815. It was projected by Mr.
" George Castor. By his persuasion Mrs. Martha
" Dungan commenced the school in the month of
" April of that year. Its first session was held by the
" stove in the church, but afterwards in the gallery.
" Mrs. Dungan had associated with her Mrs. Patter-
" son*—the only other teacher. The scholars were
" for a time all girls—at first only seven in number.

" Of the Rev. Thomas J. Biggs, whose pastorate here
" was longer than any other previous to the present,
" we happily have enough information to enable us to
" appreciate the high excellency of his character and

____

*This Mrs. Patterson was Hannah Neff.

                                  ministry.

" ministry. He was born in this city November 29, 1787,
" became a member of the Old Pine Street Church in
" 1807, when the Rev. Dr. Archibald Alexandre was
" its pastor; graduated at Princeton College in 1815,
" some of his classmates being Drs. Daniel Baker,
" Charles Hodge, S. C. Henry, and Bishop John
" Johns; was for a time tutor in Princeton College;
" studied at Princeton Theological Seminary, and was
" ordained by the Presbytery of Philadelphia, and be-
" came pastor of this church in 1818.

" After remaining here thirteen years he accepted a
" professorship in Lane Theological Seminary, at Cin-
" cinnati.   That office he held for seven years, and be-
" came President of Cincinnati College in 1839.   In
" that position he continued for six years, and for
" three years more was President of Woodward Col-
" lege in Cincinnati.   In 1852 he was installed pastor
" of the Fifth Church of that city, and after four
" years resigned that charge.   From that time he
" ceased from active service.   In 1864, at the age of
" seventy-seven, he fell asleep in Jesus.   Of this good
" man the memory is most fragrant with all those who
" remember him as pastor of this church.   None
" ever speak of him in other words than those of ven-
" eration and love.   There are those still with us who
" call him blessed for having been instrumental in
" bringing them into the kingdom.   The best tribute
" to him I have seen is that of Bishop McIlvaine
" of the Episcopal Church in Ohio. It was spoken
" at his funeral:

                                            " ' I have

"'I have known the deceased for fifty years. I entered
" the college of New Jersey in 1814. The first time I saw
" him was when he came forward in the chapel to lead the
" singing, which he was accustomed to do. Dr. Green was
" then president of the college. The students were generally
" irreligious, and opposed and persecuted the few who pro-
" fessed religion. The latter, only twelve or thirteen in num-
" ber, one of whom was young Biggs, were very faithful.
" They were accustomed to meet every evening at nine
" o'clock for prayer in the room of one of their number, and
" in these meetings they prayed earnestly for a revival of re-
" ligion in the college. Prior to this there had never been a
" revival of religion in the college, and it required great
" faith to expect it. At length, in answer to prayer, the
" Spirit of God was poured out, so that in two or three days
" the largest room in the college was filled with the pre-
" viously irreligious, asking for the prayers of the pious.
" The twelve or thirteen were now fully occupied in minister-
" ing to their fellow-students. The first prayer meeting I
" ever attended was in the room of young Biggs and Daniel
" Baker. Many were brought into the kingdom in connection
" with this revival. Among the rest were Dr. Armstrong,
" late Secretary of the American Board of Foreign Missions,
" and Dr. Hodge, who had previously seemed to be almost a
" Christian. Since Dr. Biggs came to the West in 1832
" until his death, our acquaintance was intimate. We did
" not know each other as Episcopalian or Presbyterian. A
" beautiful trait in his character was the largeness of his
" Christian regards. He was beautiful too in his faith, and
" the joyfulness of his hope. He never seemed to see God
" in the pillar of cloud, but always in the pillar of light.
" Christ was so near to him that he felt no doubts. Great

                                              lovingness

" lovingness of mind and heart characterized him beyond what
" is usual. It beamed from his countenance, it spoke from
" his voice, and was expressed in his whole manner. He
" *must* have been useful, as he was."

" These twenty-two years were a period of progress
" in the church. Especially during the ministry of
" Mr. Biggs many were added to the kingdom of
" Christ, most of whom have gone with their beloved
" pastor to the blessed congregation above. The
" church became then better established, and all her
" ordinances prepared for the work of the generations
" that were to succeed."*

The old church records of those early days which
were viewed with interest, regarding the building of
the first edifice, are all written in German, and the
name of Rudolph is seen on nearly every page—on
many more than once. It would seem that he had
been a member of an auditing committee, to pass upon
all matters relative to the building of the church and
its interests, as well as a donator to this worthy object.

The quotations and references in regard to the
church have progressed a little too far for the narrative, and a return must be made to Rudolph and his
surroundings.

It has been observed that Rudolph possessed much
of the quiet, slow disposition of the German character, which aroused was equal to all emergencies.

---

* From " The Presbyterian Church of Frankford," by Rev.
Thos. Murphy, pp. 50, 56, 63, 68, 71, 75, 77, 80.

                                    The

The previous part of this history of the ancestors reveals the fact that the Neffs in their native land were noted warriors.

It will not be surprising to find an iron spirit in each and all of the descendants. To the descendants of Rudolph in this country of activity and quickness of thought will be transmitted his peculiarities, as a native of Switzerland, coupled with the vivacity and determination of Hannah.

A digression here may be pardonable to question, whether it is ever found even in the descendants of pure Germans, their children and grandchildren in our country continuing their slow peculiarities of thought and action? If not, may it not be concluded, that the atmosphere breathed, and the life it produces, with the geographical peculiarities, have largely to do with the men produced.

At this particular time of our national history, and Rudolph's own experience, his quiet, patient waiting resulted in the greatest good: not being in a hurry to accomplish his ends, he would, after plans carefully matured and determined upon, wait patiently for their accomplishment. These plans were often the result, in the first place, of Hannah's quick perceptive suggestions. In this way he added largely to his wealth, and was soon able to give up active labors, and engage in many benevolent and philanthropic schemes; always, however, dealing heavily in real estate; and a common saying was, that " all lands he handled turned out well."

As

As these chronicles will henceforth be principally devoted to the descendants of Rudolph Neff through the line of Peter Neff, the succeeding chapter will be devoted to giving, in brief, an account of Jacob Neff, brother of Rudolph, and also of Samuel Neff, brother of Peter Neff, and son of Rudolph; together with a short account of some of the other families of Neff now in this country, before finally leaving them, trusting that down to the latest day they may ever be found venerated and esteemed.

CHAPTER VII.

The purpose of this chapter is to assist the reader
in the history of the Neffs in general in this country.

The names of Neiff, Näff, Naef, Noef, Näf, and
Naff occur frequently in the cantons of Switzerland,
especially in the Protestant cantons.

Prior to 1749, when Rudolf and Jacob Näf arrived
in this country, many Swiss, bearing the name of
Neiff, Naef, Neyf, Nef, and Neff, are recorded as having landed in this country.* They subsequently all
became Neff; hence the confusion arising regarding
relationship and descent. To quote also from a letter
from Canton Zurich, it would appear that the same
difference of spelling the name, which is seen even
there, does not always denote a marked family distinction, but is rather the result of location. Says
the writer: "The different ways of writing Näf,
" Näff, Neff, are, to my mind, without significance ;
" nearly the same change has taken place here also ;
" true Näf is usually written, and the old records have
" this spelling only."†

---

*See Rupp's " 30,000 names of Immigrants in Pennsylvania."

† Letter of Rev. Arnold Näf, of Ruschlikon, Canton Zurich,
dated July 17, 1883.

 Relative

Relative to the immigrations of the Swiss, particularly those bearing the name of Neff in some form, a few interesting extracts will be made, bearing more particularly upon the three of the name Neiff, viz: Francis Neiff, Heinrich Neiff, and Johann Heinrich Neiff, who settled in Lancaster County, Penn., prior to 1715.

"At this critical juncture [1683], the Mennonites
" were persecuted in Switzerland and driven into
" various countries—some to Alsace, above Strasburg,
" others to Holland, etc.—where they lived simple and
" exemplary lives—in the villages as farmers, in the
" towns by trades—free from the charge of any gross
" immoralities, and professing the most pure and sim-
" ple principles, which they exemplified in a holy con-
" versation. Some of those about Strasburg, with
" other High and Low Germans, transported them-
" selves about the year 1683, by the encouragement of
" William Penn, to Pennsylvania and settled princi-
" pally at Germantown: the greater part of whom
" were naturalized in 1709. The French army hav-
" ing crossed the Rhine, the distressed Palatines, per-
" secuted by their heartless Prince, plundered by a for-
" eign enemy, fled to escape from death, and about six
" thousand of them, for protection to England, in con-
" sequence of encouragement they had received from
" Queen Anne, by proclamation in 1708. Among
" these was a number to be mentioned in the sequel
" of our narrative.

" Many also had, prior to the issuing of Anne's proc-

lamation,

" lamation, determined to seek refuge in America.
" The Canton of Berne in Switzerland had employed
" Christopher de Graffenreid and Louis Mitchel,
" or Michelle, as pioneers, with instructions to search
" for vacant lands in Pennsylvania, Virginia, or Caro-
" lina.

" One of these, Michelle, a Swiss miner, had been
" in America prior to 1704 or 1705, traversing the
" country to seek out 'a convenient tract to settle a
" colony of their people on.'

" Many of the ancestors of those who first settled in
" this county [Lancaster, Penn.], whose lineal de-
" scendants still possess the lands purchased and im-
" proved by them, were beheaded, some beaten with
" many stripes, others incarcerated, and some banished
" from Switzerland. Of those who suffered, and who
" might be mentioned, were Hans Landis, at Zurich,
" in Switzerland, Hans Miller, Hans Jacob Hess, Ru-
" dolph Bachman, Ulrich Miller, Oswald Landis,
" Fanny Landis, Barbara Neff,* Hans Meylin, and
" two of his sons—all these suffered between 1638 and
" 1643. Those who emigrated to Pennsylvania had
" fled from the Cantons of Zurich, Berne, Shaffhausen,
" Switzerland, to Alsace, above Strasburg, where
" they remained for some time, thence they came to
" the province of Pennsylvania."

Of Francis Neiff, it is recorded, as follows:

---

* This is undoubtedly the ancestor whose suffering martyrdom
has been a tradition in the family.

                                                    "And

"And Francis Neiff took up lands on the west
" branch of the little Conestoga prior to 1715.

"Not to weary the reader with general details of
" individual settlers, we shall present a public docu-
" ment, possessing more than ordinary interest to the
" numerous descendants of those whose names are
" recorded in it. . . . . It is an act passed Anno
" Regni Georgii II., Regis Magnae Britanniae, Fran-
" ciae et Hiberniae tertio October 14, 1729:

" Whereas, By encouragement given by the Hon-
" orable William Penn, Esq., late Proprietary and
" Governor of the province of Pennsylvania, and by
" permission of his Majesty, King George the First,
" of blessed memory, and his predecessors, Kings and
" Queens of England, etc., divers Protestants, who
" were subjects to the Emperor of *Germany*, a Prince
" in amity with the Crown of Great Britain, trans-
" ported themselves and estates into the province of
" Pennsylvania between the years *one thousand seven
" hundred* and *one thousand seven hundred and eighteen :*
" and since they came hither have contributed very
" much to the enlargement of the British Empire, and
" to the raising and improving sundry commodities
" fit for the markets of Europe, *and have always
" behaved themselves religiously and peaceably*, and have
" paid a due regard and obedience to the laws and
" government of this province: *And, whereas,* many
" of said persons, to-wit, Martin Mrylin, Hans Graaf,
" and others, all of Lancaster County in the said prov-
" inces, in demonstration of their affection and zeal for

91   his

" his present Majesty's person and Government, quali-
" fied themselves by taking the qualification and sub-
" scribing the declaration directed to be taken and
" subscribed by the several Acts of Parliament made
" for the security of His Majesty's person and Govern-
" ment, and for preventing the dangers which may
" happen by Popish Recusants, etc., and thereupon
" have humbly signified to the Governor and Repre-
" sentatives of the freemen of this province, in Gen-
" eral Assembly, that they have purchased and do
" hold lands of the proprietary and others, His
" Majesty's subjects within this province, and have
" likewise represented their great desire of being made
" partakers of those privileges which the natural born
" subjects of Great Britain do enjoy within this prov-
" ince ; and it being just and reasonable that those
" persons who have *bona fide* purchased lands and who
" have given such testimony of their affection whatso-
" ever, as any of His Majesty's natural born subjects
" of this province can do or ought to enjoy by virtue
" of their being His Majesty's natural born subjects of
" His Majesty's said province of Pennsylvania, and
" obedience to the Crown of Great Britain, should as
" well be secured in the enjoyment of their estates as
" encouraged in their laudable affection and zeal for
" the English Constitution.

" *Be it enacted by the Hon. Patrick Gordon, Esq.,* Lieut.
" Governor of the province of Pennsylvania, etc., by
" and with the advice and consent of the freemen of the
" said province in General Assembly met, and by the

 authority

" authority of the same, that Martin Meylin, Hans
" Graaf, etc., Francis Neiff,* Francis Neiff, Jr., etc.,
" Henry Neiff, etc., John Henry Neiff,† John Henry
" Neiff, Jr., etc. [the names are numerous], all of Lan-
" caster County, be and shall be to all intents and
" purposes deemed, taken and esteemed His Majesty's

" * Francis Neff, his sons Francis, Jr., Henry and Daniel, and
" the sons of Daniel, namely: Henry and Daniel, grandsons of
" Francis, the elder, were all natives of Switzerland. On account
" of religious persecutions, being Mennonites, they fled from their
" Vaterland to Alsace, thence they emigrated to America and
" settled at a very early date on a small stream, Neff's run, which
" empties into the west branch of the Little Conestoga, where the
" great ancestor took up a large tract of land, and which is still
" owned by some of the lineal descendants of the male and female
" issue. As it may be interesting to the numerous descendents of
" one of the first families in this part of the country, we insert a
" brief genealogy of Francis Neff's progeny as furnished us *verbally*
" by *Mrs. Magdalen Sehner*, aged 79, the great granddaughter of
" Francis, the elder, and granddaughter of Daniel Neff, who had
" four sons and two daughters, viz.: Henry, Daniel, John, Jacob,
" the grandfather of Jacob K. Neff, M.D., of Lancaster; Barbara,
" who intermarried with Musselman, and Ann married to Isaac
" Kauffman; Henry, the oldest son of Daniel Neff, married a Miss
" Oberholtzer, their children were John, Daniel, David, Jacob,
" Henry, and one daughter, Mrs. Keller, Dr. John Eberli's grand-
" mother.
" The original homestead is now principally owned by Gott-lieb
" Sehner and Jacob Neff. We seek for the descendants of Francis
" Neff in the male lineage, the numerous Neffs in Lancaster and
" Huntingdon County, Pennsylvania, and in Virginia. In the
" female, the name of Musselman, Kauffman, Miller, Mayer,
" Henneberger, Schwar, Sehner, Ruth, Cassil, Florey, *Keller*,
" *Eberle*,—the two last are noticed in the sequel—Bear, Brandt,
" Shelly, Bowman, and others, principally in this county.

" † John Henry Neff, known as the 'Old Doctor,' a brother
" of Francis Neff named. He was undoubtedly the first regularly
" bred physician in Lancaster County. Who has not heard of

93   natural

" natural born subjects of this province of Pennsyl-
" vania, as if they and each of them had been born
" within the said province; and shall and may, and
" every one of them shall and may within this prov-
" ince take, receive, enjoy, and be entitled to all rights,
" privileges and advantages of natural born subjects
" as fully, to all intents and constructions and purposes
" whatsoever, as any of His Majesty's natural born
" subjects of this province can, do, or ought to enjoy
" by virtue of their being His Majesty's natural born
" subjects of His Majesty's said province of Pennsyl-
" vania." *

We also find record of the naturalization of Henry
Neaf, Jr., in Lancaster County.† Out of all these
facts it is interesting to gather that the name has ever
been one commanding respect.

" Doctor Hans Heinrich Neff? So well was Dr. Neff known, that
" when the boundaries of townships were fixed upon, June 9th,
" 1729, one of the lines of Manheim Township is thus defined:
" ' Thence down the said creek to the *Old Doctor's Ford.*' ' Hans
" Henry Neff, Doctor of Physic, had taken up land on the Cones-
" toga, a few miles from the present site of Lancaster city. Among
" his descendants are, besides the Neffs, Millers, Tchantzs, Ken-
" digs, Weavers, Bears, and others. The Neffs were of those " who
" *many years* since came into this province under a particular
" agreement with the late Honorable Proprietor, William Penn,
" at London, and had regularly taken up lands under him. 'And
" who it appears to me,' said Gov. Gordon, January 13th, 1729, 'by
" good information, that they have hitherto behaved themselves
" well, and *have generally so good a character for honesty and industry as*
" *deserves the esteem of this Government and a mark of regard for them.*' "

* History of Lancaster County. Pages 69, 70, 71, 72, 119, 121
to 128.

† History of Lancaster County. Page 271.

                                The

The relationship if any of these Neiffs of Lancaster County, to the subjects of this narrative, Rudolph and Jacob Näf, will strike the reader as very remote, and one that can only be claimed prior to the coming of the ancestors to America.

A little paragraph which is here quoted, may serve as an insight into the character and success of these worthy Mennonites.

" Holding peace principles, and taking very little if
" any part in the affairs of government, they taught
" their young men that the first great duty of life was
" for each man *to mind his own business.* Practicing
" upon this maxim they encouraged industry by their
" own examples, and discouraged ambition by a rep-
" resentation of the evils necessarily following in its
" train. Devoting themselves and their families to
" religion thy labored and were happy." *

This sentiment must have been embodied and taught by those of the German Reformed belief, as well as the Mennonites, for it is so truly a characteristic of the Neff family " to attend to their own business," which they equally expect to find those doing with whom they are brought in contact. As a consequence, when others do take it upon themselves to attend to other business than their own, and that other, being any thing relating to a Neff; they usually find that they have aroused a spirit of defensive resentment that will not hesitate at obstacles that would baffle others not inheriting these traits.

------

* History of Lancaster County.   Pages 438 and 439.

                                    From

From the extracts made, the reader will observe that the Neff's of Huntingdon County, Pennsylvania, and the family in Virginia, are all descendants of this immigration to Lancaster County, Pennsylvania, prior to 1715; it is also more than probable that the other Neffs around and about Philadelphia, Pennsylvania, who were not descendants of Rudolf or Jacob Näf, are also descended from this Lancaster County immigration. In Ohio, too, are found those of the name, who trace their lineage back to either Huntingdon or Lancaster Counties, Pennsylvania.

That the Neffs generally command respect and esteem, though not rising or even aspiring to great prominence, is evident from the following quotation from a communication of one who himself bore one of the offices named in the extract. "The name is "getting very numerous; scattered over the whole "country; and while no one of the name has reached "any very prominent position, it is gratifying to know "that for good citizens and general respectability and "thoughtfulness they will compare favorably with "any other of equal numbers. Some years ago there "was a Neff each in the Legislatures of Illinois, "Indiana, Michigan, Pennsylvania, and Ohio, and "Secretary of State in Indiana at the same time. "Five adjoining States you see." *

---

* From B. Neff, New Carlisle, Ohio, member of Ohio Legislature named above.

                                        Genealogy

"   Genealogy of the Neff Family
"   from Public Documents.
"   Anno Regni,
"   Georgius II Regis.
"   Magnea Britanniae, Franciae Hiberniae Tertio.
    "Francis Neiff was banished from Switzerland on
" account of his religious opinions [Mennonites], and
" was amongst the earliest settlers of Lancaster
" County, about the year 1717, and was naturalized in
" the year 1729, settled in what they called Manor
" land, now Manor Township, Lancaster County,
" Pennsylvania." *
    The following is a list of his descendants:
                Francis Neiff,
        His children:
                Daniel,
                Henry,
                Jacob,
                John,
                3 daughters.

— — — — — — — —

                ×Daniel Neff,
        Children:
                Henry N.
                Daniel,
                ×John,
                Jacob,
                2 daughters.

---

* The above regarding the Neff family of Lancaster and Huntingdon Counties, Penn., from papers furnished by D. J. Neff, of Altoona, Penn.

                                Henry

— — — — — — —

Henry Neff,
Children :
Henry N.
5 daughters.
The son, Henry, moved to Virginia, twelve miles above Wheeling.*

— — — — — — —

Jacob Neff,
Children :
Henry N.
John,
Jacob,
5 daughters.

— — — — — — —

John Neff,
Descent not known.

— — — — — — —

We continue the line of descent through the family of Daniel :
Henry Neff,
Children :
Christian N.
Henry,
Daniel,
John,
David,
Jacob,
3 daughters.

---

* This determines the line of descent of the Virginia Neffs.

Daniel Neff,
Children :
    1 daughter.

ˣJohn Neff,
Married to Fanny Kauffman.
Children :
    John,
    Andrew,
    Jacob,
    ˣDaniel,
    Isaac,
    Henry,
    1 daughter.

Jacob Neff,
Children :
    Daniel N.
    Jacob,
    John,
    5 daughters.

Daniel Neff,
Married to Mary Huzette, was son of John Neff,
grandson of Daniel Neff, and great grandson of
Francis Neiff.
Children :
    Henry N.

John

John H.
xDaniel J.
William,
David A.
3 daughters.*

* To the courtesy of Daniel J. Neff, for the foregoing genealogy,
thanks are due, and his line of descent is marked thus X, which
you observe throughout the generations.

1 FRANCIS NEIFF.
Born.
Married,
Died.

AND

1   NEIFF.
Born.
Married.
Died.

(Residence, Lancaster County, Pennsylvania.)

<table>
<tr><td>Children of</td><td></td><td></td></tr>
<tr><td>1</td><td>Daniel,
Born.
Married
Died.</td><td>Erb.</td></tr>
<tr><td>2</td><td>Henry,
Born.
Married.
Died.</td><td></td></tr>
<tr><td>3</td><td>Jacob,
Born.
Married.
Died.</td><td></td></tr>
<tr><td>4</td><td>John,
Born.
Married.
Died.</td><td></td></tr>
<tr><td>5</td><td>A daughter,
Born.
Married
Died.</td><td>Steiner.</td></tr>
<tr><td>6</td><td>A daughter,
Born.
Married
Died.</td><td>Keller.</td></tr>
<tr><td>7</td><td>A daughter,
Born.
Married
Died.</td><td>Florey.</td></tr>
</table>

11 DANIEL NEFF.
Born.
Married.
Died.

AND

11   ERB NEFF.
Born.
Married.
Died.

Children of

1 | Henry,
Born.
Married Anna Oberholser.
Died.

2 | Daniel,
Born.
Married.
Died.

3 | John,
Born   1761.
Married Fanny Kauffman.
Died September 28, 1819.

4 | Jacob,
Born.
Married.
Died.

5 | Barbara,
Born.
Married D. Musselman and
Dwit. [P. Levine.]
Died.

6 | Anny,
Born.
Married Isaac Kauffman.
Died.

111 HENRY NEFF.
Born.
Married.
Died.

AND

111 ANNA OBERHOLSER NEFF.
Born.
Married.
Died.

Children of

1 Christian,
Born April 24, 1773.
Married Elizabeth Boas.
Died June 12, 1861.

2 Barbara,
Born February 26, 1776.
Married Henry Brubacher.
Died.

3 Magdalena,
Born December 6, 1778.
Married Isaac Kauffman.
Died.

4 Henry,
Born August 24, 1781.
Married Barbara Rützel.
Died   1817.

5 John,
Born April 14, 1784.
Married Elizabeth Sehner.
Died May 12, 1873.

6 Daniel,
Born February 27, 1787.
Married.
Died.

7 Nancy,
Born March 15, 1789.
Married Joshua Kehler.
Died January 19, 1874.

8 David,
Born July 20, 1791.
Married Leah Kauffman and
    Julia Herr.
Died January 26, 1866.

9 Jacob,
Born December 15, 1793.
Married.
Died June, 1877.

1115 JOHN NEFF.
> Born April 14, 1784.
> Married.
> Died May 12, 1873.

AND

1115 ELIZABETH SEHNER
NEFF.
> Born.
> Married.
> Died.

(Residence of above parties, about
Dayton, Ohio.)

	Children of
1	Susanna, Born April 25, 1811. Married. Died.
2	Nancy, Born March 27, 1813. Married. Died.
3	Henry, Born July 7, 1814. Married. Died.
4	Jacob, Born November 20, 1815. Married. Died.
5	Elizabeth, Born October 14, 1817. Married. Died.
6	Nancy, Born November 1, 1819. Married. Died.
7	Magdalena, Born April 22, 1822. Married. Died.
8	John, Born April 18, 1824. Married. Died.
9	Daniel, Born July 14, 1826. Married. Died.
0	John, Born July 14, 1826. Married. Died.
1'	David, Born January 21, 1831. Married. Died.

Twins. (9 and 0)

1118 DAVID NEFF.

Born July 20, 1791.
Married February 1, 1818.
Died January 12, 1866.

AND

1118 LEAH KAUFFMAN NEFF.

Born December 12, 1796.
Married February 1, 1818.
Died March 23, 1840.

Children of

1 Benjamin,
Born March 16, 1821.
Married Elizabeth L. Hay
and Harriet J. Hay.
Died.

2 Isaac,
Born September 9, 1824.
Married Jane Brunner and
Parmelia Smith.
Died   1871.

3 Barbara Ann,
Born March 18, 1827.
Married Martin Eshleman.
Died April 16, 1850.

4 Mary Elizabeth,
Born April 2, 1830.
Married J. J. Scarff.
Died.

5 Cyrus,
Born February 8, 1833.
Married Harriet Cory.
Died.

6 Rebecca,
Born October 12, 1835.
Married George W. Neff.
Died.

7 Matilda,
Born June 7, 1838.
Married Jacob Kissinger.
Died.

1118 DAVID NEFF.

Married June 4, 1843.

AND

1118 JULIA HERR NEFF.

Born March 14, 1811.
Married June 4, 1843.
Died.

Children of

8 Charlotte,
Born March 4, 1844.
Married Wm. H. McClure.
Died.

9 Harriet A.
Born February 8, 1846.
Married Frederick Hogen-
dohler.
Died.

0 Fannie C.
Born September 5, 1849.
Married James Smith.
Died.

1' David Henry,
Born March 6, 1852.
Married.
Died.

105

11181 Benjamin Neff.
Born March 16, 1821.
Married May 18, 1848.
Died.

AND

11181 Elizabeth L. Hay Neff.
Born.
Married May 18, 1848.
Died July 29, 1849.

Children of

1   Mary E.
Born February 22, 1849.
Married John S. Patterson.
Died.

11181 Benjamin Neff.
Married October 11, 1851.

AND

11181 Harriet J. Hay Neff.
Born.
Married October 11, 1851.
Died.

(Residence of above parties, New
Carlisle, Clark County, Ohio.)

Children of

2   Charles H.
Born November 19, 1852.
Married Corinna Weakly.
Died.

3   Jennie,
Born April 9, 1855.
Married Thorton M. Perrine.
Died.

4   Frank Judson,
Born November 25, 1858.
Died February 14, 1865.

5   William M.
Born October 18, 1860.
Died February 14, 1868.

6   J. Grant,
Born November 22, 1863.
Died.

7   Henry H.
Born April 21, 1868.
Died April,   1870.

113 JOHN NEFF.
Born   1761.
Married.
Died September 28, 1819.

AND

113 FANNY KAUFFMAN NEFF.
Born.
Married.
Died March 11, 1806.

1 John,
Born November 3, 1784.
Married Magdalena Stoner
and Mary Mong.
Died July 12, 1862.

2 Andrew,
Born August 20, 1787.
Married Elizabeth Grove.
Died.

3 Jacob,
Born.
Married Eliza Weight.
Died.

4 Anny,
Born December 31, 1790.
Married H. Swoope and J.
Herncame.
Died February 8, 1877.

5 Daniel,
Born January 19, 1793.
Married Mary Huzette.
Died October 17, 1865.

6 Isaac,
Born April 26, 1795.
Married Susan.
Died.

7 Henry,
Born December 8, 1 97.
Married Mary Wallace.
Died October 4, 1842.

1131 JOHN NEFF.
Born November 3, 1784.
Married April 2, 1812.
Died July 12, 1862.

AND

1131 MAGDALENA STONER.
Born.
Married April 2, 1812
Died December 10, 1815.

1 Anna,
Born.
Married.
Died.

2 Fanny,
Born.
Married.
Died.

Children of

1131 JOHN NEFF.
Married May 29, 1817.

AND

1131 MARGARET MONG.
Born August 26, 1794.
Married May 29, 1817.
Died.

3 Mary,
Born April 9, 1818.
Married.
Died.

4 Isaac,
Born October 18, 1819.
Married.
Died May 13, 1884.

5 Margaret,
Born March 5, 1822.
Married.
Died.

6 Eliza,
Born July 9, 1824.
Married.
Died June 3, 1849.

7 Samuel,
Born July 18, 1826.
Married.
Died November 10, 1875.

8 John,
Born March 6, 1829.
Died July 29, 1830.

9 Benjamin,
Born February 24, 1831.
Married.
Died.

0 Henry,
Born July 30, 1836.
Married.
Died.

Children of

1132 ANDREW NEFF.

Born August 20, 1787.
Married.
Died.

AND

1132 ELIZABETH GROVE.

Born June 13, 1796.
Married.
Died.

Children of

1 | Benjamin,
Born September 14, 1816.
Married.
Died.

2 | Andrew,
Born September 13, 1818.
Married   Franke.
Died.

3 | Jacob,
Born October 12, 1820.
Married   Franke.
Died.

4 | Elizabeth,
Born September 27, 1822.
Married Samuel Hatfield.
Died.

5 | John Grove,
Born November 24, 1824.
Died March 10, 1833.

6 | Mary,
Born November 13, 1826.
Married Dr. M. Orlady.
Died.

7 | Daniel G.
Born August 24, 1828.
Married Susan Neff.
Died.

8 | David,
Born October 20, 1830.
Married Knode.
Died   1869.

9 | Henry,
Born March 11, 1833.
Married Francis Sprankle.
Died.

1133 JACOB NEFF.
  Born.
  Married.
  Died.

AND

1133 ELIZA WEIGHT NEFF.
  Born.
  Married.
  Died.

1 John A.
  Born.
  Married.
  Died.

2 Henry K.
  Born.
  Married Mary Miller.
  Died.

3 Edwin W.
  Born
  Married Lavinia Dorland.
  Died.

Children of

1134 HENRY SWOOPE.

> Born January 20, 1795.
> Married.
> Died October 9, 1829.

AND

1134 ANNY NEFF SWOOPE,

> Born December 31, 1790.
> Married.
> Died February 8, 1877.

Children of

1 | John N.
> Born May 21, 1823.
> Married.
> Died.

2 | Peter S.
> Born March 17, 1825.
> Died November 13, 1827.

3 | Henry W.
> Born January 8, 1827.
> Married Frances Neff.
> Died.

4 | Ann Elizabeth,
> Born February 27, 1829.
> Died August 9, 1830.

1134 JACOB HERNCAME.

> Born.
> Married   1835.
> Died.

AND

1134 ANNY NEFF SWOOPE HERNCAME.

> Married   1835.
> Died.

Children of

1135 DANIEL NEFF.
  Born January 19, 1793.
  Married November 25, 1819.
  Died October 17, 1865.

AND

1135 MARY HUZETTE NEFF.
  Born December 8, 1798.
  Married November 25, 1819.
  Died April 26, 1842.

Children of

1 Anna E.
  Born February 26, 1821.
  Married Abram Harnish.
  Died.

2 Henry,
  Born March 16, 1822.
  Married Isabella Oakes and
    Mrs. Amelia Neff.
  Died.

3 Susan,
  Born October 25, 1823.
  Married.
  Died.

4 Fanny,
  Born July 29, 1825.
  Married.
  Died June 8, 1871.

5 John H.
  Born October 9, 1827.
  Married Catherine Musser.
  Died.

6 Daniel J.
  Born January 3, 1831.
  Married Susanna B. Gray.
  Died.

7 William,
  Born October 18, 1833.
  Married Margaret Cordelia
    Howard.
  Died.

8 David A.
  Born April 15, 1836.
  Married.
  Died.

11351 ABRAM HARNISH.
    Born February 1, 1820.
    Married December 14, 1847.
    Died April 20, 1868.

AND

11351 ANNA E. NEFF HAR-
    NISH.
    Born February 26, 1821.
    Married December 14, 1847.
    Died

1 | Mary H.
        Born November 18, 1848.
        Married Rev. John A. Peters.
        Died.

2 | Emma S.
        Born November 4, 1851.
        Married.
        Died.

3 | S. Reid,
        Born March 5, 1854.
        Married.
        Died.

4 | Daniel N.
        Born June 4, 1856.
        Married.
        Died.

5 | William Harry,
        Born February 19, 1859.
        Married.
        Died.

6 | Blanche,
        Born October 4, 1860.
        Married.
        Died.

7 | John N.
        Born February 15, 1863.
        Died January 16, 1871.

Children of

11352 HENRY NEFF.

> Born March 16, 1822.
> Married December 31, 1861.
> Died.

AND

11352 AMELIA NEFF.

> Born.
> Married December 31, 1861.
> Died.

1 | Children of

Anna K.

> Born October 22, 1863.
> Married.
> Died.

11355 JOHN HUZETTE NEFF.
    Born October 9, 1827.
    Married February 6, 1851.
    Died.

AND

11355 CATHERINE MUSSER
        NEFF.
    Born.
    Married February 6, 1851.
    Died.

1

2

Children of

Mary F.
    Born January 5, 1852.
    Married Joseph Oburn.
    Died.

Ada,
    Born September 1, 1863.
    Married.
    Died.

11356 DANIEL J. NEFF.
Born January 3, 1831.
Married September 24, 1873.
Died.

AND

11356 SUSANNA B. GRAY NEFF.
Born May 3, 1854.
Married September 24, 1873.
Died.

1 | Children of

Pauline Louise,
Born April 19, 1885.
Married.
Died.

(Residence of above parties, Altoona, Pennsylvania.)

11357 WILLIAM NEFF.

Born October 18, 1833.
Married December 28, 1865.
Died.

AND

11357 MARGARET CORDELIA
HOWARD NEFF.

Born.
Married December 28, 1865.
Died.

1 Charles D.
Born October 21, 1867.
Married.
Died.

2 William Mason,
Born March 19, 1870.
Married.
Died.

3 Mary H.
Born June 2, 1872.
Married.
Died.

4 Amelia C.
Born July 10, 1874.
Married.
Died.

5 John Frederick,
Born January 2, 1878.
Married.
Died.

6 Paul Howard,
Born July 8, 1880.
Married.
Died.

7 Joseph Huzette,
Born February 11, 1884.
Married.
Died.

Children of

117

1136 ISAAC NEFF.
Born April 26, 1795.
Married.
Died.

AND

1136 SUSAN   NEFF.
Born.
Married.
Died.

Children of

No.		
1	Edwin, Born. Married. Died.	
2	William, Born. Married Died.	Mong.
3	Isaac, Born. Married. Died.	
4	Frances, Born. Married. Died.	
5	Susan, Born. Married Died.	John Morton.

1137 HENRY NEFF.
Born December 8, 1797.
Married October 25, 1827.
Died October 4, 1842.

AND

1137 MARY WALLACE NEFF.
Born January 5, 1806.
Married October 25, 1827.
Died September 14, 1882.

Children of

1 Ann Caroline,
Born August 8, 1828.
Married Perry Moore.
Died.

2 Frances Mary,
Born November 14, 1830.
Married Henry W. Swoope.
Died March 4, 1883.

3 Michael Wallace,
Born September 23, 1832.
Died June 25, 1837.

4 John Henry,
Born December 18, 1834.
Died November 8, 1842.

5 Susan Gemmill,
Born January 14, 1837.
Married William K. Black.
Died.

6 Thomas Calvin,
Born March 27, 1839.
Married.
Died.

7 Laura Wallace,
Born February 8, 1842.
Married.
Died.

Having thus briefly touched upon the immigration to Lancaster County, Pennsylvania, turn now to Jacob, who, with Rudolf, came to this country in 1749, as has been before stated.

As noted in a previous chapter, Jacob had married, and was settled on the Oxford road, near Frankford, as a farmer.

The loving union of the brothers continued until death, and they were scarcely separated in the tomb, for, within a few feet of each other, in the little grave-yard back of the old church in Frankford, repose all that is earthly of Jacob and Rudolph Neff.

The stones that mark the graves of Jacob and Ann, his wife, are plain and neat; the inscriptions on them are in German. In the same grave-lot, nearest the mother, repose the remains of their son Jacob. These are the only graves of any of the family of Jacob or his descendants bearing his name to be found in this little old grave-yard; the dates are as follows:

———

" Jacob Neff,
" Died 3rd September, 1793, aged
" 67 years and 6 months.

———

" Ann Neff,
" Died 24th February, 1805, aged
" 65 years, 8 months.

———

                                                        Jacob

———   ———   ———   ———   ———   ———

"   Jacob Neff,

"   Died 17th November, 1808, aged

"   35 years, 10 months, 17 days.

———   ———   ———   ———   ———   ———

The descendants of Jacob are numerous, and seem to have settled, principally, in and about Philadelphia. An insight into the character of Jacob may be obtained by a reference to his will, a copy of which is given here. By it the reader will ascertain the number of his children as well as their names. It would be impossible in a work of this kind to reach out and relate all that might be gathered concerning the descendants of Jacob, who are scattered here and there. This chapter is a mere suggestion—a statement of some facts. It is hoped it may be a basis, for some one in any one of the lines of the descent, to take up the history and work more in detail.

"WILL OF JACOB NEFF, DECEASED.

"In the name of God, Amen, I, Jacob Neff, of
" Oxford Township, in the county of Philadelphia, in
" the state of Pennsylvania, farmer, being of sound
" mind, memory, and understanding, praised be the
" Lord for the same and all other his mercies, do
" hereby make my last Will and Testament in manner
" following, that is to say:

"*First.* I will that all my just debts and funeral ex-
" penses shall be duly paid and satisfied as soon as
" conveniently can be after my decease.

121

"Item.

"*Item.* It is my will that my beloved wife, Ann
" Neff, shall have the use, interest, and income of all
" my real and personal estate during the term of her
" natural life, if she so long remain my widow un-
" married, subject, nevertheless, to the payment of my
" just debts and the taxes, and to the support and
" maintenance of my afflicted son David. But in case
" my said wife again intermarries, then it is my will
" that from the day of her intermarriage she shall
" have and receive the one-third part only of the
" rents, interest, and income of my real and personal
" estate, and no more, during her natural life, and the
" remaining two-thirds of said rents and income shall
" be received and applied by my executors and the
" survivor of them for and towards the support and
" maintenance of my said son David, if he so long
" live during the natural life of my said wife, and
" the overplus, if any, to go to the residium of my
" estate.

"*Item.* After the decease of my said wife I give and
" devise unto my son Jacob Neff, Junior, all that my
" dwelling-house, with all that part of my land on
" that side of the road, being the westwardly side of
" the great road in Oxford Township, containing
" about seventy-three acres, more or less, together
" with the appurtenances; to hold to him, my said
" son Jacob, his heirs and assigns, forever, subject,
" nevertheless, and charged and chargeable with the
" maintenance, " clothing," and support of my said
" son David, during all the term of his natural life;

                                    and

" and it is my express will and intent that my said son
" David, during his natural life, shall be provided and
" supplied with good, wholesome, and sufficient meat,
" drink, apparel, boarding, lodging, and washing, and
" the devise hereby made to my said son Jacob is upon
" this express condition of so maintaining and provid-
" ing for my said son David, and that my executors,
" or the overseers of the poor for the time being, shall
" have a right and authority to inspect and see from
" time to time that my said son David is so main-
" tained and provided for by my said son Jacob; and
" in case of neglect or refusal on the part of my said
" son Jacob, his heirs or assigns, to maintain and sup-
" port my said son David as aforesaid, that then my
" executors, or the overseers of the poor for the time
" being, shall enter into and take possession of the
" said messuage and land, and the same to let and
" demise, and use and employ the rents, issues, and
" profits thereof for and towards the maintenance
" and support of my said son David during his nat-
" ural life, so, nevertheless, that the overplus of the
" rents and profits, if any, after the maintenance and
" support of my said son David, shall be paid to and re-
" ceived by my said son Jacob, his heirs and assigns.
"*Item.* After the decease of my said wife I give and
" devise unto my son Rudolph Neff, his heirs and
" assigns forever, all my lands on the eastwardly side
" of the great road aforesaid, containing about forty
" acres, more or less, with the appurtenances, subject

123   to

" to the payment of the sum of Five Pounds to my
" daughter Elizabeth, as hereinafter mentioned.

"*Item.* I give and bequeath unto my daughter
" Esther the sum of One Hundred Pounds, and to
" my daughter Ann the like sum of One Hundred
" Pounds, to be paid to them within two years next
" after the decease of my said wife by my said son
" Jacob, and I do hereby charge all the real and per-
" sonal estate in this, my will, given to my said son
" Jacob with the payment of the said two legacies of
" One Hundred Pounds each to my said two daugh-
" ters, Esther and Ann.

"*Item.* I give unto my daughter Elizabeth the sum
" of Five Pounds, to be paid her by my said son Ru-
" dolph out of the land devised to him as aforesaid,
" which, with what I have heretofore given and ad-
" vanced for my said daughter, and the amount of her
" husband's, Christopher Madery's, bonds to me, which
" I hereby release and discharge, is in full of her share
" and dividend in my estate.

"*Item.* I will that after my wife's decease my per-
" sonal estate shall be converted into money, which,
" with all the residue and remainder of my estate, real
" and personal, whatsoever, shall be equally divided
" between my five children, Jacob, Rudolph, David,
" Esther, and Ann, their respective heirs and assigns,
" part and share alike, as tenants in common, and
" that my son David's share shall be received by my
" son Jacob, and applied to the use and support of my
" said son David. Provided always, and it is my mind .

124   and

" and will that in case any or either of my said
" children happen to depart this life in his or her mi-
" nority, without lawful issue, then the part and share
" of my real and personal estate hereinbefore given
" and intended for such descendant shall go to and be
" equally divided amongst all my surviving children
" and the lawful issue of such as shall be then de-
" ceased, their respective heirs and assigns, part and
" share alike, as tenants in common, so, nevertheless,
" that such issue take and receive such part and share
" only which his, her, or their deceased parent might
" have had and taken if then living. Provided, also,
" that what I have hereinbefore given or intended for
" my said wife is in lieu and full satisfaction of all her
" dower or thirds in my estate, and not otherwise;
" and further that neither my wife nor my executors
" shall have any right to cut or sell any growing trees
" or timber off my land, and shall not permit or suffer
" any other person or persons to cut or destroy any
" except only what shall be absolutely required for
" keeping up the fences and making the necessary re-
" pairs of the premises and for fuel for my said wife
" and tenants on the farm after the dead and fallen
" wood shall be first used, any thing hereinbefore con-
" tained to the contrary notwithstanding.

"*Item*. I do hereby nominate and appoint my said
" wife Ann, so long as she remains my widow un-
" married, but no longer, executrix, and my brother,
" Rudolph Neff, and cousin, Adam Stricker, execu-
" tors of this my last Will and Testament.

                                          "*Lastly.*

"*Lastly.* I do hereby revoke all other Wills and
" Testaments by me heretofore made and published,
" and do declare these presents only to be and contain
" my last Will and Testament.

" In witness whereof, I have hereunto set my hand
" and seal this twenty-sixth day of July, in the year
" of our Lord one thousand seven hundred and ninety-
" three.

"   (Signed),   JACOB NEFF.* [SEAL.]

" Signed, sealed, published, and declared by the said
" Testator, Jacob Neff, for and as his last Will and
" Testament, in the presence of us, who, at his re-
" quest and in his presence, have hereunto subscribed
" our names.

"   (Signed),   SAM'L WHELER,
"   R. WHITEHEAD,
"   ROBT. WHITEHEAD.

" Richard Whitehead and Robt. Whitehead, two of
" the witnesses to the foregoing will, on oath, do
" depose and say that they saw and heard Jacob Neff,
" the Testator, duly sign, seal, publish, and declare
" the same as and for his last Will and Testament,
" and that at the doing thereof he was of sound mind,
" memory, and understanding, to the best of their
" knowledge and belief.

" Sworn the 25th day of June, 1794, before Geo.
" Campbell, Reg'r.

" The foregoing will being proved, Probate thereof

---

* Fac simile of signature, see page 171.

                                      was

" was granted unto Ann Neff, executrix, and Rudolph
" Neff and Adam Stricker, executors therein named,
" they being first duly sworn well and truly to per-
" form the same, exhibit a true inventory, and render
" a just and true account when thereunto lawfully
" required.

" Given under the seals of office the day and date
" aforesaid.

"   (Signed),   Geo. Campbell,
"   *Register.*"

The son Jacob, spoken of so frequently, and in
whose trust so much seemed to be placed, is the Jacob
who died at the age of 35 years, and whose grave is
found near that of his parents, in the little old church
yard of the Presbyterian Church at Frankford. From
the records of the courts, which are given below, this
son Jacob left several children.

RECORD OF THE ORPHANS' COURT OF PHILADELPHIA.

"   21.) O. C., November, 1824.
"   No. 88.—Jacob Neff's Estate.
" On the petition of Rudolph Neff and Mary Brock,
" formerly Mary Neff, and Daniel Brock, her hus-
" band, etc.—
" Setting forth that in the year 1808 Jacob Neff, of
" Oxford Township, in the county of Philadelphia,
" farmer, died intestate, seized of personal and real
" estate, leaving a widow, Mary Neff, now Mary
" Brock, one of the petitioners, and six children, viz:

                                    Jacob

" Jacob Neff, Samuel Neff, Elizabeth Neff, Daniel
" Neff, Charles Neff, and Mary Neff."

To turn to Samuel Neff, the brother of Peter and son of Rudolph.

Early in life Samuel married and lived to quite an advanced age, leaving nine children, three of whom were sons—Jacob, Robert, and Benjamin.

He was a wheelwright by occupation, and as such established himself in business in connection with certain blacksmith shops of Peter Neff; the enterprise not resulting well financially, was given up, and his subsequent business is not known.

There are some of his descendants known to be living in and about Frankford. Many more are scattered over different states; their tables of descent, as far as possible to be obtained, are given in their chronological order (see pages 308–317).

Succeeding chapters will treat of the Neffs in America through the line of Peter Neff, son of Rudolph Neff.

1 JACOB NÄF.

    Born March 3, 1726.
    Married 3rd February, 1756.
    Died September 3, 1793.

AND

1 ANNA BUSER NÄF.

    Born June 24, 1739.
    Married 3rd February, 1756.
    Died February 24, 1805.

Children of

1 Elizabeth,
    Born November 4, 1756.
    Married Christopher Madera,
      April 30, 1776.
    Died December 21, 1821.

2 David,
    Born March 30, 1760.
    Died   1823.

3 Esther,
    Born January 20, 1766.
    Married Jacob Folkrod.
    Died October 8, 1811.

4 Ann,
    Born August 10, 1769.
    Married David Newell.
    Died January 8, 1844.

5 Jacob,
    Born December 30, 1772.
    Married Mary Wolfe.
    Died November 17, 1808.

6 Rudolph,
    Born August 29, 1776.
    Married Margaret Rugan.
    Died June 11, 1857.

11 Christopher Madera.*
Born 1750.
Married.
Died February 19, 1825.

AND

11 Elizabeth Neff Madera.
Born November 4, 1756.
Married.
Died December 21, 1821.

(Residence, Philadelphia, Penn.)

----

* Variously spelled in this country. "Madera, Madery, Madury, Madara, Madeiry, Madeira, and Madöri, were originally Madöri of Spain, Protestants of Andalusia, who, at a time of persecution, passed over France into Holland, and from there sailed to America."

Children of

1 Jacob,
Born 1777.
Married.
Died December 21, 1825.

2 Christopher,
Born 1778.
Married Martha Campbell.
Died October 10, 1829.

3 Hester,
Born.
Married William Ross.
Died.

4 Elizabeth,
Born.
Married Arnold Baker.
Died.

5 Ann,
Born.
Married Francis Asbury Cassidy.
Died.

6 David,
Born January 21, 1797.
Married.
Died September 9, 1820.

7 John,
Born January 12, 1800.
Married.
Died February 4, 1824.

130

13 JACOB FOLKROD.
Born.
Married.
Died.

AND

13 ESTHER NEFF FOLKROD.
Born January 20, 1766.
Married.
Died October 8, 1811.

1 Children of

Ann,
Born.
Married Jacob H. Gardner.
Died.

(Residence, Philadelphia, Penn.)

131

14 DAVID NEWELL.
Born.
Married.
Died.

AND

14 ANN NEFF NEWELL.
Born August 10, 1769.
Married.
Died January 8, 1844.

1 William,
Born.
Married.
Died.

2 Ellen,
Born.
Married David W. Clark.
Died.

3 Elizabeth,
Born.
Married.
Died.

Children o

15 JACOB NEFF.
Born December 30, 1772.
Married.
Died November 17, 1808.

AND

15 MARY WOLFE NEFF.*
Born.
Married.
Died.

Children of

1 Jacob,
Born,
Married.
Died.

2 Samuel,
Born.
Married.
Died.

3 Elizabeth,
Born.
Married.
Died.

4 Daniel,
Born.
Married.
Died.

5 Charles,
Born.
Married.
Died.

6 Mary,
Born.
Married.
Died.

All died in Phialdelphia.

Emigrated to Ohio.

*Afterward became Mary Brock.

133

16 RUDOLPH NEFF.
Born August 29, 1776.
Married December 4, 1802.
Died June 11, 1857.

AND

16 MARGARET RUGAN NEFF.
Born May 24, 1780.
Married December 4, 1802.
Died January 23, 1861.

Children of

1 John,
Born April 12, 1804.
Married Margaret Davidson.
Died September 3, 1869.

2 Jacob,
Born May 29, 1805.
Married Jane McAllister and
Adaline King.
Died July 3, 1839.

3 William,
Born February 10, 1807.
Died July 9, 1814.

4 Elizabeth,
Born June 23, 1808.
Married Samuel Baugh.
Died.

5 Rugan,
Born January 29, 1810.
Married Elizabeth Madera.
Died January 9, 1861.

6 Charles,
Born October 22, 1811.
Married Margaretta Rugan.
Died.

7 George,
Born December 22, 1813.
Married Elizabeth Rugan.
Died

8 William P.,
Born April 1, 1815.
Married Mary A. Williams.
Died.

9 Thomas,
Born July 17, 1817.
Married Julia Hazleton.
Died January 23, 1850.

0 Henry,
Born January 4, 1821.
Married Mary A. Fisler.
Died November 9, 1859.

1' Samuel,
Born June 20, 1822.
Married Annie Houlston.
Died.

161 JOHN NEFF.
    Born April 12, 1804.
    Married January 9, 1834.
    Died September 3, 1869.

AND

161 MARGARET DAVIDSON
    NEFF.
    Born November 11, 1805.
    Married January 9, 1834.
    Died.

1   Annie,
    Born June 13, 1836.
    Married.
    Died February 3, 1883.

2   Margaret,
    Born December 17, 1843.
    Married George W. Hunterson.
    Died.

Children of

(Residence of above parties, Philadelphia, Penn.)

135

162 JACOB NEFF.
Born May 29, 1805.
Married August 17, 1827.
Died July 3, 1839.

AND

162 JANE McALLISTER NEFF,
Born.
Married August 17, 1827.
Died.

1 Children of

Rudolph,
Born August 31, 1828.
Married Emma Louisa
Stinger.
Died May 6, 1859.

162 JACOB NEFF.
Married June 29, 1830.

AND

162 ADALINE KING NEFF.
Born July 8, 1809.
Married June 29, 1830.
Died

(Residence of above parties, Philadelphia, Penn.)

2 Children of

Harmanus,
Born March 27, 1831.
Married Amanda Glading.
Died March 9, 1877.

136

1621 RUDOLPH NEFF.
Born August 31, 1828.
Married February 11, 1852.
Died May 6, 1859.

AND

1621 EMMA LOUISA STINGER
NEFF.
Born January 21, 1829.
Married February 11, 1852.
Died December 1, 1862.

1 Albert Barnes,
Born March 3, 1853.
Married.
Died November 3, 1884.

2 Jane McAllister,
Born February 11, 1855.
Died December 24, 1869.

3 John Chestnut,
Born July 26, 1857.
Died May 21, 1872.

4 Rudolph,
Born November 13, 1859.
Married.
Died.

Children of

1622 HARMANUS NEFF.
Born March 27, 1831.
Married November 5, 1850.
Died March 9, 1877.

AND

1622 AMANDA GLADING NEFF.
Born.
Married November 5, 1850.
Died

1 Mary Ann,
Born August 26, 1851.
Married.
Died.

2 Adaline,
Born January 7, 1853.
Married.
Died.

3 Robert P. King,
Born August 5, 1859.
Married.
Died.

4 Harmanus,
Born March 10, 1861.
Married.
Died.

5 William Turner,
Born October 30, 1864.
Married.
Died.

6 Lyleete,
Born January 30, 1866.
Married.
Died.

7 John Thomley,
Born August 16, 1868.
Married.
Died.

8 George Glenn,
Born January 1, 1870.
Married.
Died.

9 Amanda Susanna Hagner,
Born September 4, 1872.
Married.
Died.

Children of

164 SAMUEL BAUGH.
　Born October 12, 1803.
　Married August 23, 1832.
　Died

AND

164 ELIZABETH NEFF BAUGH.
　Born June 23, 1808.
　Married August 23, 1832.
　Died

Children of

1 Margaret,
　Born June 15, 1835.
　Married William Alexander Millar.
　Died.

2 Henry Neff,
　Born October 4, 1837.
　Married Sarah Owen.
　Died.

3 Elizabeth,
　Born October 8, 1839.
　Married.
　Died.

4 Rudolph Neff,
　Born March 28, 1845.
　Married Lulu Post Allin.
　Died.

(Residence of above parties, Philadelphia, Penn.)

139

165 RUGAN NEFF.
>Born January 29, 1810.
>Married September 8, 1853.
>Died January 9, 1861.

AND

165 ELIZABETH MADERA NEFF.
>Born September 21, 1818.
>Married September 8, 1853.
>Died.

1 | Children of

Thomas R.,
>Born December 5, 1859.
>Married.
>Died.

(Residence of above parties, Philadelphia, Penn.)

166 Charles Neff.
    Born October 22, 1811.
    Married June 6, 1839.
    Died.

AND

166 Margaretta Rugan
    Neff.
    Born February 14, 1816.
    Married June 6, 1839.
    Died April 30, 1849.

1 G. Rugan,
    Born September 24, 1840.
    Married Julietta Sagendorf.
    Died.

2 Charles W.,
    Born July 17, 1842.
    Married.
    Died November 17, 1861.

3 Catherine R.,
    Born February 5, 1845.
    Married.
    Died.

4 William Ashford,
    Born August 18, 1848.
    Died June 10, 1850.

Children of

(Residence of above parties, Philadelphia, Penn.)

141

1661 GEORGE RUGAN NEFF,
Born September 24, 1840.
Married October 11, 1865.
Died.

AND

1661 JULIETTA SAGEN-
DORF NEFF.
Born November 19, 1840.
Married October 11, 1865.
Died.

1 Charles S.,
Born September 15, 1866.
Died April 26, 1867.

2 George S.,
Born June 14, 1869.
Married.
Died.

3 Henry S.,
Born September 19, 1871.
Married,
Died.

4 Florence Julietta,
Born November 20, 1877.
Married.
Died.

5 Frank Rugan,
Born May 28, 1885.
Married.
Died.

Children of

167 GEORGE NEFF.
    Born December 22, 1813.
    Married October 9, 1845.
    Died.

AND

167 ELIZABETH RUGAN NEFF,
    Born July 18, 1818.
    Married October 9, 1845.
    Died July 8, 1883.

1   Susanna R.,
    Born June 29, 1847.
    Married Phillip Edgar Ack-
      ert.
    Died.

2   John R.,
    Born April 14, 1849.
    Married Emma Virginia
      Rhoades.
    Died.

Children of

(Residence of above parties, Pough-
keepsie, N. Y.)

143

1672 JOHN RUGAN NEFF.
Born April 14, 1849.
Married August 12, 1874.
Died.

AND

1672 EMMA VIRGINIA
RHOADES NEFF.
Born.
Married August 12, 1874.
Died.

1 Children of

Elizabeth,
Born July 20, 1877.
Married.
Died.

168 WILLIAM P. NEFF.
　　Born April 1, 1815.
　　Married February 27, 1839.
　　Died.

AND

168 MARY A. WILLIAMS NEFF.
　　Born November 3, 1819.
　　Married February 27, 1839.
　　Died.

(Residence of above parties, Philadel-
　　phia, Penn.)

Children of

1 Catherine,
　　Born July 20, 1840.
　　Married Edwin Quig.
　　Died.

2 Rudolph,
　　Born August 25, 1842.
　　Married Mary Emma Col-
　　　sher.
　　Died.

3 Samuel Williams,
　　Born October 19, 1844.
　　Married Rebecca Monaco
　　　Barcus.
　　Died.

4 Edward,
　　Born August 12, 1848.
　　Married.
　　Died.

5 Emma,
　　Born November 26, 1852.
　　Married Henry Phillip Har-
　　　mann.
　　Died.

1682 RUDOLPH NEFF.
Born August 25, 1842.
Married January 26, 1869.
Died.

AND

1682 MARY EMMA COLSHER
NEFF.
Born April 24, 1846.
Married January 26, 1869.
Died.

1 Frank Colsher,
Born August 25, 1869.
Died January 15, 1872.

2 Edward,
Born January 21, 1872.
Married.
Died.

3 Gertrude,
Born July 12, 1874.
Died September 29, 1875.

4 Blanche,
Born October 30, 1876.
Married.
Died.

5 Anna Colsher,
Born June 10, 1878.
Married.
Died.

6 Marion Dunlap,
Born September 2, 1881.
Married.
Died.

7 William Peddle,
Born July 25, 1884.
Married.
Died.

Children of

1683 SAMUEL WILLIAMS
NEFF.
Born October 19, 1844.
Married September 21, 1871.
Died.

AND

1683 REBECCA MONACO BAR-
CUS NEFF.
Born February 15, 1845.
Married September 21, 1871.
Died.

1 Howard Barcus,
Born July 26, 1872.
Married.
Died.

2 William Stephen,
Born May 15, 1879.
Married.
Died.

Children of

169 THOMAS NEFF,
Born July 17, 1817.
Married June 23, 1843.
Died January 23, 1850.

AND

169 JULIA HAZLETON NEFF.
Born March 8, 1827.
Married June 23, 1843.
Died October 27, 1875.

1   Eliza,
Born November 6, 1844.
Married.
Died May 6, 1881.

2   Jacob,
Born June 12, 1848.
Married Sarah Louisa Yount.
Died.

3   Francis,
Born July 24, 1850.
Married Alphonse Lamartine Beck.
Died.

Children of

1692 JACOB NEFF.
  Born June 12, 1848.
  Married November 21, 1872.
  Died.

                    AND

1692 SARAH LOUISA YOUNT
  NEFF.
  Born May 2, 1847.
  Married November 21, 1872.
  Died.

(Residence, Spring City, Chester Co.,
  Penn.)

Children of

1 Paul Jacob,
  Born December 9, 1876.
  Married.
  Died.

2 Charles Hazleton,
  Born March 16, 1880.
  Married.
  Died.

149

160 **HENRY NEFF.**
Born January 4, 1821.
Married October 17, 1844.
Died November 9, 1859.

AND

160 **MARY A. FISLER NEFF.**
Born March 15, 1823.
Married October 17, 1844.
Died.

1 William R.,
Born November 1, 1846.
Married Isabella McKee.
Died.

2 Marceline,
Born March 23, 1850.
Married.
Died.

3 Howard I.,
Born January 23, 1853.
Married Amelia Warner.
Died.

4 Emma L.,
Born November 12, 1855.
Married Irwin S. Cliver.
Died.

5 Frank,
Born May 1, 1859.
Married.
Died.

Children of

(Residence of above parties, Camden County, N. J.)

150

1601 WILLIAM R. NEFF.
Born November 1, 1846.¹
Married September 14, 1870.
Died.

AND

1601 ISABELLA McKEE
NEFF.
Born January 14, 1852.
Married September 14, 1870.
Died.

Children of

1 Sarah R.,
Born July 10, 1871.
Married.
Died.

2 Mary A.,
Born September 16, 1873.
Married.
Died.

3 Florence M.,
Born February 24, 1877.
Married.
Died.

4 Emma L.,
Born September 25, 1878.
Died September 3, 1879.

5 Elizabeth P.,
Born October 28, 1879.
Married.
Died.

6 Henry,
Born February 24, 1882.
Married.
Died.

151

1603 HOWARD I. NEFF.
    Born January 23, 1853.
    Married July 1, 1879.
    Died.

AND

1603 AMELIA WARNER NEFF.
    Born December 7, 1854.
    Married July 1, 1879.
    Died.

1 Howard I.,
    Born June 11, 1880.
    Married.
    Died.

2 Marceline W.,
    Born August 11, 1881.
    Died September 3, 1881.

3 Mary L.,
    Born February 5, 1883.
    Died March 23, 1883.

4 Leonard W.,
    Born January 25, 1884.
    Died March 25, 1884.

Children of

161' SAMUEL NEFF.
 Born June 20, 1822.
 Married February 27, 1851.
 Died.

AND

161' ANNIE HOULSTON NEFF.
 Born October 13, 1833.
 Married February 27, 1851.
 Died.

1 Emma V.,
 Born November 16, 1851.
 Married John K. Garrett.
 Died.

2 Howard L.,
 Born April 15, 1853.
 Married.
 Died.

3 Helen P.,
 Born May 20, 1866.
 Married.
 Died.

Children of

(Residence of above parties, Philadelphia, Penn.)

153

CHAPTER VIII.

Years have rolled on, and Peter having completed his education according to the best advantages of his surroundings, chose to learn a trade, and selected that of a blacksmith.

His position as laborer at the forge did not long continue, and shortly he assumed superintendence of all his work, which consisted finally, in the oversight and management, of several blacksmith shops. His ability was great enough to see correctly that all points fit, and his wise administration of business soon exhibited rewards in large financial returns.

In a few years, while yet a very young man, his business worth, coupled with great integrity, seemed likely to prove him a rival of his father.

About the time of Peter's increasing prosperity, there is observed an unusual stir at the brick house occupied by Rudolph and Hannah, together with their unmarried children. What can it all mean? The occupant of the other half of the house has moved out. Painters are at work following up the labors of the carpenters in repairs. Over it all Rudolph and his son Peter keep careful watch that every particular may be as they desire. There is another, too, whose

                                        taste

taste is often consulted and referred to about all this, who seems to be living at somewhat of a distance, judging from the time consumed by Peter when a conference is necessary. Perhaps time will explain this mystery.

The outside work is all accomplished, carpets are being put down, and other efforts being made that suggest the possibility of an early occupant.

The reader may no longer be kept in suspense, the explanation of all this preparation may be found on little cards, written somewhat in this style:

Aaron Scout and Wife

Will be glad to see you

At the marriage of their daughter,

Rebecca,

to

Peter Neff,

on the

4th day of March, 1784.*

It must be apparent now what all the work at the brick house meant. The invitations, about twenty-five in number, were sent to the friends and relatives of Peter and Rebecca, who were present at the cere-mony performed by the pastor of the Little Brick

---

*The names and dates are as given in the Family Bible of Peter and Rebecca, now in possession of Peter Rudolph Neff, Cincinnati, Ohio.

155church.

church. It was not necessary to inform the friends that they would not receive presents, for wedding gifts were not customary, save from the parents of the contracting parties. Rebecca Scout, now Rebecca Neff, is the daughter of Aaron and Sarah Scout, of Bucks County, who were what is commonly called Pennsylvania Dutch. Rebecca was the third child of ten children,* consequently, though her father was very comfortably off, she could not expect a large portion from him; he, however, provided her with all the items thought necessary for a bride, with which to furnish her house and home. The ample provision furnished by Peter rendered their beginning of home and married life a step higher in the scale of comfort and elegance than had been that of his father, Rudolph. After a few hours spent with their friends, concluding the festivities of the day, they do not start off on a wedding tour of length and expense, but quietly take a carriage, and drive to their home, every detail of which is of interest to Rebecca.

The enjoyment of investigating and appropriating all the delights centering in and about this new home can not be intruded upon, but let it be left to their own minds and eternity the pleasures they there realized.

There is an old saying, that "matches are made in Heaven;" yes, they used to be, but somehow of late

* Family Bible of Peter and Rebecca Neff, now in the hands of Peter Rudolph Neff, Cincinnati, Ohio.

people say they get sadly mixed in coming down. Not so with Peter and Rebecca; they are evidences of the truth of the first saying, for they began life with love, and so death found and severed them.

Rebecca was born on the 27th of April, 1764, and was consequently only two months younger than her husband; they are at this time past twenty, and the future looks very bright before them. In appearance Rebecca was rather tall, and not so fleshy as her husband and his family.* Her face, how can words be found to describe it? There is a serene light beaming from her eyes of softest blue, a firm yet loving expression about the mouth, that indicates the strength of character to be evinced from time to time.

Peter, you remember, is in appearance like his mother, bright black eyes, and a quick, vivacious, determined manner. They are both noble and good, and constant attendants upon the brick church, though neither of them are members.

The routine of home life, with its pleasures, crosses, and vexations, came to them as to others; the various anxieties connected with outside friends and relations, every thing, and all that is common to human nature, they met, and, in united strength, surmounted.

As the daughters of Rudolph and Hannah have by this time married, and settled in and about Philadelphia, or Frankford, securing homes of comfort for

---

* This from Mrs. Rebecca Neff Biggs.

157   themselves,

themselves, Rebecca very naturally becomes doubly dear to the new parents, who still occupy the other half of the brick house.

In this daily discharge of duties, days have rolled on, until it is found that *Old Time* has scored 1787.

In this year occurs an eveut to break the monotony of daily duties, for another member, on the 8th of June, enters this home of love, and in testimony of love is named Hannah.

By this time Rudolph's steps begin to totter, which is equally true of his beloved wife, Hannah. They both, however, find that, though the step may often be weary and slow, yet the heart is active, and the distance to the home of Peter and Rebecca is so short, that they often cross the threshold of the new home, to renew, as it were, the hopes gone by, in hours spent with the little Hannah, whose life is all before her, whether of weal or woe.

Among the friends of Peter and Rebecca, grim death had often been present, to snatch some loved one from them, yet a sorer trial was before them, that of parting from their mother, Hannah, who died on the 10th of January, 1789, after a short illness, in her sixty-eighth year. Some cares and anxieties had weighed upon her, and weakened her physical nature, so that after a short illness she was carried beyond the cares of this life into an untried future.

This event made many changes; the home of Rudolph must be broken up, and, although he has many daughters of his own, he chooses to live with Peter,

Rebecca

Rebecca having grown so dear to him. It was a saying of his, "I could live with Rebecca always."

Before her death it had been a constantly expressed
wish of Hannah's, that a son might be given to Peter
and Rebecca. This wish found fulfillment, not long
after her death, as, on the 12th of January, 1789, a
son was born to them.

In the morning, as the dear old grand-parent, Rudolph, went to see the baby boy, Rebecca told him
how that the night before, in a dream, she saw his
wife Hannah, who came to her and took the child in
her arms, and called him John Rudolph. The old
man's eyes filled with tears, when he told Rebecca his
christian name *was* John Rudolph, though in this
country he had been known only as Rudolph.

Thus it appears that romance enters into this family
history, and probably continues, which, in succeeding
generations, would become of intense interest to the
descendants, if the record were only preserved as the
events occur.

If these chronicles should serve to inspire some of
those living to continue the records, these pages will
not have been written in vain.

This historical fact has been guarded in the family
with great interest, and handed down, in one or two
branches, for a definite purpose, as it would now seem,
to quote from the "Family Tree of the Families of
" Näf, of Zurich and Cappel, showing the succeeding
" generations, by Emil Näf, Architect in Zurich (11
" Y.), New Year, 1881," we find the following:

John Näf, born 1727.
Jacob Näf, " 1729.
brothers.

	Sons of Jacob Näf.	No. 39
No. 39	Son of Heinrich "	28
28	" " Jacob "	23
23	" " Hans "	10
10	" " Hans "	5
5	" " Heini "	2
2	" " Adam Näf,	

who fought with Zwingli, rescuing the banner, as has
been described.

The dates throughout this history, regarding Rudolph and Jacob, are all made from the records of their tombstones, as being the only way possible of obtaining data regarding their ages. It is well known how unreliable all such tombstone records are, in the first place, by a want of certainty on the part of those erecting the memorial, and secondly, the inroads that time makes on such records, destroying a line here and there, that an interpretation of them is not likely to be correct, after having been a few years exposed to the elements. Take, for instance, the tombstone of Jacob Neff, in Frankford; should the 67 years be 64 (see page 120), it would make his birth agree with the table just quoted, and an error of the kind could so easily occur, for, by the obliteration of the cross-line in the figure 4, a seven is readily indicated. There is also a discrepancy between the records in the church of his death and that on the tombstone; and while it

does

does not prove his age to have been 64 years at the time of his death, it yet shows that there was doubt in the matter. The church record and the tombstone of Rudolph agree in the main (see page 168). Every evidence goes to prove that these two brothers, John and Jacob Näf, of Switzerland, are the Rudolf and Jacob Näf of this history, which seems to be further strengthened when we remember the fact that Rudolf Näf had a son, whom he called Johannes, that lived but a short time. Subsequent communications will determine the matter, but this history having been written, continues according to the records on the tombstones, which indicate Jacob as the older.

From 1789 we pass on to the birth of William, on the 7th of February, 1792. Thus is found the home circle growing and increasing, and for each addition, whole realms of love and wisdom are waiting to control and counsel each—for Rebecca, though young, has wonderful tact and management to govern and direct them, though doing it by love.

The management of the children and the home was her care. Peter found that providing for the little household, together with his business, as well as the outside work produced by his public spirit, quite enough for his hands. He was largely engaged in all improvements, such as the making and repairing of roads, bridges, etc., and *home* was the haven of rest and comfort that he always looked forward to, after his day of labor with the rougher and more un-

friendly

friendly world. He seems not to have been wanting in a real sense and enjoyment of humor. It is related that at one time there was a meeting of some political interest, at a place not far from Frankford, but separated from it by a stream of water, not at all times very high, but subject to a sudden rise, if a storm came up. During the meeting such a storm did come up; the question then was how to cross the stream. Peter was provided with long, heavy boots, quite equal to the time and the emergency, which, being observed by a large, fleshy Irishman, with his usual Hibernian perception and credulity, accepted the offer made by Peter to carry him across the stream on his back. Here pause to picture to yourself the situation—on the bank of a swollen stream, possibly surrounded by several spectators from the late meeting, see Peter, a man of medium size, with laughing dark eyes, standing, with his heavy top boots on, ready for the start, and the fleshy Irishman, of avoirdupois about two hundred pounds, also ready for the ride. They did start, and when in about the middle of the swollen stream, Peter informed his burden that it was impossible to proceed further, so deposited his load then and there. The Irishman, who was a neighbor of Peter's, and a man of some wealth, departed to his home a wiser and less credulous man, none the less a friend and good neighbor.

On the 26th of June, 1794, Sarah was born—a bright little heart, only lent for a short time, for her race was soon run, when, at the age of eleven months,

 she

she died. Thus the first break in the home circle
here on earth was made, and the first link of the
chain was gathered in Heaven.

The influence of the Quakers, on all those living in
or near Philadelphia, was manifest even in this house
and home, for Rebecca, although not herself a Quaker,
early adopted their style of dress. Her children and
grandchildren remember seeing her in her sombre
robe, with the plain cap, and the little shawl of white,
with a silk shawl over it, about the shoulders. One
set of these three articles, which belonged to her, is
still in existence, and is in the possession of Mrs. Peter
Neff, of Gambier, Ohio. In looking at them, one can
picture the sweet, calm, but resolute face of Rebecca,
smiling from under the cap through all troubles.

Are there not some lives that seem to attest the
power of Christian love and fellowship long before it
is even known by the possessor, or a public acknowl-
edgment of faith has been made before the world?
If such there be, Rebecca's was such an one.

The household cares and duties have gone on with
quiet regularity, the *three* children to gladden the
hearthstone, until Rebecca is ushered into this world,
filled with trials and crosses. Hers was a May-day
blessing to the household, for she came to them on
the first of May, 1796.

Time can not be given to dwell upon their childhood days; they must have been much like those of
other children that are seen about us now—each turn
in their every-day life being of interest, and noted by

                                   both

both parents for the time, and then passed on, and forgotten.

Peter, George Washington, and Mary Amanda follow Rebecca in succession—Peter, born on the 31st of March, 1798; George Washington, on the 19th of May, 1800; and Mary Amanda, on the 16th of December, 1802. Two years after the birth of Mary Amanda, an event occurred that changed and shaped the destiny of each member of the family. The household at this time, July, 1804, numbers ten in all. There is the venerable old grandfather, Rudolph, whose advanced age is plainly observed in his tottering steps and in the childishness that in this year began to show itself in many little ways, and which continued until his death. Rebecca has grown older, with her cares and seven children about her, though only in her fortieth year. Peter, too, is really in the prime of manhood, being but two months his wife's senior, but his physical nature has sustained a shock that seems likely to prove too great for his endurance. About two years previous to this time, a fire occurred in the neighborhood, when Peter, with his usual consideration for the misfortunes of his neighbors, went and took with him a ladder—he was at this time quite fleshy—and this load, together with his haste and great exertion, caused the rupture of a blood-vessel, and on this account he was prostrated for a time by illness, during which he was attended by his friend and physician, Dr. Benjamin Rush, of Philadelphia. In a short time he recovered his strength. From an acci-

 dent

dent caused by falling against a gate of a picket fence, he subsequently ruptured this vessel again; possessing, however, great vitality, he rallied, but, in 1804, from some trivial cause, the same vessel was again ruptured, this time causing more serious trouble, that ended in his death, which occurred on the 14th of August, 1804.

As was customary in previous years, for persons to wait until they thought themselves likely to die before making any will for the disposition of property, so it was with Peter. Cut off in his prime, no act of the kind was left to govern and protect those dear to him, by securing to them their lawful rights, without the interposition of the Courts.

Consequently are found notices in the Orphans' Court, of Philadelphia, when sales of property were necessary to be made, thus: "8th April, A. D. 1807, " No. 485," * is found "a petition for sale." Also, from the Orphans' Court Docket, No. 24, page 269, April 15, 1814, can be found a full account of the property left by Peter, as there is filed a petition for further sale of the property, enumerating the same.

On the evening of the 18th of August, 1804, a daughter, Matilda, was born, who lived but two weeks. Before closing this chapter, linger a moment to consider Rebecca, who was surrounded with a world of care and anxiety, yet she assumed control with a firm resolution, and as each trial and obstacle was presented, her courage enabled her to rise above and sur-

---

* Orphans' Court Docket, No. 22 [1805–1807], page 199.

mount

mount them, aided by her valued and trusted children,
as they, one by one, became able to assist her.

The property left by Peter, comprising the following lots of land in Frankford, is shown by the following entry:

"O. C., June 18, 1813, No. 725. On the petition of
"John R. Neff, eldest son of Peter Neff, late of the
"borough of Frankford, and county of Philadelphia,
"yeoman, deceased, setting forth, that the petitioner's
"said father lately died *intestate*, leaving a widow, to
"wit, Rebecca Neff, and issue, seven children, to wit,
"the petitioner and Hannah, William, Rebecca, Peter,
"George, and Mary Neff, the four last named of
"whom are still in their minority, and that the said
"intestate died seized in his demesne as of fee of and
"in all those certain lots and messuages hereinafter
"described, to wit:

"No. 1. A lot on Bristol road, containing $3\frac{3}{4}$ acres,
"more or less.

"No. 2. A lot on Bristol road, containing 10 acres,
"more or less.

"No. 3. A lot on Bristol road, containing 1 and
"$35\frac{2}{10}$ pr., more or less, with a two-story frame erected
"thereon.

"No. 4. A lot on the Bristol road, containing 7
"acres, more or less.

"No. 5. A lot on the Bristol road, containing $\frac{3}{4}$
"acres, more or less, with 2 small stone and one frame
"house erected thereon.

"No. 6. A lot on Bristol road, containing 1 acre
                                        and

" and 5 pr., or thereabouts, with a two-story frame
" and blacksmith shop erected thereon.

"No. 7. A lot on Bristol road, containing 1 acre
" and 19½ pr., more or less, with a two-story frame
" house erected thereon.

"No. 8. A lot on Paul Street, containing 3 acres,
" or thereabouts.

"No. 9. A lot on Adams Street, containing 46 pr.,
" with a two-story frame erected thereon.

"All of which said described lots and messuages
" are situated in the borough of Frankford, Oxford
" Township, and county of Philadelphia; also another
" lot, situated on the road leading from the Frankford
" road to Point no Point, containing 1¼ acres, more or
" less, with the appurtenances."

This, together with Peter's personal property, made
an estate sufficiently large for each daughter's portion
to be a help to her as she began married life; for the
sons, enough to give them an education suitable to
prepare them for business life; while to Rebecca was
secured, during her life, a comfortable and cheery
home, in which the grandfather, Rudolph, had his
share, until his death, on the 14th of February, 1809,
at the good old age of eighty-two years.

An incident in the life of Rudolph is related by one
of the grandchildren, who states that, as he grew
older, he became childish, and when he wished to at-
tract the attention of any one of them, he would, instead of speaking, throw at them his large-brimmed
hat, which he always wore.

If this mode of address was disregarded by them, as
it seems frequently to have been the case, he would
be greatly displeased. To gratify him in his childishness, Rebecca would, when she left for Philadelphia,
tell the old grandfather that he must take charge of
the young people, whom she left in his care. His
success in the government of them was not great, and
he would in hopeless terms express to Rebecca, on her
return, his inability to do any thing with them.

A custom of Rudolph's was to sit outside the front
door, and drink his daily glass of good cheer, placing
the glass, when not in use, on a little ledge at the side
of the door, off which place it would frequently fall
and break. That he might enjoy his old custom,
without the repetition of the oft-recurring accident,
Peter, before his death, had manufactured for his
father two silver cups, of peculiar size and shape,
from which ever after he took his beverage. These
cups were for many years in the possession of Peter
Neff, now deceased, of Cincinnati. They were stolen
from his house at one time, bnt found, subsequently,
in Mill Creek bottom; a second time they were stolen,
and though never recovered, they were traced to where
they were melted. Rudolph, having revoked, before
his death, all wills made by him, his estate was distributed in accordance with the statutes. A copy of
the paper is given on page 170. The settlement
was tedious, since it was not finally disposed of until
the 18th of August, 1826.

In the grave-yard at Frankford, back of the old
                                          church,

church, Hannah and Rudolph are buried, side by side. On the headstone at the grave of Hannah, is inscribed the following:

" In Memory of
" Hannah Neff,
" wife of
" Rudolph Neff,
" who departed this life
" January 10th, 1789. Aged 68 years."

On the footstone the initials—

"H. N."

On the headstone at the grave of Rudolph is inscribed the following:

" In Memory of
" Rudolph Neff,
" who departed this life
" February 14, 1809.
" Aged 82 years."

On the footstone the initials—

" R. N."

As this chapter closes, there are remaining in life, as members of the family, the following:

Rebecca Neff,
Her children,

Hannah,	Rebecca,
John Rudolph,	Peter,
William,	George Washington,

Mary Amanda.

169

" Whereas,

"Whereas, I, Rudolph Neff, of the Borough of
" Frankford, in the County of Philadelphia, wheel-
" wright, have, on mature reflection, determined to
" revoke all wills and testimentary dispositions by
" me heretofore made, in order that the first and
" equal distribution may be made in case of intestacy
" by the Laws of Pennsylvania may take effect in re-
" gard to such property as I may die seized or pos-
" sessed of or entitled to. . . . . .

"Now these presents witness that I, the said Ru-
" dolph Neff, in consideration of the premises, have
" revoked, and by these presents do revoke, annul,
" and make void all and every will or writing in the
" nature of a will by me heretofore made.

" Witness my hand and seal this 16th day of Oc-
" tober, in the year of our Lord one thousand eight
" hundred and four. 1804.

" Sealed and delivered
" in the presents of
" John Keylerz,
" Matthias Giller, [X]
" Joshua Sullivan.

RUDOLPH NEFF. [SEAL.]

(For fac simile of signatures, see following page.)

" Phila., *June* 9, 1885.

" I, Charles Irwin, Clerk, Office of Register of Wills
" for the City and County of Philadelphia, Pennsyl-
" vania, do certify that the foregoing paper, marked
" C. I., and attached to this sheet, is a true and cor-

170   rect.

" rect copy of an original paper filed with the admin-
" istration papers, etc. (original), in the Register's
" Office, Philadelphia County, in the estate of Ru-
" dolph Neff, deceased 1809, as the same remains on
" file.

" Witness my hand the above date.

"   .   CHAS. IRWIN,
"   1847 *N. Front St., Phila., Pa.*"

(*a*)

(*b*)

"REGISTER OF WILLS,
" No. 421 Chestnut Street,
" Philadelphia, May 19, 1885.

" State of Pennsylvania,   }
"   County of Philadelphia. } *ss.*

" Personally appeared before me, a Notary Public
" for the County and State aforesaid, Charles Irwin,
" who, being duly sworn according to law, deposes
" and says, that he is clerk in the Register of Wills
" Office, Philadelphia County, Penna., and has access

171   to

" to and charge of all original papers in said office;
" that the foregoing, marked *a*, is a photograph of
" the original signature and seal of Jacob Neff to
" his original will, made on the 26th day of July,
" A. D. 1793, and admitted to probate on the 25th
" day of June, A. D. 1794, (Ann Neff, Rudolph Neff,
" and Adam Stricker, Executors); said photograph
" being taken by Louis N. Greenig, Photographer,
" Philadelphia, on the 19th day of May, A. D.
" 1885.

"Also, that the foregoing, marked *b*, is a photo-
" graph of the original signature and seal of Rudolph
" Neff to an original paper, made and signed by him
" on the 16th day of October, A. D. 1804, and which is
" of itself a document revoking all previous wills
" made by him, in order that distribution may be
" made according to the laws of Pennsylvania, which
" paper is filed with the original administration bond,
" said estate of Rudolph Neff being administered on
" by John H. Worrell, of Oxford Township, Phila-
" delphia County, on the 20th day of February, A. D.
" 1809, said photograph being taken by Louis N.
" Greenig, photographer, Philadelphia, on the 19th
" day of May, A. D. 1885.

" Further, that both original documents are on
" file (the foregoing being of record and the latter on
" file) in the Office of Register of Wills, Philadelphia
" County, Pennsylvania.
"
"   CHARLES IRWIN,
"   1847 *N. Front St., Phila., Pa.*

172   " Sworn

"Sworn and subscribed to before me, this 19th day
" of May, A. D. 1885.
"   [NOTARY PUBLIC SEAL.]   FRANK M. CODY,
"   *Notary Public.*

"I certify that I am acquainted with the above-
" named Charles Irwin, and that he is clerk in the
" above-named office.
"   FRANK M. CODY,
"   528 *Walnut St.*"

The following certified copy from the church records
of the Market Square German Reformed Church of
Germantown, gives what is there contained regarding
the Näf families.

The Heinrich Näf, here spoken of, does not enter
into this volume; the only descendant at present
known of resides in Kutztown, Pennsylvania—Miss
Hannah Neff.

The discrepancies regarding the dates in the tombstone records, and those of the church, indicate an in-
accuracy, that suggests again the fact that neither the
tombstones nor the church records are quite correct
in this country, which strengthens the belief, that
when absolute certainty is reached, the records from
Switzerland, as quoted on page 169, will be found to
be the true dates regarding Rudolph and Jacob Näf,
who were known in Switzerland as John and Jacob
Näf, and thus the connection with the family in Switzerland will be established and complete:

"I hereby certify that the following is a correct
173   copy

" copy from the records of the Market Square German
" Reformed Church, Germantown, Pennsylvania, the
" same having been examined by me; that the said
" Book of Records, as therein stated, was commenced
" in the year 1753, and is now in the possession of
" the authorities of the said church:

"   MARRIAGES.

" 1754, January 29.   Heinrich Näf married Johanna
" Neger.

" 1756, February 3.   Jacob Näf married Anna
" Buser.

" Original German:

„Den 29. Januar 1754 wurden getraut.
„Heinrich Näf mit Johanna Neger.
„Den 3. Februar 1756, wurden getraut Jakob Näf und
„Anna Buser.

"   BIRTHS.

" 1769, August 10.   Anna Neff, daughter of Jacob
" and Anna Neff.

„Den 10. August 1769 wurde geboren Anna Neff,
Tochter von Jakob und Anna Neff.

"   DEATHS.

" 1793, September 27.   Jacob Neff, from Frankford,
" aged 69 years and 7 months.

" 1809, February 14.   Rudolph Neff, aged 81 years,
" 4 months, 18 days.

„Den 27. September 1793 starb Jakob Neff von
Frankfurt, 69 Jahre und 7 Monat alt.
„Den 14. Februar 1809 starb Rudolph Neff, 81 Jahre,
4 Monate und 18 Tage alt.

"   H. GRAHN, *Pastor.*
" PHILADELPHIA, *September* 24, 1885.

174   "Before

"Before me, the subscriber, a Notary Public in and
" for the City of Philadelphia, personally appeared
" the above-named Rev. H. Grahn, who, being duly
" sworn according to law, did declare that the above
" copy of records, as written, was a true and correct
" copy of the original entries in the above-mentioned
" Book of Records of the Market Square German
" Reformed Church, of Germantown, Pennsylvania.
"Witness my hand and official seal, this twenty-
" fourth day of September, A. D. 1885.
" [NOTARY PUBLIC SEAL.]   E. L. MINTZER, JR.,
"   *Notary Public.*"

A full examination has been made of the records of
the church situated on Wallace Street, formerly on
Race Street, below Fourth, known as the First (*German*) Reformed Church, Philadelphia, Pennsylvania,
Rev. Dr. David Van Horne, Pastor. To these records
reference was made as having been those of the church
which Rudolf Näf attended for a time, prior to the
building of the church in Frankford in 1770.

On these records the names of both Rudolf and Jacob
Näf appear in connection with baptisms, either of
their own children or the children of others. They
are in fault as to names, in some cases, as well as to
dates, yet they approach the truth of other records so
nearly as to identify the reference.

Thus: "Rudolph Näf and wife, Anna, child born
" April 27, 1759, baptized May 18th, 1760.

"Also, Jacob Näf and wife, Anna, had a son, Dan-

                                         iel

" iel (*Duvid?*), baptized at the same time, born March
" 10th, 1759; on the margin is the Latin ' Obit.'

" Rudolph Näf and wife had a child, Sarah (*Mary?*),
" February 6th, baptized April 30th, 1762; the same
" marginal entry here is ' Obit.' "

The above is quoted to show the difficulty experienced in investigating and reconciling old records, and to indicate the thoroughness of the efforts to secure all information from every quarter.

The following certified copy explains itself. Notice is directed to the name of the son, which, here given, is Daniel, in place of David, as in the will. A slight change in the formation of a letter or two renders such an error possible, and the old records are so nearly obliterated that perfect accuracy is almost impossible:

" The State of Ohio,
"   Cuyahoga County. } *ss.*

" Before me, Louis H. Winch, a Notary Public
" within and for said county and state, personally ap-
" peared Peter Neff, Jr., to me well known, who,
" being by me first duly sworn, upon his oath deposeth
" and saith that the document hereto attached, and
" marked " Exhibit A," is a correct and literal trans-
" lation done into English from the original German
" of a manuscript leaf said to have been taken from
" a family Bible now in the possession of the descend-
" ants of Jacob Näf, said manuscript leaf being a
" record of the births and christenings of the chil-

                                    dren

" dren of the said Jacob Näf, and further affiant
" saith not.   PETER NEFF, JR.

"Subscribed by the said Peter Neff, Jr., in my
" presence, and sworn to by him before me, this
" twenty-third day of November, A. D. 1885.
" In testimony whereof, I have hereunto subscribed
" my name, officially, and affixed my Notarial Seal,
" the day and year last above written.
"   [NOTARIAL SEAL.]   LOUIS H. WINCH,
"   *Notary Public*,
"   Cuyahoga County, Ohio.

"   *'Exhibit A.'*
" The 30 March, 1760, my son, Daniel, was born,
" Sponsors at whose christening were Daniel Bechli *
" and his wife.

"February 20, 1766, my child, Esther, was born,
" Sponsors at whose christenings Jacob Zöbli and his
" wife, Esther.

"Anno Domini, 1769. The 10 August was born to
" me, into this world, a daughter, whereupon, she re-
" ceived in holy baptism, the name of Ana, Sponsors
" at whose christening were I, her Father, Jacob Näf,
" and her Mother, Ana Näf.

---

* Some read Yechli.

177"1772,

"1772, on the 30* day of December, was my son,
" Jacob, born, at whose christening Sponsors were
" Jacob Zöbli and his wife, Esther.

" 1776, the 20 day of August, my son, Rudolf, was
" born, Sponsors at whose christening, Rudolf Nef
" and his wife, Ana.†"

* 31, some read.

† This is very uncertain; the writing is very faint, and *the
paper torn.* Some think it a contraction for Hannah—space very
limited.

2 RUDOLF NÄF.
    Born September 26, 1727.
    Married January 6, 1752.
    Died February 14, 1809.

AND

2 *HANNAH MORSE NÄF.
    Born   1721.
    Married January 6, 1752.
    Died January 10, 1789.

Children of

1 **Elizabeth,**
    Born November 8, 1752.
    Married A. Baker, March 15, 1773.
    Died June 6, 1829, aged 76 years, 6 months, 28 days.

2 **Barbara,**
    Born February 2, 1754.
    Married Adam Stricker, July 18, 1779.
    Died.

3 **Hannah,**
    Born May 6, 1759.
    Married Phillip Buckius.
    Died.

4 **Mary,**
    Born January 26, 1762.
    Married John H. Worrell.
    Died January 26, 1842, aged 80.

5 **Peter,**
    Born February 15, 1764.
    Married Rebecca Scout, March 4, 1784.
    Died August 14, 1804.

6 **Johannes,**
    Born September 22, 1766.
    Died July 6, 1767.

7 **Samuel,**
    Born June 27, 1768.
    Married Eleanor Helveston.
    Died   1839.

---

* Some records give her name as Anna.

CHAPTER IX.

At the time of Peter's death, he was building for himself and family a large stone house (the house is still standing), intending shortly to leave the old brick house, the cellar of which, being the first work his father, Rudolph, together with his uncle, Jacob, had been engaged upon in this country. The contracts for the new house and home were such that Rebecca continued the work, and with womanly nobility of character, directed all, and soon settled with her family in the new home. Can you not imagine the sadness with which she took up her abode in this new home, and remembered the happy "Hanging of the Crane," when she, with Peter, began life, in the half of the old brick house? But it is now no time for regrets; life is too real for the living to waste it foolishly mourning for the dead. In her purpose and effort to carry out the wishes of her husband in the training of their children, in the determination to impress upon them the principles and character of their father—to reproduce his life in theirs—she reared a more beautiful and lasting monument to his memory, and gave a nobler and a grander expression of her undying affection for him.

Hannah,

Hannah, who married William Patterson, of New Jersey, the first of the children to marry, as the eldest, had been, in trying moments, her mother's comfort and assistant. Happy it proved for the mother, that her daughter, after her marriage, could and did remain with her. This daughter was always known in the family by the name of "Aunt Patty," as she greatly disliked the good old name of Hannah.

Two of Rebecca's sons received a collegiate education—in part, at least—John Rudolph spending two years, and George Washington being graduated from Princeton College. John Rudolph, afterward marrying Miss Bird, located in Philadelphia. George Washington, receiving his degree from Princeton in his eighteenth year, and in the year 1818, subsequently studied law with the late Hon. Horace P. Binney, of Philadelphia, was admitted to the bar, but, later, abandoned the profession, and adopted a business life.

William and Peter embraced the opportunities offered them at the academy in Frankford. William, early developing business talent, assumed at once an active life, as will appear in the chapter detailing his subsequent career. Peter also went no further than the academy, and entered business life. Rebecca received her education in Philadelphia, and in her twenty-fifth year, married Rev. Thomas J. Biggs, pastor of the church of which her grandfather, Rudolph, had been one of the founders.

A brief account of Dr. Biggs will be given in the

chapter

chapter giving the account of Rebecca's life. Let us
here digress for a moment to tell of the happy influence of this new son-in-law. Neither of the parents
had made any profession of religion, although Christians at heart. Through the influence of the Rev. Dr.
Biggs, Rebecca became an earnest member of the
Frankford church. From her sixteenth year she had
suffered much from rheumatism, which greatly increased as she grew older. For the last twenty years
of her life she was almost helpless; having lost the
use of her limbs, she was taken about the house in a
chair on wheels. Her hands, too, were greatly affected, the joints of her fingers having been drawn
out of place by the contraction of her muscles.

When thus suffering and confined, Dr. Biggs would
have prayer meetings at her house. These meetings
are remembered by those who attended as precious
seasons, when her bright Christian face, full of love
and patience, shone through all her trials. She ever
kept her eye towards her Saviour, bright with his re-
flected light as the eagle's to the sun. There was
in the town of Frankford about this time, jewelers, by
the name of Woolworth, who had four apprentices.
The name of one was M. W. Baldwin. He was an
industrious, intelligent young man, who attended well
to his business duties, while he carefully remembered
his higher obligations. To these prayer-meetings, at
Mrs. Neff's house, he came, and who can tell the
worth those meetings were to him. Time has gone
on, and now it is M. W. Baldwin, of locomotive fame.

                                        Only

Only a few years previous to his death, Mr. Baldwin, to one of the descendants, referred with pleasure to those meetings of prayer and praise. William married a Miss Wayne, of Savannah, Georgia, and they made for themselves a home in Cincinnati, Ohio. Mary Amanda married Kirkbride Yardley, at her home in Frankford, shortly after a visit to her brother, in the west, where she first met Mr. Yardley. She returned with him to his home in Cincinnati. Her history, although brief, will be given in a subsequent chapter. Rebecca, after her marriage, resided for a time in Frankford, and subsequently removed, with her husband, to Cincinnati. Peter, who was in business in Baltimore for some time, married Mrs. Isabella Lamson of that city, also removed to Cincinnati, where he entered into business with his brothers, and remained there until his death. George Washington, marrying Miss White, of Philadelphia, also removed to Cincinnati. In subsequent years it will not be surprising to find the name of this family numerous in and about Cincinnati. The three brothers, having settled and reared their families there, where they each were known and individually appreciated, in the early days of that city. What a record for a family reared by a mother, without the counsel and assistance of a father. Each one of the four sons commanded respect in his line of business, and each died respected and beloved—not one of the four brothers ever indulging in the humiliating, degrading, and almost universal vices of intemperance, etc., that in their

day,

day, as well as ours, were rife in the land. What an example for succeeding generations, and with what feelings of gratitude can descendants look back upon such a record. Thus five of the children had settled in the then far west, leaving their mother, Rebecca, with her daughter, Hannah, living in the homestead in Frankford.

The character of love, trust, and energy is shown by Rebecca in every act. To have her children so far away from her, would have been, to a person wanting in resolution, a separation too terrible to have been thought of or endured. Knowing, as she must have known, that life for her could not be long, she would bid them good-bye, with a hearty God speed, and an abiding faith in the future each would make. From her invalid chair, from day to day, would her sweet, loving face look forth, to gladden all who saw her— her's being a perfect example of patience throughout all those twenty years of her life, when her limbs had refused to perform their office. The rheumatism, which so afflicted her, was more terrible in its effects at that time, possibly, than at the present, on account of the treatment, which was largely that of experi- ment. Rebecca was a remarkably sweet singer, and it is said that at one time she knew a ballad for every day in the year. The days in the cheery sick room passed on, with letters from the absent ones, with yearly visits from her children in the west, together with frequent calls from John Rudolph, the only son now living in Philadelphia. Hannah's two children served to glad-

184den

den the long and weary days for Rebecca, who received from the hands of Hannah kind and loving attentions in her invalid state.

Thus cared for and surrounded, she lived until the cold and trying days of the unfriendly March, of the year 1834, came, when, on the 23rd day of that month, she passed peacefully to her rest, full of years and honors, having spent an useful life of 69 years, 10 months, and 26 days.

Her body was borne in reverence and love to the little old grave-yard back of the old brick church, in Frankford, where lay the remains of Rudolph and Hannah Neff. By the side of her beloved husband, Peter, all that was mortal was placed, and the same tombstone covers the graves of both. It is of some kind of granite; the sides, head, and foot are slabs about $2\frac{1}{2}$ feet high, which support a horizontal slab of the same stone, on which is inscribed the following [time is doing its usual and successful work in obliterating the lettering]:

"   In memory of
"   Peter Neff,
"   Who was born 15th of February, 1764,
"   And departed this life the
"   14th of August, 1804,
"   Aged
"   40 years, 6 months, and 10 days."

                                    "Also

"   Also,
"   Rebecca Neff,
"   relict of Peter Neff,
"   who departed this life
"   March 23rd, 1834, aged
"   69 years, 10 months, 26 days."

— — — — — — — — — —

The following is a fac simile of the signature of
Rebecca Neff, wife of Peter Neff, the son of the senior
Rudolph Neff, taken from the records of the Orphan's
Court, Philadelphia, Pennsylvania:

25 PETER NEFF.

Born February 15, 1764.
Married March 4, 1784.
Died August 14, 1804.

AND

25 REBECCA SCOUT NEFF.

Born April 27, 1764.
Married March 4, 1784.
Died March 23, 1834.

Children of

1   Hannah,
Born June 8, 1787.
Married William Patterson.
Died November 11, 1862.

2   John Rudolph,
Born July 12, 1789.
Married Caroline Bird.
Died July 23, 1863.

3   William,
Born February 7, 1792.
Married Elizabeth Clifford Wayne.
Died November 25, 1856.

4   Sarah,
Born June 26, 1794.
Died June 11, 1795.

5   Rebecca,
Born May 1, 1796.
Married Thomas J. Biggs.
Died August 24, 1885.

6   Peter,
Born March 31, 1798.
Married Isabella Lamson.
Died July 20, 1879.

7   George Washington,
Born May 19, 1800.
Married Maria White.
Died August 9, 1850.

8   Mary Amanda,
Born December 16, 1802.
Married Kirkbride Yardley.
Died July 11, 1849.

9   Matilda,
Born August 18, 1804.
Died September 1, 1804.

CHAPTER X.

Hannah Neff, the oldest child of Peter and Rebecca Neff, who was born in the old brick house, in Frankford, became quite a remarkable woman. Very early in life, when about eighteen years old, which was soon after her father's death, she married William Patterson, of New Jersey. Life so shaped itself for her, that nearly all the time after her marriage, until the death of her mother, which occurred in 1834, she spent in the homestead, a comfort and support to her invalid parent; her shrewd management, and comprehensive ability in all business matters, rendered her a valued counselor in all matters of family concern. The younger children, throughout life, always sought for and appreciated her judgment.

She subsequently moved, with her family, to St. Louis, Missouri, her daughter having previously married George K. Budd, of Philadelphia, who accompanied them to the west, settling in business in the same city.

The investments in this part of the new world, suggested and entered into by Hannah, resulted favorably, and later years attested her appreciation and

ability

ability to seize all favorable circumstances for the advantage of herself and children.

Truly, her memory is one to be revered. Early in life she united with the Presbyterian Church, becoming an active member and earnest worker, her name being associatied with the first Sabbath-school teachers in America. In the fellowship of this same church she died.

The following, from her diary, with the notices of her death, together with the number and names of her descendants, was furnished the compiler by her daughter, Rebecca Budd.

"As the aged wife of her dear pastor, Dr. Biggs
" [her own dear sister], is still living, in her 89th
" year, and in full use of all her faculties, I append
" some portions of her diary, feeling it will comfort
" her :

"January, 1818, she writes of the interesting group
" of children which composed her Sabbath-school
" class, and of the Rev. Backus Wilber preaching to
" them. They were then without a pastor, for she
" adds, 'how much do we need a faithful pastor to in-
" struct and comfort us.'

" September 29, she writes, 'my heart rejoices that
" our Heavenly Father has provided a pastor to pre-
" side over this little flock,' and Oct. 2nd, she adds,
" 'this day, in commemoration of our blessed Lord,
" we again partook of the emblems of his broken
" body and shed blood. Dr. Janeway preached and

                                     administered

" administered the sacrament, and the Rev. Mr. Biggs
" assisting in the holy ordinance.'

"November 10, 1818, she adds, 'how solemn have
" the proceedings of this day been. The Rev. Mr.
" Biggs ordained and installed our pastor—the charge,
" how great. May God grant him grace and strength
" to perform his duties, and may we be enabled by
" grace divine to fulfill ours!'

"January, 1819, she writes, 'we again assemble at
" our Lord's table to commemorate his dying love.
" It is the first time our worthy and beloved pastor
" has administered the ordinance, and we rejoice that
" there were added to our little company!'

"'Six years,' she adds, 'have now elapsed since the
" seal was set to the covenant made between God and
" my soul—to be *his* and *his* only.'

"It was then, in January, 1813, that she made a
" profession of religion at Frankford, Penn., and how
" faithfully she lived up to that profession, all can
" testify who knew her.

" From my earliest recollections she was the most
" self-sacrificing and devoted Christian, abounding in
" all good works, a tender and loving mother, unsur-
" passed in devotion, trust, and love, and I feel as-
" sured she has received the plaudit, ' Well done, good
" and faithful servant, enter ye into the joy of your
" Lord!'

St. Louis, Mo.

Obituary.

" Our paper of Wednesday contained the simple notice of the decease, on the previous day [Nov. 11th], of Mrs. Hannah Neff Patterson.

" Funeral services were held at the house of her son-in-law, George K. Budd, Esq., after which her remains were attended by a number of friends across the river, to be conveyed thence to Cincinnati, for intermennt, in charge of her brother, Peter Neff, Esq., of that city.

" Mrs. Patterson had been a resident of our city for twenty-six years, and had a large circle of friends among our citizens. She was a most amiable woman, and an active, consistent, and exemplary Christian. She was a member of the First Presbyterian Church, in which she attended upon public worship with great constancy and faithfulness, and was regarded by her pastor and fellow-worshipers with more than ordinary esteem and veneration. She had been a consistent professor of the Christian faith for over half a century, and is believed to have been one of the earliest Sabbath-school teachers in America.

" Who can estimate the amount of good accomplished by such a life? The applauses of the world are wont to be given to those who act on more conspicuous arenas, but many of our readers will agree with us in the wish to honor, by a modest tribute,

                                              the

" the memory of this godly woman, whose quiet,
" and peaceful, and happy life among us has just
" closed. There is no danger of overestimating the
" value of such lives. We do well to study such
" characters. Mrs. Patterson was a person of whom
" those who knew her will be reminded by many
" passages in Solomon's charming description of 'the
" virtuous woman,' whose price he wisely describes to
" be ' above rubies.'

" ' She openeth her mouth with wisdom : and in her
" tongue is the law of kindness.'

" ' She looketh well to the ways of her household
" and eateth not the bread of idleness.'

" ' Her children arise up and call her blessed.'

" ' Favor is deceitful and beauty is vain, but a woman
" that feareth the Lord she shall be praised.'

" Mrs. Patterson was sustained during her sickness
" by a steadfast hope in the Saviour of sinners, in whom
" alone she trusted for salvation.

" She was anxious to depart, she said, and be with
" Christ, but she added, I will wait patiently God's
" will, and she did. 'Blessed are the dead who die in
" the Lord.'

" The Philadelphia Evangelist, in copying this obit-
" uary, prefaces it with, ' we copy from the St. Louis
" Democrat, of the 14th inst., the following notice of
" the death of Mrs. Hannah Neff Patterson, formerly
" of Frankford, in this county, where she was born,
" and resided for more than forty years. The de-
" ceased was a member of the Rev. Dr. Nelson's

                                   church,

" church, St. Louis, in which city she had resided for
" more than twenty-five years:
"   'Funeral of Mrs. Nannah Neff Patterson,
"   'November 12, 1862, by Rev. Dr. Nelson.'
" Man *that is* born of a woman *is* of few days and
" full of trouble.
" He cometh forth like a flower, and is cut down :
" he fleeth also as a shadow, and continueth not.
" Job xiv : 1, 2.
" The days of our years *are* three-score years and
" ten ; and if by reason of strength *they be* four-score
" years, yet *is* their strength labour and sorrow ; for
" it is soon cut off, and we fly away.   Ps. xc : 10.
" For what *is* your life ?   It is even a vapour, that
" appeareth for a little time, and then vanisheth away.
" James iv : 14.
" A tale that is told—thin vapour, that speedily van-
" ishes from view the unsubstantial shadow ; such
" are the Scriptural emblems of this earthly life.
" Honor thy father and thy mother ; that thy days
" may be long upon the land which the Lord thy God
" giveth thee.   Exodus xx : 12.
" Happy *is* the man *that* findeth wisdom.
" Length of days *is* in her right hand ; *and* in her
" left hand riches and honour.   Proverbs iii : 13, 16.
" The hoary head *is* a crown of glory, *if* it be found
" in the way of righteousness.   Poverbs xvi : 31.
" The righteous shall flourish like the palm tree:
" he shall grow like a cedar in Lebanon.

193   " Those

"Those that be planted in the house of the Lord
" shall flourish in the courts of our God.

"They shall still bring forth fruit in old age: they
" shall be fat and flourishing.

"To show that the Lord *is* upright: *he is* my rock,
" and *there is* no unrighteousness in him. Ps. xcii:
" 12, 13, 14, 15.

"And *even* to *your* old age I *am* he; and *even* to hoar
" hairs will I carry *you:* I have made and I will bear;
" even I will carry, and will deliver *you.* Isaiah
" xlvi: 4.

" To such comfort in old age and such divine sup-
" port may they look forward who lead lives of Scrip-
" tural piety by faith in the Lord Jesus. Such a se-
" rene and quiet evening, such a lovely and hopeful
" sunset may they enjoy whose morning and noon of
" life have dutifully and devotedly been given to God.
" Little do I need to say to those who knew her, how
" pleasantly Mrs. Patterson had these Scriptures ful-
" filled to her. Those who frequented the sanctuary
" where she worshiped, and observed how regularly
" and how early she was seen in her accustomed seat,
" and how devoutly she attended upon God's word
" and ordinances; those who often felt the friendly
" pressure of her hand and the kindly beaming of her
" face upon them, and who sometimes heard her hum-
" ble and fervent words, expressive of deep Christian
" feeling, and who observed her blameless life and
" knew her simple trust in Jesus, feel that the palm
" tree, green and fruitful and casting a wide and

                              pleasant

" pleasant shade, was her proper emblem. Who has
" not felt that to pause for a half hour, and rest from
" life's toil in pleasant conversation with such an aged
" Christian, gathering the rich clusters of ripe ex-
" perience, and feeling the restful influence of such
" Christian society, is like turning aside from a dusty
" and wearisome march to rest beneath the grateful
" shadow of a green and thrifty tree? How happy
" are they, over whose home such a palm tree casts
" its refreshing shadow, and within whose chambers
" its delicious and wholesome fruits are garnered:

" The memory of the just *is* blessed. Proverbs
" x: 7.

" The righteous shall be in everlasting *remembrance.*
" Ps. cxii: 6.

" Precious in the sight of the Lord *is* the death of
" his saints. Ps. cxvi: 15.

" Mark the perfect *man,* and behold the upright:
" for the end of *that* man *is* peace. Ps. xxxvii: 37.

" And I heard a voice from heaven saying unto me,
" Write, Blessed *are* the dead which die in the Lord
" from henceforth: Yea, saith the Spirit, that they
" may rest from their labours: and their works do
" follow them. Revelation xiv: 13.

" They shall hunger no more, neither thirst any
" more; neither shall the sun light on them, nor any
" heat.

" For the lamb which is in the midst of the throne
" shall feed them, and shall lead them unto living

fountains

" fountains of waters: and God shall wipe away all
" tears from their eyes.   Revelation vii: 16, 17.

"For if we believe that Jesus died and rose again,
" even so them also which sleep in Jesus will God
" bring with him.

" Wherefore comfort one another with these words.
" 1 Thessalonians iv: 14, 18.

" Hannah Neff Patterson, daughter of Peter and
" Rebecca Neff, was born in Frankford, Penn., June
" 8, 1787, and died November 11, 1862.

"Her remains were carried from her brother Peter's
" residence, on Walnut Street, Cincinnati, and interred
" in Spring Grove Cemetery, representatives from
" each branch of her family acting as pall-bearers.
" At the early age of eighteen she was married to
" William Patterson, of New Jersey, and had two
" children—
"   Charles Neff Patterson,
"   Rebecca Patterson.

"Charles died unmarried, and Rebecca married
" George K. Budd, of Philadelphia, Penn., now de-
" ceased, and had five children, grandchildren of Han-
" nah Neff Patterson, all now living.

" Their names are:
"   Marcia D.
"   Charles P.
"   Helen W.
"   Wayman C.
"   Isabella Neff

                                    " Wayman

"Wayman married, in San Francisco, California,
" Annabella Parks, and has four children.

" Isabella Neff Budd married Captain Buchannan
" Wade, of the United States Army, now deceased,
" and has three children, great grandchildren of Han-
" nah Neff Patterson."

251 WILLIAM PATTERSON,
Born.
Married October 24, 1805.
Died.

AND

251 HANNAH NEFF PATTER-SON,
Born June 8, 1787.
Married October 24, 1805.
Died November 11, 1862.

Children of

1 Charles Neff,
Born October 18, 1806.
Married.
Died June 6, 1850.

2 Rebecca,
Born.
Married George K. Budd.
Died.

2512 GEORGE K. BUDD,

Born February 12, 1802.
Married April 29, 1830.
Died September 24, 1875.

AND

2512 REBECCA PATTERSON
BUDD,

Born.
Married April 29, 1830.
Died.

(Residence, St. Louis, Mo.)

1 Marcia D.,
Born.
Married.
Died.

2 Charles P.,
Born.
Married.
Died.

3 Helen W.,
Born.
Married.
Died.

4 Wayman C.,
Born.
Married Annabella Parks.
Died.

5 Isabella Neff,
Born.
Married Robert Buchanan
Wade.
Died.

Children of

199

25124 Wayman C. Budd,
Born.
Married.
Died.

AND

25124 Annabella Parks
Budd,
Born.
Married.
Died.

(Residence, Chicago, Ill.)

1   Georgia Knight,
Born.
Married.
Died.

2   Wayman Clifford,
Born.
Married.
Died.

3   Britton I.,
Born.
Married.
Died.

4   Blanche,
Born.
Married.
Died.

Children of

200

25125 ROBERT BUCHANNAN
WADE,
   Born.
   Married.
   Died January 8, 1884.

AND

25125 ISABELLA NEFF BUDD
WADE,
   Born.
   Married.
   Died.

1 Robert Budd,
   Born.
   Married.
   Died.

2 George K. Budd,
   Born.
   Married.
   Died.

3 McKean Buchannan,
   Born.
   Married.
   Died.

Children of

(Residence, St. Louis, Mo.)

201

JOHN RUDOLPH NEFF.

The eldest son of Peter and Rebecca Neff, John Rudolph Neff, was born in the old brick house in Frankford, on the 12th of January, 1789, and was, consequently, but fifteen years old when his father died, in 1804. Cares and responsibilities thus early in life thrust upon him, matured him rapidly, and he soon assumed management, with his mother, of all their business interests, not, however, without fully preparing himself by a school education, to which he added two years at Princeton. His management of his father's estate is attested by the Records of the Orphan's Court, Philadelphia. His business relations and success are noted in the obituary attached to this chapter. As will appear in subsequent chapters, his own mercantile advancements he turned to the profit of his brothers, as well, with whom he was associated in the west. Marrying Caroline Bird, of Philadelphia, his married life was spent in that city. On May 29, 1843, Caroline died very suddenly, and thus, for him, began a long and lonely period of twenty years, until his death, in 1863. A portion of this time, his house and home were presided over by the queenly

dignity

dignity of his daughter, Jane, until her marriage, on
the 10th of June, 1847; after this he still continued
housekeeping, with valued and trusted servants and
the companionship of a devoted friend and amanuen-
sis, Alexander Boyd. Shortly before his death, John
R. Neff, Jr., removing, with his wife and family, to
Philadelphia, occupied the house with him, and were
thus there at the time of his death.

The following memoirs, and list, with names, etc.,
of his descendants, are as given by Josephine M. C.
Neff, wife of John R. Neff:

"On the 23rd of July, in the present year (1863),
" died, at his residence, No. 328 Spruce Street, in the
" city (Phila.), John R. Neff, in the 75th year of his
" age, an old and respected merchant. Mr. Neff com-
" menced life with but few advantages, and he is in-
" debted to his energy and mercantile talent for that
" advancement which took him through life success-
" fully, and enabled him to enjoy, in his old age, the
" ease and comfort which are secured by affluence.
" He was born in the village of Frankford, in Phila-
" delphia County, in the year 1789. He received a
" fair education for the time in which he lived, but
" enjoyed no extraordinary advantages beyond the
" ordinary tuition of the common school. His prefer-
" ences inclined to the mercantile profession, and, at
" a proper age, he was placed in the counting-house
" of Messrs. Israel, shipping merchants, Front Street,

                                                           where

" where he acquired a thorough knowledge of the
" shipping business and of the general principles reg-
" ulating trade. After he was of age, he continued
" in the position of clerk, until he had acquired suffi-
" cient headway to trust to his own efforts. This
" happy time for him arrived about the year 1815,
" when he was in the 26th year of his age. He sought
" an entrance into the western trade, and established
" himself near the center of that traffic, at No. 266
" Market Street, which was near Eighth; but he
" did not long remain in that location, but resolved
" to turn his attention to shipping interests. In 1817
" he entered into partnership with his brother, Will-
" iam Neff, and the firm established itself at the well-
" known property of Latimer and Murdock, which
" extended from the wharf to No. 67 North Water
" Street, and was on the north side of the second
" alley above Arch Street. The two brothers kept
" their dwelling at No. 295 Market Street, from which
" John R. Neff removed, some years afterwards, to
" No. 7 South Ninth Street. The firm of John R.
" and William Neff afterwards removed to No. 37
" North Water Street, which was below Arch Street,
" in the square occupied by Stephen Girard, Sam'l
" V. Anderson, Gustavus and Hugh Calhoun, Mont-
" gomery and Newbold, Smith and Ridgway, and
" others. About 1822 the firm of J. R. and W. Neff
" was dissolved, with a view to the formation of a new
" firm—Neff and Brothers, of Cincinnati, Ohio, which
" was composed of J. R. Neff, William Neff, and

                                          another

" another brother. The two latter removed to Cin-
" cinnati. In the west this house was principally en-
" gaged in the shoe business, and it was one of the
" largest concerns in Ohio. Subsequently, the busi-
" ness was extended to Louisville, in Kentucky, where
" it was represented by Neff, Wanton and Company.
"At No. 37 North Water Street Mr. Neff remained
" for several years, but, finally, he removed to No. 6
" North Wharves, which was, we believe, the last es-
" tablishment occupied by him.
"The business of the Neffs in this city and in the
" western states was extensive and prosperous, and
" yielded all the partners very profitable returns. The
" shipping branch was managed by John R. Neff,
" who established connections with Savannah and
" other southern ports. His vessels were known as
" regular packets, and the care and attention bestowed
" upon the line won general confidence. The brig
" Francis was a favorite in this line, and was for many
" years safely navigated from port to port by an old-
" fashioned seaman, faithful and careful, whose name
" we will omit, for prudential reasons. The Captain
" died while in the employment of Mr. Neff, leaving
" his family in fair circumstances. But the widow
" unexpectedly found a generous friend in John R.
" Neff. He had kept a regular account of the earn-
" ings of the brig, and knew how much he had been
" indebted for its profitable voyages to the care and
" prudence of the Captain. After the death of this
" faithful seaman, Mr. Neff balanced the account of
205   the

" the earnings of the brig, and footed up what he
" thought was due, not legally, but generously, as the
" Captain's share. We need not say that when Mr.
" Neff waited upon the widow, and presented her
" with a check for several thousand dollars, as a debt
" which, in his own mind, he considered that he owed
" the Captain, she was overwhelmed by this noble
" act, which she had no right to expect, as the Cap-
" tain had always been paid according to his agree-
" ment. There are few instances that can be named
" of similar liberality, and the simple narration of the
" circumstances tells more than volumes could of the
" kindness and generosity of John R. Neff.

"Henry Sloan and Charles P. Relf, two of our most
" estimable citizens, were clerks, about 1821, in Mr.
" Neff's store. The excellent qualifications of Mr.
" Neff, and his standing as a merchant, naturally drew
" him into public positions of trust and responsibili-
" ties. He was a Director of the Bank of the United
" States in its best days, and enjoyed the friendship
" and esteem of the leading men who were then en-
" gaged in the management of the institution. He
" was a Director of the old Saving Fund, that venera-
" ble and responsible society which has ever been
" managed with justice and with a prudent and hon-
" est regard to the interest of the worthy poor people
" who have intrusted their little accumulations to the
" care of its officers. He was also connected with the
" well-established and ever-reliable ' Insurance Com-
" pany of North America,' and gave to its concerns

                                                much

" much of his valuable time and attention. The
" Provident Society and associations of benevolence
" and charity also engaged his care. To all them he
" was a valuable and liberal friend.

"In political life he enjoyed some of the honors of
" his fellow-citizens. He was a member of the Legis-
" lature when that trust was honorable alike to the
" delegate and to his constituents. He served in the
" General Assembly for two terms. He was also a
" member of the City Councils, during the good old
" times when the city was bounded north by Vine
" Street and south by Cedar Street, and he was a
" member of the committee on Girard estates at the
" time when measures were taken to construct the
" magnificent college edifice which the merchant and
" mariner had bounteously provided for.

" Mr. Neff attached himself, at an early age, to the
" First Presbyterian Church, of which Rev. James P.
" Wilson was pastor. He worshiped in the old edi-
" fice at the corner of Bank and Market Streets.
" When the congregation removed to Washington
" Square, Mr. Neff went with them, and he sat for
" many years under the preaching of the now ven-
" erable successor to Dr. Wilson, the Rev. Albert
" Barnes. To every society of a benevolent char-
" acter under Presbyterian control he was a liberal
" giver; but he did not confine his charities to the
" sect with which he was affiliated. He was an open
" friend of all good works, no matter by what sect

                                        they

" they might be projected, and his hand and his heart
" were always ready to alleviate the distressed.

" Mr. Neff married Miss Bird, a daughter of the
" well-known citizen, Charles Bird, hardware mer-
" chant, who was once established in active business
" at No. 98 Market Street. Mr. Bird brought up
" many excellent young men, who afterward became
" noted among our first merchants. We may men-
" tion in this connection the fact that the brothers
" Earp—Thomas, Robert and George—were brought
" up in that store. They were the founders of the
" well-known firms of Earps and Baxter and Earps
" and McMain.

" John R. Neff leaves behind him that most precious
" bequest of the merchant—a good name. He was
" kind, generous, and just. During the latter years
" of his life he suffered much from disease, but he
" bore his afflictions with a noble fortitude, and proved
" how meek and cheerful the true Christian can meet
" alike the smiles of health and the trials of sickness.
" He left a large property to his representatives, which
" is computed to be worth at about half a million of
" dollars—all honestly earned, and remaining, after
" many generous and continued benefactions.

" While attempting a slight tribute to the memory
" of this lamented gentleman, it would be impossible,
" within the limits proposed, to offer any fine analysis
" of character, or to enter on any extended biography;
" while, on the one hand, the space usually assigned

                                                                 to

" to a newspaper article of this description, would
" forbid this, upon the other a consideration for views
" and tastes which were his well-known characteris-
" tics would equally operate to restrain us.

"Born in the year 1789, at Frankford, the village
" which, just north of the city, then had an independ-
" ent existence, Mr. Neff, in boyhood, entered the
" service of a mercantile house [here in Philadel-
" phia] which was then among the most prominent.
" Prompt, accurate, and careful, his advancement was
" rapid and success early assured. Viewing the ex-
" perience and incidents of this mercantile pupilage
" as contributing largely to the formation of his char-
" acter, they continue to be among the most pleasant
" recollections of his latest days. Enterprises on his
" own account, entered upon in early manhood, it is
" believed, were alike successful; but, in conjunction
" with his brothers, in the cities of Cincinnati, Ohio,
" and Louisville, Kentucky, some forty-five years
" ago, he commenced large mercantile establishments,
" whose business, through a series of years, proved
" eminently remunerative. These houses—Neff and
" Brothers, of Cincinnati, Ohio; Neff, Wanton and
" Company, of Louisville, Kentucky—enjoyed a rep-
" utation among the highest. These engagements,
" however, in a private capacity, did not prevent his
" early call to public service—first, as representative
" of the city in the State Legislature, and, subse-
" quently, as a member of both branches of the City
" Council. It is believed by the writer that he was
209   at

" at the head of the committee in select council with
" whom originated the splendid edifice provided by
" Stephen Girard's munificence. Identified, too, with
" institutions, both of a business and benevolent char-
" acter, he devoted to their services, conscientiously
" and unselfishly, all those powers, mental and moral,
" which contributed to his success in a private ca-
" pacity, and, it is believed, his record in connection
" with the Provident Society, the Philadelphia Sav-
" ing Fund Society, and Insurance Company of North
" America, will exhibit nothing to be regretted.
" While retaining, until the close of life, a warm in-
" terest in these latter institutions, his active partici-
" pation in their business had ceased, through bodily
" infirmity, several years since.

" Through a series of years Mr. Neff was connected
" as a Director with the Bank of the United States;
" but, whatever unhappy memories may be associated
" with that institution, no measure of policy ad-
" vanced by him ever contributed to its decay. Pos-
" sessing the unlimited confidence of the distinguished
" gentleman who was its presiding officer for so many
" years, his counsel was peculiarly valued on many
" trying occasions, and, it is believed, results fully
" proved this estimate of his sagacity. Unless the
" writer is greatly mistaken in his recollection, the
" presidency of the institution was at one time within
" his reach, but his private business, independent of
" other considerations, constrained his declinature
" of it.

                                      " While

"While no sectarian, Mr. Neff was yet a decided
" Christian and warmly attached to the denomination
" within whose pale he was born and reared, and
" hence the various institutions pertaining to that
" branch of the Christian Church [the Presbyterian],
" and, no less so, those of a more general character,
" enjoyed largely of his sympathy, and towards them,
" constantly, for many years, flowed his many bene-
" factions. Much more might be written in regard to
" this aspect of his character, but it can be more ap-
" propriately furnished by other hands.

"An invalid for some years, and enjoying a compe-
" tency, Mr. Neff sought and secured within his
" peaceful home that great requisite to his bodily
" comfort, as he was wont to term it, peace of mind.
" Tumultuous as were passing events [during the civil
" war], their disturbing influences were not permitted
" to reach him, and thus, amidst this voluntary se-
" clusion, the latter years of his life were passed.

"Not more serenely do evening shadows fall when
" the day is o'er than closed his earthly existence,
" leaving, as we are persuaded, memories the most
" pleasant among all who were associated with him,
" either in business or social life.   A."

This article appeared in a Philadelphia newspaper,
on August 11, 1863, and was written by Alexander
Boyd.

Mr. Neff died July 23, 1863 ; was buried at Laurel
Hill Cemetery.

                                    John

John Rudolph Neff, son of Peter and Rebecca Neff, was born January 12, 1789; died July 23, 1863.

On the 23rd September, 1817, he married Caroline Bird, of Philadelphia, Penn.

Their children were:

Jane Bird Neff,	Deceased,
William Peter Neff,	"
Rebecca Neff,	Deceased in childhood,
John Rudolph Neff, Jr.,	" " "
Charles Neff,	Deceased,
George Washington Neff,	Deceased in childhood,
James P. W. Neff,	Deceased,
John R. Neff, Jr.	

Grandchildren of John Rudolph Neff.

M. Jennie Williams, daughter of Jane B. Neff, who married Cyrus M. Williams.

———

Rudolph Neff,	Deceased,
Clark Williams Neff,	
Frank Neff,	Deceased,
Mary C. Neff,	
Percy Neff,	
Caroline B. Neff,	Deceased,
Charles Neff,	

Children of William Peter Neff, who married Narcissa Williams.

———

Caroline Neff,	Deceased,
Joseph Seal Neff,	

Children of Charles Neff, who married Mary Seal.

                                    Fannie

Fannie B. Neff,

Child of Charles Neff, who married Louisa Badger, a
second wife.

———

Rudolph Lee Neff,
Narcissa Neff,
Sarah Josephine Neff,
Jonathan Cilley Neff,

Children of John R. Neff, Jr., who married Josephine
M. Cilley.

———

Great-grandchildren of John Rudolph Neff.
Edith Cole,
Natalie Cole,

Children of M. Jennie Williams, who married George
B. Cole.

———

Leonora Gurley,

Child of Caroline B. Neff, who married Henry Gurley.

———

William Neff Armel,

Child of Mary C. Neff, who married William J. Armel.

252 **John Rudolph Neff,**
Born January 12, 1789.
Married September 23, 1817.
Died July 23, 1863.

AND

252 **Caroline Bird Neff,**
Born December 4, 1799.
Married September 23, 1817.
Died May 29, 1843.

Children of

1 Jane Bird,
Born August 17, 1818.
Married Cyrus M. Williams.
Died March 28, 1850.

2 William Peter,
Born November 14, 1819.
Married Narcissa Williams.
Died November 19, 1877.

3 Rebecca,
Born January 1, 1821.
Died January 4, 1823.

4 John Rudolph,
Born April 10, 1824.
Died April 4, 1826.

5 Charles,
Born May 25, 1825.
Married, 1st, Mary Seal;
2nd, Louisa Badger.
Died September 20, 1871.

6 George Washington,
Born July 8, 1826.
Died September 27, 1832.

7 James P. W.,
Born September 4, 1827.
Married.
Died September 24, 1855.

8 John Rudolph,
Born October 2, 1828,
Married Josephine M. Cilley.
Died.

2521 CYRUS M. WILLIAMS,
   Born March 15, 1822.
   Married June 10, 1847.   **1**
   Died June 20, 1884.

              AND   **2**

2521 JANE BIRD NEFF WILL-
      IAMS,
   Born August 17, 1818.
   Married June 10, 1847.
   Died March 28, 1850.

Caroline Neff,
   Born November 18, 1848.
   Died November 18, 1848.

M. Jennie,
   Born March 21, 1850.
   Married George B. Cole.
   Died.

Children of

25212 GEORGE B. COLE,
Born January 26, 1833.
Married February 25, 1880.
Died.

AND

25212 M. JENNIE WILLIAMS
COLE,
Born March 21, 1850.
Married February 25, 1880.
Died.

1 Edith,
Born June 5, 1881.
Married.
Died.

2 Natalie,
Born February 9, 1884.
Married.
Died.

3
Born November 29, 1885.
Married.
Died.

Children of

(Residence, Baltimore, Md.)

216

2522 WILLIAM PETER NEFF,
Born November 14, 1819.
Married December 14, 1846.
Died November 19, 1877.

AND

2522 NARCISSA WILLIAMS NEFF,
Born January 25, 1826.
Married December 14, 1846.
Died.

(Residence, Cincinnati, O.)

Children of

1 John Rudolph,
Born November 1, 1847.
Married.
Died January 31, 1876.

2 Clark Williams,
Born September 7, 1849.
Married.
Died.

3 Frank Livingston,
Born October 8, 1851.
Died November 26, 1867.

4 Mary C.,
Born July 5, 1853.
Married William J. Armel.
Died.

5 Percy Hastings,
Born July 17, 1855.
Married.
Died.

6 Caroline B.,
Born June 20, 1857.
Married Henry Gurley.
Died September 6, 1884.

7 Charles S.,
Born November 13, 1860.
Married.
Died.

8 James P. W.,
Born February 1, 1863.
Died July 18, 1865.

217

25224 WILLIAM J. ARMEL,
Born November 24, 1844.
Married December 31, 1883.
Died.

AND

25224 MARY C. NEFF ARMEL,
Born July 5, 1853.
Married December 31, 1883.
Died.

1 | Children of

William Neff,
Born November 16, 1884.
Married.
Died.

(Residence, Cincinnati, O.)

25226 Henry Gurley,
Born January 2, 1857.
Married April 22, 1880.
Died.

AND

25226 Caroline B. Neff
Gurley,
Born June 20, 1857.
Married April 22, 1880.
Died September 6, 1884.

Children of

1 Leonora,
Born February 11, 1882.
Married.
Died.

2 Infant daughter,
Died September 6, 1884.

219

2525 CHARLES NEFF,
Born May 25, 1825.
Married June 19, 1849.
Died September 20, 1871.

AND

2525 MARY SEAL NEFF,
Born.
Married June 19, 1849.
Died March 22, 1854.

1 Caroline,
Born April 12, 1850.
Married.
Died June 18, 1873.

2 Joseph Seal,
Born February 27, 1854.
Married Harriet Ludlow.
Died.

Children of

2525 CHARLES NEFF,
Married April 19, 1859.

AND

2525 LOUISA BADGER NEFF,
Born.
Married April 19, 1859.
Died.

3 Fannie Badger,
Born.
Married Samuel Evans Ewing.
Died.

Children of

25252 JOSEPH SEAL NEFF,
Born February 27, 1854.
Married June 12, 1879.
Died.

AND

25252 HARRIET LUDLOW
NEFF,
Born.
Married June 12, 1879.
Died.

(Residence, Philadelphia, Penn.)

25253 Samuel Evans Ewing,
    Born.
    Married April 9, 1885.
    Died.

AND

25253 Fanny Badger Neff
    Ewing,
    Born.
    Married April 9, 1885.
    Died.

Children of

2528 JOHN RUDOLPH NEFF,
Born October 2, 1828.
Married May 6, 1852.
Died.

AND

2528 JOSEPHINE M. CILLEY NEFF,
Born April 10, 1832.
Married May 6, 1852.
Died.

Children of

1 | Rudolph Lee,
Born August 13, 1 53.
Married.
Died.

2 | Narcissa,
Born December 8, 1856.
Married.
Died.

3 | Sarah Josephine,
Born October 16, 1861.
Married.
Died.

4 | Jonathan Cilley,
Born August 22, 1866.
Married Mary Bell Wampole.
Died.

25284 JONATHAN C. NEFF,
Born August 22, 1866,
Married December 27, 1884.
Died.

AND

25284 MARY BELL WAMPOLE
NEFF,
Born.
Married December 27, 1884.
Died.

(Residence, Philadelphia, Penn.)

Children of

CHAPTER XII.

The following biography of William Neff, written by his son, Peter Neff, was furnished by him at the compiler's request:

" Was born on the 7th day of February, 1792, at
" Frankford, Penn. His parents were Peter and Re-
" becca Neff.

"In his early boyhood, he attended, with his
" brothers and sisters, a small school, taught by an
" old man named Samuel Morrow. It was his cus-
" tom to use the rod pretty freely, and he would
" throw it at the boy to be chastised, and make him
" bring it up to him to be used in the punishment
" that followed. William's sister, Rebecca (Mrs.
" Thomas J. Biggs), relates what she witnessed—
" that, on one occasion, William went out to the pump
" for water, and stayed too long; and, as usual under
" such circumstances, the teacher threw his rod at
" William, to bring up and take the whipping, which
" he did, and then walked to his seat, picked up his
" hat and books, and turning to ' Old Sammy,' said,
" ' Good morning,' and walked out of the school-

room,

" room, and he did not return to it. He afterwards
" attended a 'Classical School,' taught by one Riley,
" as principal, and a Mr. Glass, assistant in the class-
" ics. At this school he passed several years in study,
" and graduated with a thorough English course.
" William was twelve years old when his father died.
" In his sixteenth year, 1808, he began work as an
" office boy in the commission house of Messrs. Gus-
" tavus and Hugh Calhoun, in Philadelphia, Penn.
" With this firm he served out his apprenticeship fully
" and acceptably to his employers, and he was re-
" warded by being sent by them to Lisbon, Portugal,
" in 1813, as supercargo of a ship loaded with cotton.
" The following is a copy of his original letter, and is
" expressive of his love and attachment for his home,
" his invalid mother, suffering from rheumatism, and
" for his brothers and sisters:

"   'NEW YORK, *Jan'y* 19, 1813.
" 'MRS. REBECCA NEFF, FRANKFORD, PENN.—
"   '*Dear Mother, Brothers, and Sisters:* I have now a
" task before me, which seems almost beyond my un-
" dertaking—the bidding farewell to mother, brothers,
" and sisters (I may almost say to every thing), to all
" that is dear to me in this world. On leaving Frank-
" ford, I did not show much dissatisfaction, but, I as-
" sure you, it was a task for me to leave it as I did.
" I, however, now feel perfectly reconciled to leave
" all, both relatives and friends, for a country where
" I may have greater need for them, and find none;

                                   where

" where every soul will be a stranger; where I will
" have business to transact, and know not with whom,
" whether friend or foe. I expect to leave this place
" for Savannah to-day, from whence you will hear
" from me repeatedly. I hope not to be more than
" ten days on our way from here there, and expect to
" remain there about the same number of days; to
" proceed from thence to Lisbon, and, if fortunate, to
" be in Frankford five or six months hence. John
" has promised to write me often to Savannah, Geo.,
" and I hope that the rest of you will not forget me.
    " 'I beg to be remembered to all my friends, and
" remain an affectionate son and brother,
"   'WILLIAM NEFF.
" 'P. J. O.
    " '20th. Why should I think the task too hard to
" leave my relatives and friends?—'t is but for a mo-
" ment, as it were, and then we shall meet again. Why
" should I think it hard, when we all know 't is for
" my benefit? I cheerfully resign myself to the will
" of Providence, and trust to his goodness and mercy.
" The British fleet are now at the Hook, and I expect
" they will capture us. If they do, I shall see you
" sooner than I expected. It now blows a fine N. W.
" wind, and we proceed to sea immediately. Adieu.
" Still affectionately,   WILLIAM NEFF.'

    " The good ship escaped the perils of the sea and
" the British cruisers, and its cargo was safely dis-
" charged. In Lisbon he found a friend in the Amer-

ican

" ican Consul. He remained at Lisbon several months,
" and fully executed the orders of his employers.
" Returning home, he took passage on another vessel,
" but was not so fortunate in escaping the British,
" for the vessel was captured on the high seas, and
" William was taken a captive on board a British
" man-of-war, and into Halifax, a prisoner. The
" British officer at the Port of Halifax was found to
" have been a friend of Peter Neff, of Frankford.
" Embracing William, he asked how he came to be
" there a prisoner (a happier conversation, my father
" has told me, he never had). A parole was given
" him, and he entered into the pleasures of the place.
" An incident occurred while there which William
" was always proud to relate; it was being invited to
" a ball on board a British man-of-war. He was
" taken from shore in the officers' gig, but when he
" reached the steps of the gangway to board the ship,
" he saw that the stars and stripes of his country was
" the carpet he would have to tread. At once he or-
" dered the cockswain to put him ashore, and gave
" his reason that he would not walk on the flag of his
" country. The next day the officer, his friend, called
" to explain, as an apology, that such a custom was
" usual in times of war. To which William replied,
" that it was not necessary to have invited him to the
" ball. He was always very precise and neat in his
" dress, and he frequently spoke of the prunellas and
" knee-breeches, with gold buckles and silk stock-

                                        ings,

" ings, which he wore on that occasion. The ruffled
" shirt bosom he always wore till late in life.

"In the early fall of 1818, he was released, and re-
" turned in the noble ship, Koran, to Philadelphia.
" He met all he had so reluctantly parted with in
" January, finding himself the most changed of all,
" by an experience of trials and responsibilities. His
" mother and family rejoiced with William home
" again, and likewise did the Calhouns rejoice over
" the profits he laid on their desk, as the closing act
" of his services in their commission house, resulting
" from this successful adventure to Lisbon through
" the British blockade. The future was now engaging
" his thoughts. With satisfaction over the past, he
" laid his plans midst the enjoyments of his home,
" where, as a filial son, he had for so many years
" shared its responsibilities and rejoiced in its happy
" circle of domestic life. While he was at work in
" Philadelphia, he went home regularly each week.
" At this time, he was home only for a season, and it
" seemed a dearer home than ever before. The man-
" liness of his filial affection was beautiful.

"After a few months of leisure at home, he entered
" upon a new career in life—old associations to be
" severed, home and friends parted from, for a life
" among strangers. His oldest brother, John Ru-
" dolph, being established as a merchant in Phila-
" delphia, took him into partnership in the winter of
" 1818, and their card was printed.

                                   (*Copy*).

"   (*Copy*).
"   'John R. and William Neff,
"   Philadelphia, Penn.
  " On the reverse side—
"   William Neff,
"   Commission Merchant,
"   Savannah, Geo.'

"Arriving at Savannah, in the winter of 1813–14,
" the following card was issued:

"   (*Copy*).
"   'William Neff,
"   Commission Merchant,
"   Savannah, Geo.
"   References to:
" John C. Jones, Esq.............................. Boston.
" Messrs. Divie, Bethune & Co................New York.
" Messrs. Gustavus and Hugh Calhoun...Philadelphia.
" Frederick C. Graf, Esq.......................Baltimore.
" Christopher Fitzsimons, Esq...............Charleston.'

" He remained in Savannah till spring of 1825, be-
" ing eleven years there, engaged in business as a com-
" mission merchant and cotton factor. He enjoyed
" the respect and confidence of all who knew him.
" Many associations and friendships were formed,
" which continued through life. As for pastimes and
" pleasures, incident to the times, he enjoyed hunting
" and fishing. He was a member of Judge Berrien's
" famous horse troop, and was very expert, winning
" enviable distinction as a swordsman. He was ath-

230   letic

" letic and a great jumper. The varied pursuits of
" his southern home engaged his interests and ener-
" gies. Attentive to all the details of business, he
" met with prosperity and success; reverses and losses
" incident to business enterprises were shared. One
" of their ships, loaded with cotton, was never heard
" from, all aboard perishing in mid ocean; as is sup-
" posed, the ship was struck by lightning and burned
" up, as it was reported that a fire at sea was ob-
" served, during a storm, at about the longitude their
" ship should have been in at the time. His summers
" were spent in the north and at Frankford, and the
" journey he sometimes made in stage coaches. An
" encounter with highwaymen one night caused him
" to make the journey afterwards in sailing vessels.
" The adventure was in this wise: while the stage
" was jogging along, through a dismal forest in Vir-
" ginia, and the only passenger, he heard a whistle.
" This indicated trouble. He at once climbed out the
" window to the top of the stage, and observed a man
" climbing up the ' boot; ' he fired his flint-lock pistol
" at the man, and the driver refusing to whip up the
" horses, he seized the reins and put the horses to
" their speed. Words ensued with the driver, but he
" was overawed, and so the danger passed. He was
" always convinced that this driver was in league
" with the parties in the woods, and that his fearless
" and prompt action saved the treasure he was con-
" veying, and probably saved his life. Even to a

231   much

" much later day, such risks were taken in trans-
" porting money.

"Misfortunes in business resulted in their adven-
" tures in cotton, and William began to plan a busi-
" ness life at the north in the far west. His desire to
" leave the south was, at this time, strengthened by
" what he knew and saw of slavery. He felt that
" he would not rear a family midst slaves; neither
" could he own a slave. On one occasion, while on a
" hunting trip at a friend's plantation, some distance
" up the river, the slave that was usually appointed
" by his master to be William's servant while a guest
" he found bound in the stocks, and suffering from a
" terrible whipping, given him by the overseer. He
" could, of course, do nothing but inquire into the
" case, and ask for the poor slave's release. During
" the night death came to the poor fellow's relief.
" The sad story, and its sequel, broke all his attach-
" ment for plantation life. This trying experience in-
" creased his desire to move to the north, and business
" not proving as successful as they had hoped, he de-
" cided to close out their business in Savannah, and
" to return north. This was early in the year 1825.
" During his sojourn in Savannah, he formed an at-
" tachment which bound him to the place. There
" were two sisters, the Misses Wayne (whose parents
" were dead), who lived with their uncle, Geo. An-
" derson, Esq. Their charms were of such a different
" character, and so marked, that they were desig-
" nated as ' night ' and ' morning.' Elizabeth Clifford

" Wayne reciprocated William's attention and at-
" tachment, and on the eve of his departure from Sa-
" vannah, they became finally engaged to be married,
" and arrangements were made for it when he should
" be settled in his new business. He then left for the
" north with a buoyant heart and strengthened de-
" terminations.

" When he arrived at Philadelphia, the details of
" business to be carried on in Cincinnati, Ohio, were
" not long delayed in arranging. John Rudolph Neff,
" the royal brother and capitalist in the new enter-
" prise, took, as partners, William, Peter, and George
" W. Neff, his three brothers, and William soon ar-
" ranged for the long journey into the 'far west.'
" His mother, with her sagacity and forethought,
" asked her son whether he was engaged to be mar-
" ried? William told her of his plans regarding this,
" and she told them to the brother, John Rudolph,
" who advised him to write Miss Wayne, and inquire
" if she would not 'so far change the arrangement as
" to consent to be married, and at once go west. The
" advice was acted upon, and her consent was given,
" so that William sailed for Savannah much sooner
" than they had expected; and on the 19th May, 1825,
" William Neff married Elizabeth Clifford Wayne,
" daughter of Richard Wayne, Esq., ot English de-
" scent.

" They received a hearty welcome in the old stone
" house, at Frankford, from all the family. A short
" time was passed in making the final preparations

                                             for

" for the move to Cincinnati. Meanwhile Clifford
" won the affections of all the family, so that when
" they departed it was the loss also of a daughter to
" Rebecca and a sister to the children. The long and
" weary journey ended, they soon began housekeep-
" ing in the brick building at the south-east corner of
" Sycamore and Fifth Streets, which was, at that
" time, in the suburbs of Cincinnati, Ohio. In 1827,
" they bought the middle one of the three brick
" houses which stand on the south side of Fifth
" Street between Sycamore and Broadway, and nearly
" opposite the M. E. Church (then the old stone
" building), Wesley Chapel. Here they resided till
" 1851, when they moved to his residence, old No. 419
" West Sixth Street, west of Park Street. At this
" residence William Neff died, in 1856.

" It was ever a sad reflection of theirs, that they
" never revisited their southern home, and *there* met
" their numerous friends and relatives. Almost yearly
" they visited the east, taking their children with
" them, journeying by slow stages, generally in their
" private carriages; frequent stops were made along
" the Old National Road to enjoy fishing or hunting.
" The hospitable landlords of the wayside inns af-
" forded most enjoyable and comfortable quarters for
" travelers. At Laurel Hill, among the mountains,
" several days were usually passed. Their friends and
" relatives from the south were met during their
" visits at Philadelphia and other eastern places, and
" they also had the pleasure of their occasional visits

                                          in

" in their Ohio homes. Approaching Baltimore, in
" 1833, they quitted the carriage to try the novel mode
" of riding in the railway coach.

" Their last visit to the old homestead and family,
" in Frankford, was made in 1833. Their return
" journeys were often shortened by taking a steam-
" boat at Pittsburg or Wheeling, carrying aboard,
" also, the carriages and horses.

" The mercantile and business firm of 'Neff and
" Brothers' was established in 1825, doing a general
" wholesale trade in hardware, queensware, boots and
" shoes, which proved very successful to all the broth-
" ers. The firm occupied the building on the south-
" west corner of Main and Columbia Streets. The
" ground lease, for 99 years, was made by William
" for his brother, John R. Neff, who continued to re-
" side in Philadelphia. The buildings, which still
" stand there, he erected on the ground lease.. Dur-
" ing the flood of 1832, the water stood about five feet
" on the first floor of this building, and entrance was
" made through the second-story window by rowing
" in a yawl from Pearl Street.

" Drays and transportation wagons were little used
" in those days. There were no railroads, and no
" 'commercial travelers' employed. Merchants came
" in their canvas-covered 'Conastoga wagons,' some-
" times called 'prairie schooners,' to make their semi-
" annual purchases of goods, and carried their mer-
" chandise back with them to their country stores, and
" in many cases distant towns. The ways of con-
235ducting

" ducting business, as well as the modes of living,
" were, in many respects, essentially different from
" what they now are. However, the sum of pleasure
" and enjoyment, both in business and living, was not
" the less on account of those modes which we would
" *deplore*, if they could be now restored.

"In 1836 William withdrew from the firm of 'Neff
" and Brothers,' and engaged in the pork and beef-
" packing business, establishing himself at the north-
" west corner of Court and Vine Streets, and subse-
" quently at the south-east corner of Vine and Canal
" Streets, before the canal basin was abandoned. For
" nearly nineteen years he was engaged in the pork
" business. He then became a partner in the steam
" sugar refinery, on Pearl Street between Elm and
" Plum Streets, closing, at the end of life, a year of
" successful business in sugars.

" William Neff died on the 25th November, 1856,
" and was entombed in his burial lot in Spring Grove
" Cemetery, Cincinnati, Ohio.

" During the residence of William Neff in Cincin-
" nati, covering a period of thirty-one years, he was
" active in public enterprises and zealous in good
" works and investments for the prosperity of the
" city.

" In 1829 he was a Director of the U. S. Branch
" Bank, etc., associated with Peter Benson, Robert
" Buchanan, and other pioneers. He served as di-
" rector and president of turnpike and bridge com-
" panies; at one time, as President of the O. & M. R. R.

                                          He

" He was an importer and breeder of fine stock—
" Durham cattle, Berkshire hogs, and Southdown
" sheep—on his once famous Cheviot farm (after-
" wards the home of the late Hon. Chas. Robb).

"For full accounts of his farming operations and
" horticulture, refer to the volumes of the 'American
" Farm and Garden,' published at Cincinnati, 1832 to
" 1842.   His devotion to agriculture, horticulture,
" and raising of fine stock extended to his large farm
" in Edgar County, Illinois, from 1836 to 1852; also,
" to his Yellow Springs farm, in Greene County,
" Ohio, from 1842 up to the time of his death.   Here,
" as well as enjoying the pleasures of his farm and
" rural home, he so generously and happily dispensed
" his hospitalities to relatives and numerous friends,
" in whose memory the couplet, William Neff and
" the Yellow Springs, awaken recollections of happy
" associations, joyous days of the past, which can
" not be lived over again, yet are fresh in memory's
" store-house of pleasures that never will be for-
" gotten.

" William Neff was not an aspirant in politics—an
" old-line Whig, a conservative, and had a well-bal-
" anced mind; his judgment was good.   He was on the
" committee which located the 'Methodist Episcopal
" Book Concern' at the corner of Eighth and Main
" Streets, though he urged the corner of Fourth and
" Main Streets as a better site for it; also, to locate
" the Custom House at the corner of Fourth and
" Vine Streets, with Josiah Lawrence and others.   He

                                        was

" was one of the incorporators of the Spring Grove
" Cemetery, January, 1845. He was an active mem-
" ber of the ' Cincinnati Chamber of Commerce.' On
" the great questions of his time—temperance and
" slavery—he had his share of duty and responsibility.
" With reference to the temperance question, he acted
" on the Apostolic injunction, to be 'temperate in all
" things;' looking at prohibition, in its moral, polit-
" ical, and legal aspects, he firmly concluded that the
" traffic in liquors should be regulated, restrained, and
" controlled by legislative enactments, and that the
" public intemperate man should be punished. He
" believed, that if a pure, unadulterated wine could
" be produced, so cheap that all could be supplied,
" this would afford an efficient check to the evils of
" strong drink. He would have the young reared
" midst the evils and temptations of intemperance,
" with the same vigilant care and watchfulness as are
" exercised over them regarding the various other
" social evils and temptations. He believed that legal
" enactments, prohibiting intemperance and the com-
" mission of crime, do not work out reformation of
" character; but that laws were for the punishment
" of offenders, and not against opinions, but against
" acts and crimes.

" As a Christian philosopher, he felt the religion of
" Jesus Christ was the only efficient and appointed
" remedial agent for all the sins of men; that any
" other plan for saving men, body as well as soul, was
" derogatory to the Divine will and plan, and always

a

" a failure; that, until the heart is first renewed and
" made right by the power of the Holy Spirit, that no
" prohibitory legislation could legislate men to be
" temperate in any thing.

" The slavery question pressed issues upon him with
" fearful forebodings. He was opposed to the exten-
" sion of the demon of slavery into new territory;
" he was also opposed to interference with the insti-
" tution in the slave states. He could not view, with
" any allowance, the extreme measures of either the
" Abolitionists, or the pro-slavery party. He well
" knew the evils of the system; he abhorred it, and
" felt that it was encompassed with so many evils to
" the white people, that Georgia, with other southern
" states, following the example and experience of
" those northern states with their unprofitable slave
" systems, would manumit their slaves by some equit-
" able and just policy. The slave property, which,
" by inheritance, fell to his estimable wife, was freed
" under the laws of the state of Georgia, for she
" shared her husband's feelings and sympathies on
" this subject. While he would not countenance the
" abduction of slaves, yet, when appealed to for aid
" in behalf of a poor fugitive, he was ready to give
" help for the fugitive's present necessity, and for his
" journey onward into Canada. He was more ready and
" willing to aid the fugitive from slavery when he had
" escaped and gotten into a free state than he would to
" be a party to any execution of the infamous 'Fu-
" gitive slave law' for the capture of the fugitives.

                                        His

" His strong anti-slavery feelings took deep hold upon
" the poor fleeing slave, and cases were not wanting
" for him to practically exhibit his sympathies for the
" colored people. During the 'Negro mob of 1841,'
" he sheltered a number of colored people. It fre-
" quently happened that colored people were 'kid-
" naped' or arrested and hurried across the Ohio
" River, and put into jail in Kentucky. When un-
" dergoing trial, they were almost always remanded
" back to the party claiming such persons as their
" slave property. The late Chief Justice S. P. Chase,
" a friend and neighbor of William Neff, would often
" plead the cause of such poor blacks. When it be-
" came evident that the prisoner would be sent into
" slavery, whether a runaway or not, then Mr. Chase
" would, at times, confer with William Neff about
" purchasing the black man or woman, as the case
" might be, and it several times resulted in the pur-
" chase of the slave from his master. He would then
" execute the legal papers and manumit the slave.
" Such freed colored people were full of gratitude, and
" continued constant friends, and repaid their pur-
" chase money.

  "I will relate one such incident that came under
" the writer's own observation. It was the case of
" one colored man, about twenty-five years old, named
" Anderson, who had, about the year 1833, served my
" father as coachman, and journeyed with the family
" to Philadelphia, and returned, driving the baggage
" wagon. My father always drove the family car-

                                          riage.

" riage. It was observed that parties followed them
" in their journeyings. After their return to Cincin-
" nati, this Anderson was suddenly seized, while shak-
" ing carpets in the vacant lot by the grave-yard
" about Wesley Chapel, and hurried across the river
" into jail in Newport, Ky. The trial would have
" resulted in Anderson being sent back to slavery.
" My father, with Mr. Chase, went into the jail, and
" asked Anderson to tell them the truth, whether he
" was a slave or not, and who was his owner. He
" confessed that he was a slave, and the man claiming
" him was his master, and then pleaded that he might
" not be sent back into slavery. Whereupon, my
" father purchased Anderson from his master for
" eight hundred dollars, and gave him his freedom.
" Anderson proved to be a good cook, and found em-
" ployment on a New Orleans steamboat. Before he
" had fully repaid his purchase, he was drawn over-
" board, in bailing a bucket of water, and was
" drowned.

" Cynthia Pendleton, also freed by his aid, was able
" to purchase several of her family out of slavery.
" She lived to see her race set free, though it was by
" the price of the war of the Rebellion ; and also old
" ' Maum Minty,' whose recent death, at the age of
" over one hundred years, and who will be long re-
" membered by many, owed her freedom to his aid
" and protection.

" William Neff died during the agitation that pre-
" ceded the outbreak of the slave power into open war

                                    against

" against freedom and the government. He feared
" bloodshed, and said, that if the south drew the
" sword, that slavery would cease.

"In educational matters he took a deep and active
" interest. For the preparation of his own sons for
" college and business, he had a private instructor,
" Mr. Montague Phelps, at his Yellow Springs resi-
" dence. Some friends sent their sons also, and thus
" formed a private school, of about fourteen boys,
" from 1842 to close of 1846. In 1842 he was ap-
" pointed one of the committee to report as to a suit-
" able place for establishing 'an institution which
" should embrace all the branches of female educa-
" tion.' This resulted in the foundation of the Wes-
" leyan Female College of Cincinnati. He was also
" one of the first trustees of the Ohio Wesleyan Uni-
" versity, at Delaware, Ohio. He assisted O. M.
" Mitchell, in his organization of the observatory on
" Mt. Adams, etc.

"For over twenty-five years William and Elizabeth
" Clifford Neff were faithful, zealous Christians, and
" earnest members of the Methodist Episcopal Church,
" being intimately associated with the events and
" early history of Wesley Chapel, where they first
" joined. They were very tolerant and charitable to-
" wards those differing in religious opinions and prac-
" tices. Their piety was not that which judged
" others by their own standards of belief and conduct.
" In the broadest sense they lived and acted towards
" others as the Saviour did when his Disciples would

                                    forbid

" forbid those from casting out devils, because they
" 'followed not with them;' when Jesus said to them,
" 'forbid him not, for he that is not against us is for
" us.' They studied the Scriptures as their sole rule
" of faith and practice, and followed Christ as their
" pattern among men. They condemned hasty judg-
" ment as unchristian. They made their Christianity
" a joyous service, and used the good things of life
" which God gave them without abusing them. They
" wanted to make everybody about them, especially
" the young, happy and cheerful. They entered into
" the sports of young people, and 'rejoiced with them
" that did rejoice.' In non-essentials, and in things
" not forbidden in God's word, they were indulgent
" and tolerant, desiring that every one should settle
" the matters of his conduct and practice by his own
" conscience with his God, and not have all square
" their conduct by an inexorable and inflexible rule;
" while, on the fundamentals of Christianity, with-
" out which no one can serve the Lord, they were
" firm and exacting. Their faith was in the Gospel of
" Jesus Christ. With such Christian tempers, it is
" not surprising that they cast the mantle of benevo-
" lence and moderation over many of the rules of
" their church—those wherein the 'letter killeth, but
" the spirit giveth life.' They allowed differences of
" judgment and of conduct as perfectly consistent
" with Christian character, and did not claim that the
" right was always on one side; nor did they cry,
" 'The Temple of the Lord are we,' but, quietly and

                              unobtrusively,

" unobtrusively, they 'proved their faith by their
" works.' They made their home a Christian house-
" hold, bright and cheerful, and the fireside was the
" sportive place for amusements and instruction of
" their joyous children.

"These facts should be noted : that Elizabeth Clif-
" ford Wayne was confirmed, at Savannah, by Bishop
" Dehon, of the Protestant Episcopal Church, and
" that her fervent evangelical piety exerted its influ-
" ence for many years prior to her uniting with the
" Methodist Episcopal Church at the same time her
" husband, William Neff, joined it. In Savannah he
" attended Dr. Kolloch's Presbyterian Church. The
" first years of their life in Cincinnati they were
" members of Christ Protestant Episcopal Church,
" under the rectorship of Dr. Johnson; afterwards, of
" Dr. Aydelote. During the agitation of the slavery
" question, for a while, they connected themselves
" with Soule Chapel, and subsequently united with
" the Park Street Methodist Episcopal Church; and
" after his death, she quite frequently attended, with
" her children, the Protestant Episcopal Church, many
" of her friends and associates being members of
" Christ Protestant Episcopal Church, under the pas-
" torate of Rev. J. W. McCarty, Rector.

" The following was written by the late Rev. Jas.
" B. Finley, one of those wonderful pioneers of Meth-
" odism whose fame is throughout the churches, and
" was published in the Western Christian Advocate :

                              " RECOLLECTIONS

"In 1831 I became acquainted with the late Will-
" iam Neff, and have been intimately acquainted with
" him ever since. He was early instructed in the
" truths of Christianity by a pious widowed mother,
" and was a firm believer in the inspiration and di-
" vinity of the Bible; and this had its influence on
" his heart, and swayed a scepter over his feelings
" which often brought a deep conviction of the neces-
" sity of experiencing its power. I was a witness to
" the struggle of his soul seeking after God, and was
" with him when he found the Pearl of great price.
" His passage from death to life was clear, peaceful,
" and triumphant, and, as pastor, I received him into
" the church of Christ, and have been intimate with
" him as a man and Christian till his decease. As a
" Christian, he was practical and conscientious in the
" discharge of all his duties to himself, his family,
" and the church of his choice. He served in several
" official relations: as a steward, his purse was al-
" ways open in the support of the ministry and all
" benevolent enterprises, and in this he had no su-
" perior, that I know of; as a leader, he was atten-
" tive and most affectionate in teaching those com-
" mitted to his care how to fight the good fight of
" faith, and to lay hold on eternal life. But his
" greatest attachment was to his class of children, of
" whom he had a great number. He had a peculiar
" talent for instructing them and leading their youth-
" ful minds to the knowledge of God, the most of

245   whom

" whom afterwards became professing Christians and
" useful members of the church of Christ. He often
" conversed with me on the early instruction of chil-
" dren, and said that the Sabbath-school, though ex-
" cellent in its place, was not sufficient; but that they
" ought to be classed, and catechised, and prayed
" with, and taught the truth of experimental religion.
" As a trustee, he was indefatigable and liberal in his
" donations.

" Brother Neff was a great friend of the poor, white
" or black. I know whereof I speak. For the two
" years I lived in his family I was his almoner, and
" during the cold and searching weather, from ten to
" fifteen dollars per day did I, from his hand, bear to
" the homes of the needy and destitute, besides the
" relief his kitchen afforded to the hungry and the
" naked, and what his excellent wife distributed. He
" was a safe counselor, both in spiritual and temporal
" things, and often, for twenty-five years, I have
" sought his counsel, and have never regretted that I
" have followed his advice. He was a practical man;
" this is well known by the citizens of the city and its
" business men as well as the church, and the worth
" of such a man is rarely or properly appreciated in
" society. He was vigorous, as well as practical, in
" all his business undertakings, and, in general, suc-
" cessful. He was a peacemaker in society, and often
" to him was referred difficulties, both in commercial
" as well as in religious associations; for he was
" honest, and his decisions were just and righteous.

 He

" He was generous, and well do I know it. His gen-
" erosity was not of that kind which lavishes kind-
" ness on you in your presence, and as soon as your
" back is turned, speaks of you with contempt, and
" vilifies your character. He was no bigot; his soul
" was not pent up with narrow, contracted views of
" Christianity, but he extended the hand and the
" heart of fellowship to all who feared God and
" wrought righteousness.

" He was a politician; he loved his country; he un-
" derstood his own rights and his responsibilities as a
" citizen, without the desire of the emoluments aris-
" ing from office. His friendship was ardent, flowing
" from a heart filled with love to God and man. It
" was pleasant to be his associate, and of this I had
" the pleasure for many years.

" Reader, you ask, 'had your friend no faults?'
" He had his faults incident to humanity, but as few
" as fall to the lot of men; and these I covered over
" with the mantle of love, knowing my own, for love
" covers over a multitude of our shortcomings.

" But now he has gone. The Master has come and
" called for him, and he was prepared to go, and to
" go cheerfully. His faith was strong in God and the
" power of his might; his soul was anchored by hope to
" Him that was within the veil, sure and steadfast, and
" did not fail him when Jordan's waves around him
" rolled. He fully experienced God's promise recorded
" in the 41st Psalm and first three verses; read it. He
" crossed Jordan at a bold point. His afflictions

                                                        were

" were short, but no murmur escaped his lips. Hav-
" ing settled his temporal affairs and set his house in
" order, he took his leave of his affectionate wife and
" children, giving each his departing blessing and ad-
" vice; then to his relations and friends, exhorting
" all to prepare for death and to meet him in heaven.
" I can fancy I hear him singing, with the poet:

"   'O, who can tell a Saviour's worth,
"   Or speak of Grace's power;
"   Or benefits of a new birth
"   In a departing hour.

"   'Come nigh, kind death, untie life's thread,
"   I shall to God ascend;
"   In joys I there shall with him dwell,
"   Joys that shall never end.

"   'Jesus, the vision of thy face
"   Hath overpowering charms;
"   Scarce shall I feel death's cold embrace,
"   If Christ be in my arms.

"   'And when you hear my heart strings break,
"   How sweet the moments roll;
"   A mortal paleness on my cheek,
"   But glory in my soul.'

    "May God comfort the widow, and children, and
" friends, and bring them and us all to join him in
" the eternal songs of the redeemed in heaven.
"   November, 1856.   JAS. B. FINLEY.'

    " This occasion is taken to state some facts regard-
" ing our ancestors—the Wayne family, (De) Clifford,
248   Smyth,

"Smyth, and Gresham families—hoping that a full
" history may be compiled of their descendants.

"Richard Wayne came from London, England, as
" junior Major in the Royal Welsh Fusilier 23rd
" Regiment (Pierce Butler was senior Major), to the
" American Colony, in South Carolina, about the year
" 1760. The 14th September, 1769, he married Miss
" Elizabeth Clifford, or De Clifford, the daughter of
" Thomas (De) Clifford, of South Carolina, and he went
" into mercantile life at Charleston, South Carolina.
" With his family he moved to Savannah, Georgia,
" about the year 1780, where he died, in 1809. He
" was a Tory. Their children were Richard and Eliz-
" abeth Clifford (twins), Mary, James Moore, Will-
" iam Clifford, Thomas, Stephen.

"Elizabeth Clifford married George Anderson, of
" Savannah, Georgia.

" Mary married Richard Montgomery Stites, of New
" Jersey.

" James Moore Wayne married Mary Julia Camp-
" bell, of Virginia. James Moore Wayne was Asso-
" ciate Justice of the Supreme Court of the United
" States. His wife survives him, now in her 94th
" year.

" William Clifford Wayne married Ann Gordon, of
" Augusta, Georgia.

" Thomas and Stephen died in their childhood.

" Richard Wayne, the eldest child, was born at
" Charleston, South Carolina, about 1771. Towards
" the close of that century, he became a merchant at

                    Augusta,

" Augusta, Georgia, and in 1800 he married Julianna
" Smyth, of Chestertown, Kent County, Maryland.
" She was educated in England.   Her father, Thomas
" Smyth, was a Colonel in the British army, and mar-
" ried his cousin, Mary Gresham, and he was a Col-
" onist. Julianna Smyth Wayne died on the 25th
" April, 1807, at Savannah, Georgia, being 25 years
" and .8 months of age.   Richard Wayne was chief
" foreman of the Savannah, Georgia, fire depart-
" ment, and at a fire he received an injury which
" caused his death, in December, 1822, and he was
" buried on New Year's day, 1823.   Their children
" were: Mary Eliza Smyth (after the death of her
" mother she was called Mary Julia Wayne). She
" married Robert Pooler, of Savannah, Georgia.
" Richard Wayne, who married Henrietta Harden, of
" Savannah, Georgia.   Thomas Smyth Wayne, who
" married Eliza Caldwell Roe, of Savannah, Georgia.
" Stephen Wayne, died eleven days old, soon after the
" death of his mother, Julianna Smyth Wayne, in
" 1807.   Their daughter, the second child, Elizabeth
" (De) Clifford Wayne, was born at Savannah, Geor-
" gia, the 3rd January, 1803.   She married William
" Neff, the 19th May, 1825, and she died at Cincinnati,
" Ohio, the 18th October, 1864, and was laid to rest
" beside her husband in Spring Grove Cemetery.

" This chapter would be incomplete without a trib-
" ute to the memory of Elizabeth Clifford Wayne

Neff.

" Neff. All who knew her, love to cherish recollec-
" tions of her; her good influence is leavening, and
" will continue to leaven so long as a descendant shall
" remain to rise and call her blessed. Her good works
" do follow her.

" The following memorial was published, soon after
" her death, by Miss J. M. Fuller:

" It is the duty of all to acknowledge in the dispen-
" sation of Divine Providence; and while the ' rod is
" heavy that smites,' it is especially the Christian's
" privilege to bow meekly in resignation, and feel that
" ' He doeth all things well.' The hand of God has
" taken from our circle one whose blameless life and
" Christian character pre-eminently fitted her for use-
" fulness in this life, and for the blessings of that
" which is to come. One of life's brightest lights
" went out when God took to himself our beloved
" sister and friend, and we are left to cherish her
" memory and emulate her many virtues. The church
" has lost a consistent Christian, her family its guiding
" star, society an ornament, the poor a friend, and the
" Home Mission its long and faithful member.

" Her life was truly spent in the cause of her Re-
" deemer, zealous in her work, and true in all things;
" the strong staff of Christian fortitude bore her up
" when afflictions came, and as her days drew well
" nigh to a close, the hand of the Saviour led her
" safely through ' the dark valley;' and when the

251   lamp

" lamp of life was nearly spent, the light of faith
" opened the way, and her pure spirit passed tri-
" umphantly in glory to its God. To her stricken
" family, relations, and friends, we tender heartfelt
" sympathies for their irreparable loss, and unite with
" them in mourning this sad bereavement.

"   "'T is sweet to die with Jesus nigh,
"   The rock of our salvation.'

" CINCINNATI, OHIO, ⎱   J. M. FULLER,
"   October, 1864. ⎰   *In behalf of the Board of the
                             Home Missions of the M. E. Church.*

———

" We can not live over again our childhood's happy
" days under our parents' roof; memory alone can
" go over the associations of those days. Time and
" changes can not efface these recollections; and while
" we recall the pious, noble lives of our parents, let
" us, their children and grandchildren, aspire to their
" Christian faith and zeal, and seek to lay up in
" heaven 'treasures' that shall unite us all again for-
" ever.

———

" We have gathered these events in the lives of our
" parents, not for public gaze, but for the guidance of
" ourselves, taking the history of our dearest ones as
" helps to our conduct, that we may make our lives
" the more noble in all that constitutes true and
" Christian character.

252   The

The descendants of William and Elizabeth Clifford (Wayne) Neff are:

Children.

Peter,
William Clifford,
Julianna Wayne,   Deceased,
Richard Wayne,   Deceased,

Richard Wayne Neff, Lieutenant, Company L, 4th Ohio Volunteer Cavalry, was killed at the battle of Chickamauga, at Craw-fish Springs, the 20th day of September, 1863. He was buried in 1864, in Spring Grove Cemetery.

John Rudolph,   Deceased,
Elizabeth Clifford Wayne,   Deceased,
Montague Phelps,   Deceased,
Edmund Waggener Sehon,
James Moore Wayne.

Grandchildren.

Elizabeth Clifford,
Thomas J. Biggs,   Deceased,
William,   Deceased,
Rebekah,
Peter, Jr.,

Children of Peter Neff, who married Sarah A. Biggs.

Nicholas W. Thomas,   Deceased,
William,   Deceased,
Clifford Gordon,

253   Kathrina L.,

Kathrina L.,
Theodore,
Eliza Clifford,
Children of William Clifford Neff, who married Ellen
B. Thomas.

Stewart Maurice,
Child of M. Phelps Neff, who married Susan L. Wood.

Clifford Alfred,
Nina Wayne,
Edmund Eugene,
Children of Edmund W. S. Neff, who married Estelle
J. Fechet.

Nettelton G.,
Richard Wayne,
Louise A.,
Children of J. M. Wayne Neff, who married Lucille
Nettelton.

253 William Neff,

Born February 7, 1792.
Married May 19, 1825.
Died November 25, 1856.

AND

253 Elizabeth Clifford Wayne Neff.

Born January 3, 1803.
Married May 19, 1825.
Died October 18, 1864.

Children of

1 Peter,
Born April 13, 1827.
Married Sarah A. Biggs.
Died.

2 William Clifford,
Born April 8, 1829.
Married Ellen B. Thomas.
Died.

3 Juliana Wayne,
Born September 30, 1832.
Died February 8, 1837.

4 Richard Wayne,
Born January 23, 1835.
Married.
Died September 20, 1863.

5 John Rudolph,
Born June 25, 1837.
Died September 27, 1839.

6 Elizabeth Clifford Wayne,
Born January 30, 1840.
Died January 25, 1841.

7 Montague Phelps,
Born November 14, 1841.
Married Susan L. Wood.
Died February 8, 1886.

8 Edmund Waggener Sehon,
Born March 11, 1843.
Married Estelle J. Fechet.
Died.

9 James Moore Wayne.
Born April 9, 1847.
Married Lucille Nettelton.
Died.

2531 PETER NEFF.
Born April 13, 1827.
Married February 27, 1850.
Died.

AND

2551 SARAH A. BIGGS NEFF.
Born June 15, 1821.
Married February 27, 1850.
Died.

1 Elizabeth Clifford,
Born August 24, 1851.
Married.
- Died.

2 Thomas J. Biggs,
Born March 30, 1856.
Died February 19, 1860.

3 William,
Born February 1, 1858.
Died January 20, 1860.

4 Rebekah,
Born August 2, 1860.
ed.
Died.

5 Peter,
Born March 15, 1868.
Married.
Died.

Children of

(The above parties reside at Gambier,
Knox County, Ohio.)

256

2532 WILLIAM CLIFFORD NEFF.
Born April 8, 1829.
Married February 14, 1854.
Died.

AND

2532 ELLEN B. THOMAS NEFF.
Born February 14, 1834.
Married February 14, 1854.
Died.

Children of

1 Nicholas W. Thomas,
Born April 25, 1855.
Died June 28, 1855.

2 William,
Born November 6, 1856.
Died November 9, 1856.

3 Clifford Gordon,
Born July 19, 1859.
Married.
Died.

4 Katharina L.
Born August 1, 1861.
Married.
Died.

5 Theodore,
Born January 24, 1868.
Married.
Died.

6 Eliza Clifford,
Born September 17, 1870.
Married.
Died.

(The above parties reside at Cincinnati, O.)

2537 MONTAGUE PHELPS
  NEFF.
  Born November 14, 1841.
  Married February 17, 1863.
  Died February 8, 1886.

AND

2537 SUSAN L. WOOD NEFF.
  Born May 10,   .
  Married February 17, 1863.
  Died.

1 Children of

Stewart Maurice,
  Born June 3, 1866.
  Married.
  Died.

2538 EDMUND WAGGENER
SEHON NEFF.
Born March 11, 1843.
Married July 18, 1866.
Died.

AND

2538 ESTELLE J. FECHET
NEFF.
Born February 22, 1848.
Married July 18, 1866.
Died.

1 Clifford Alfred,
Born May 5, 1867, at Savannah, Ga.
Married.
Died.

2 Nina Wayne,
Born December 20, 1869, at Yellow Springs, O.
Married.
Died.

3 Edmund Eugene,
Born February 3, 1872, at Port Huron, Mich.
Married.
Died.

Children of

(The above parties reside at Cleveland, O.

2539 JAMES MOORE WAYNE **1** Nettelton,
    NEFF.
Born April 9, 1847.
Married September 30, 1868.
Died.

AND

2539 LUCILLE NETTELTON
    NEFF.
Born April 8, 1848.
Married September 30, 1868.
Died.

1 Nettelton,
Born September 25, 1869.
Married.
Died.

2 Richard Wayne,
Born April 27, 1873.
Married.
Died.

3 Louise Aguiel,
Born July 17, 1875.
Married.
Died.

Children of

(The above parties reside at Cincinnati, O.)

CHAPTER XIII.

REBECCA NEFF.

The ensuing chapter, containing the history of Rebecca Neff, the last surviving member of the family of Peter and Rebecca Neff, is contributed for the use of the compiler by her daughter, Sarah A. Biggs Neff:

"Rebecca Neff was born on the 1st day of May,
" 1796, in Frankford, Penn. She was the second
" daughter of Peter and Rebecca Neff; was educated
" at Madam George's school, Philadelphia. In her
" twenty-fifth year she married Thomas J. Biggs,
" Pastor of the Presbyterian Church, Frankford, of
" which her grandfather, Rudolph Neff, had been one
" of the founders. The marriage took place on the
" 7th of September, 1820, her sister, Mary, and Miss
" Castor, with the late Rev. Dr. Hodge, of Princeton,
" and the Rev. Dr. Steele, of Abington, Penn., being
" the attendants on the occasion. They continued to
" live in Frankford until the year 1832, during which
" time six children were born. In that year Rev. Mr.
" Biggs received a call to the Presidency of Washing-
" ton College, Pennsylvania, but declined it to accept
" a call to a Professorship in Lane Theological Sem-

inary,

" inary, Walnut Hills, Cincinnati, Ohio, where an en-
" dowment had been made, conditioned upon the Rev.
" Mr. Biggs filling the chair. The journey from
" Frankford to Cincinnati, at that time, required a
" week of tedious traveling, which they undertook,
" with five children, the oldest son, Joseph, having
" gone out with his father the year previous, where
" he remained with his relatives.

"At Walnut Hills, as a Professor, Rev. T. J. Biggs
" remained for six years. When the division in the
" Presbyterian Church took place, he resigned his
" position, and accepted a call to Cincinnati College,
" as President, in 1838. They then removed to the
" city. His administration there was successful, but
" the college building was burned down, and the col-
" lege suspended. On the 27th October, 1845, he en-
" tered upon the Presidency of Woodward College,
" and held the office until the organization of the
" Woodward High School. Later he spent a few
" years in the pastorate of the Fifth Presbyterian
" Church. The latter position he held until failing
" health necessitated his retiring from all active labors,
" except that he continued his position as President
" of the Board of Directors of the House of Refuge
" until his death, and where he loved to go as long as
" his health permitted him to ride. Some years pre-
" vious to his death he was connected with the organ-
" ization of the Seventh Presbyterian Church, on
" Broadway, Cincinnati. In short, his labors were

                              always

" always directed toward the promotion of Christ's
" kingdom.

"The following extract, from a Cincinnati paper,
" which appeared shortly after his death, gives, in
" brief, a history of his life:

"   'DEATH OF DR. BIGGS.

"'Another name is added to the long list of aged Cin-
" cinnatians, deceased within the last twelve months;
" and another vacancy occurs to remind us that the
" generation of noble men who laid the foundations
" of our city, and contributed largely to establish
" those Christian and educational institutions, the ad-
" vantages of which we now so fully enjoy, are rap-
" idly disappearing. Yesterday, Rev. Thomas J. Biggs,
" D.D., was called to his rest. This announcement
" will not surprise those who were aware of the con-
" dition of the health of the deceased for some time
" past; but the announcement of his death will, nev-
" ertheless, be received with sorrow by our citizens,
" who have known him from his long connection
" with the religious and educational interests of Cin-
" cinnati, and who esteemed and loved him for his
" many excellent qualities. Faults, he had few; vir-
" tues, he had many; enemies, he had none; friends,
" they were as numerous as his acquaintances. If he
" has not enjoyed the fame of great men, in the gen-
" eral acceptation of that term, he has been rever-
" enced as a father in Israel, and as a meek, faithful,
" and consistent Christian.

263   Dr.

"'Dr. Biggs was born in Philadelphia in the year
"1787. He graduated at Nassau Hall, and afterward
"studied for the ministry at Princeton Theological
"Seminary, then under the care of Rev. Archibald
"Alexander, D.D. He afterward was a tutor in
"Princeton College, and thence removed to Frank-
"ford, near Philadelphia, where he became Pastor of
"the Presbyterian Church, and married Rebecca Neff,
"who, after a union of over forty years, survives
"him. In 1832 he removed to Cincinnati, and be-
"came one of the professors in Lane Theological
"Seminary, at its organization. The professorship
"was endowed by friends at the east expressly for
"him. Here he remained many years, till the unfor-
"tunate division in the Presbyterian Church, when
"he resigned his professorship, and became President
"of the Cincinnati College, with the lamented Gen-
"eral O. M. Mitchell and Charles L. Telford among
"the members of the faculty. He remained Presi-
"dent of Cincinnati College till its suspension, and
"then was called to the Presidency of Woodward
"College, of which he had charge for several years.
"When Woodward College became a high school, he
"resigned the Presidency of the institution and be-
"came Pastor of the Fifth Presbyterian Church, in
"this city. The growing infirmity of age pressed
"upon him, and after one or two years of pastoral
"labor, he resigned his charge, and retired from pub-
"lic life, except that he continued to serve as Presi-
"dent of the Board of Directors of the House of

                                        Refuge.

" Refuge. He was the last surviving member of the
" convention that founded the American Bible So-
" ciety.'

"And the following letter, addressed to his son-in-
" law, describes his connection with the American
" Bible Society:

"   'NEW YORK, *Jan.* 25, 1882.
" 'PETER NEFF, ESQ., Gambier, Ohio—

" '*Dear Sir:* The American Bible Society was or-
" ganized in this city in May, 1816, by a convention
" of delegates from numerous local Bible societies.
" Among those delegates, I find enrolled the name of
" Mr. Thomas J. Biggs, representing the Nassau Hall
" Bible Society, which had been organized three years
" earlier, at Princeton, New Jersey. By vote of the
" board of managers, all the members of the conven-
" tion were made directors for life in the American
" Bible Society. In the annual report for 1820, Mr.
" Biggs's address appears as Rev. Thomas J. Biggs,
" Frankford, Penn.

" 'I do not know of any thing more than this in
" relation to his connection with the early history of
" an institution which became at once so conspicuous,
" and has flourished, with God's blessing, for two-
" thirds of a century, to the great advantage of the
" world.   Yours, respectfully,
"   'EDWARD W. GILMAN,
"   ' *Cor. Sec.*'

" Dr. Biggs's death occurred on the 9th of February,
" 1864, leaving his wife and six children, all married

" save one daughter, Rebecca, who, with her mother
" and Maria, the youngest daughter, and her husband,
" William H. Andrews, remained in the old home-
" stead, No. 332 Vine Street, Cincinnati, Ohio. The
" daughter, Rebecca, died on the 31st of August,
" 1865, and Mr. Andrews's death occurred eight
" months later. These events left the mother, Mrs.
" Biggs, and her daughter, Maria [Mrs. W. H. An-
" drews], with one child alone in the old home.
" Shortly the housekeeping there was broken up, the
" property sold, and they all removed to the home of
" the eldest daughter, Mrs. Peter Neff, Gambier, Ohio.
" At this place they remained about a year, during
" which time a second child was born to the widowed
" daughter, three months after her husband's death.

" At the close of the year, Mrs. Biggs, with her
" widowed daughter, began housekeeping again, and
" in Gambier, where they remained for three years.
" From Gambier they removed to Glendale, where
" they lived several years. The death of Mrs. Andrews,
" which occurred on the 20th of October, 1879, ne-
" cessitated another change.

" Mrs. Biggs returned to her daughter, Mrs. Peter
" Neff, Gambier, Ohio, where she is still living at this
" date, April, 1885. The two grandchildren, Rebecca
" and Jaennette Andrews, were received by their uncle,
" Rev. H. W. Biggs, who, having no children of his
" own, became a father to them indeed. At the ad-
" vanced age of nearly 89 years, Mrs. Biggs still re-
" tains all her faculties perfectly, except her hearing,

                                    which

" which is somewhat impaired. Her general health
" is good, a marvel to all who know her.

" Her trials in life have been many, having seen
" pass away, through great suffering, two sons and
" two daughters, during all of which she has been
" sustained by the widow's God.

" Mrs. Biggs was always most earnest to promote
" the comfort of her household, which often comprised
" more than her own family, for at several periods in
" her life other boys were committed to her husband's
" care to be educated and trained, usually the sons of
" old friends, of which there are several prominent
" men, now living, and filling places of important
" trust, who have reason to bless God that their young
" days were spent where they had such careful train-
" ing, both for their mental and spiritual natures,
" some of whom have been known to say they were
" indebted to the care of Dr. and Mrs. Biggs for what-
" ever good there was in their characters.

" One son, an earnest, useful Presbyterian minister,
" Rev. Henry W. Biggs, who has been settled over
" the First Presbyterian Church of Chillicothe for the
" last twenty years, and another son, the youngest
" child, Thomas J. Biggs, a merchant in Cincinnati,
" Ohio, and the oldest daughter, Mrs. Peter Neff, are
" all that are left to soothe her declining days." *

---

* To the frequently expressed recollections of those early days
by Rebecca Biggs, regarding our ancestor, may be attributed the
thought and attention which has become the incentive of these
pages.

                                    [From

[From the Philadelphia Public Ledger, 28th August, 1885.]

" OBITUARY.—Rebecca Neff Biggs, relict of the late
" Rev. Thomas J. Biggs, Pastor of the Presbyterian
" Church at Frankford from 1818 to 1832, died at the
" residence of her son-in-law, Peter Neff, at Gambier,
" Ohio, on the 24th day of August, 1885, in the 90th
" year of her age, sister of the late John Rudolph
" Neff, of Philadelphia, and the granddaughter of
" Rudolf Näf, who, with his brother, Jacob Näf, on
" their arrival from Switzerland, settled in Frankford
" in 1749, and were among the founders of the Pres-
" byterian Church there.   In 1832 Dr. Biggs removed
" to Cincinnati, Ohio, having been elected a professor
" in Lane Theological Seminary.   Burial at Spring
" Grove Cemetery, Cincinnati, Ohio."

" A statement of some facts regarding Dr. Biggs's
" parents and their children are here given.

" John Biggs and Sarah, his wife, immigrated from
" London, England, to Philadelphia, Pa., about the
" year 1782.   He was a commission dry goods mer-
" chant.   Sarah Biggs died the last of the month of
" September, 1793, of yellow fever, at Philadelphia,
" Pa. During her short and painful sickness, her
" anxiety was for the religious teaching and educa-
" tion of her children.   The same night that she died
" her husband composed the following :

" The bitterness of death, my Lord, is o'er;
" My prayer is granted, now I ask no more.
" O Lord, my God, the author of my life,
" She, next to thee, is gone, my much loved wife—

268   " Much

" Much loved, more dear than all the world beside.

" With her three times I crossed the ocean wide,

" My heart, unstrung, now lies down by her side.

" Her dying groans were sweetly mixed with prayer,

" Which rose to Heaven and found acceptance there.

" No visual signature of grief I wear;

" My heart is wounded and my mournings there.

" I 've lost a wife, in whom I could depend,

" A humble, chaste, and faithful bosom friend;

" No masculine attempt at sovereign sway,

" But ever ready, willing to obey.

" A child obedient to her parent's nod,

" Who early taught their child the fear of God.

" This marked the maiden and this marked the wife;

" The fear of God shone bright through all her life.

" Go thou, loved shade, and join thy happy peers,

" Released forever from this vale of tears;

" Religion thy pursuit and heaven thy prize,

" Go join the innocent, go join the wise."

" He adds in a note : ' She suffered extreme pain.
" I prayed for an easy descent from life to death, for
" from the moment she was taken I expected death.'
" They were not long separated, for early in the
" month of October the husband died of the same ep-
" idemic. He was buried at midnight. His daughter,
" Maria, and one female friend alone followed him to
" his grave. They were, in England, Wesleyan Meth-
" odists, devout Christian parents, who, when dying,
" committed their children to their covenant-keeping
" God. Letters of administration of the estate of
" John Biggs, deceased, were granted December 6,
" 1793. The administrator's bond was six thousand

 pounds,

" pounds, unto the Commonwealth of Pennsylvania.
" No records of the accounts and settlements of this
" estate can be found.

" Three children had died before their parents.
" John, their oldest child, was born in England. He
" died soon after his parents. The remaining six chil-
" dren, orphaned, but not friendless, were taken and
" cared for by good Christian people, and although
" separated and among strangers, they grew up cher-
" ishing the most loving attachment for each other,
" and adorned their lives by an exemplary and con-
" sistent profession of the Gospel. Their lives became
" useful. Maria Biggs was born in England. She
" did not marry. Died in Cincinnati, Ohio, August
" 11, 1845. She was connected with the first free
" school of Philadelphia, Pa., founded in 1803 by la-
" dies of the Presbyterian Church of that city. Her
" life was devoted as a Dorcas in society and in the
" church. James Biggs was born about 1784. Early
" in the nineteenth century he went to London, Eng-
" land, and studied law. In 1806 he went out from
" New York, in the Miranda expedition, as second
" lieutenant in artillery. He writes : 'Being per-
" suaded by my friend, Mr. *****, to commit myself
" to the chances of an expedition at once extraordi-
" nary and dangerous.' In 1808 he was back in New
" York, and wrote his patron and friend, Mr. R. S.
" G***n, of Philadelphia, Pa., as follows : 'After a
" long interval, I proceed to wind up my correspond-

                                    ence.

" ence. My disgust has made me willing to dismiss
" the subject from my thoughts.'

" To this friend he wrote an interesting account of
" this Miranda expedition as the events occurred.

" 1809 finds James Biggs again in London, England.
" The 11th of March, 1809, he published ' The His-
" tory of Don Francisco De Miranda's attempt to
" effect a Revolution in South America, in a series of
" letters. By James Biggs. Revised, corrected, and
" enlarged. To which are annexed Sketches of the
" Life of Miranda and Geographical Notices of Ca-
" raccas. "Thoughts tending to ambition, they do
" plot unlikely wonders."—*Shak.* London. Printed
" for the author by J. Gillet, Crown Court, Fleet
" Street, and sold by Goddard, Pall Mall, and Sher-
" wood, Neely & Jones, Paternoster Row. 1809.'
" Such is the title page of this philosophical and in-
" teresting history of one of the most remarkable
" men and expeditions of that age. The author, in
" his preface to this London edition, says : ' The
" writer of these letters had the best opportunities for
" ascertaining facts, and in his reasoning upon them
" he is confident he shall not incur the imputation of
" illiberality. Though he has freely animadverted on
" the conduct of the *hero* of this history, the most
" *conspicuous political empiric* of this age, he avers that
" no sinister views nor malicious feelings have
" prompted him to make this expose to the world.'
" Again he writes : ' This enterprise and incidents af-
" ford a curious exhibition of human nature. The

                                                        boldness

" boldness of the design and the variations of fortune
" in its progress and execution; the sufferings and
" the actions of the adventurers are not wholly un-
" worthy of the attention of those who wish to be
" instructed by a view of the obliquities of the human
" mind or amused by the perusal of eccentric ad-
" venture.' In October, 1811, he sailed from England
" for the west coast of Africa, commissioned by the
" king. On the 2d of September, 1812, he wrote that
" he was still at Sierra Leone, West Africa, engaged
" in the suppression of the slave trade. He went into
" parts of the interior of Africa, and returned to Lon-
" don in 1813. On the 16th of March, 1814, he wrote
" from London, England, to his sister, Maria, in New
" York, U. S. A., saying: ' By perusing a book which
" I send you, entitled "The Trials of the Slave
" Traders at Sierra Leone," you will learn my motive
" for having accepted the appointment of attorney-
" general and king's proctor in the court of Vice Ad-
" miralty in the British colony of Sierra Leone, West
" Africa, and you will see with pleasure that my time
" has been employed in an important, honorable, and
" benevolent manner, not unworthy of your approba-
" tion.'

" The full title of this pamphlet, by James Biggs, is
" 'The Trials of the Slave Traders, Samuel Samo,
" Joseph Peters, and William Tufft, tried in April
" and June, 1812, before the Hon. Robert Thorpe,
" LL.D., Chief Justice of Sierra Leone, etc., with
" two letters on the Slave Trade, from a gentleman
272resident

" resident at Sierra Leone to an advocate for the
" abolition in London. London. Printed for Sher-
" wood, Neely and Jones, Paternoster Row, and to be
" had of all other booksellers. 1813.' Mr. James Biggs
" also wrote numbers of the ' Explorator,' published,
" 1813–1817, in London, and although his health was
" greatly impaired by his sojourn in Africa, yet he
" is found engaged in the law and literary pur-
" suits, having his office with Hon. Robert Thorpe,
" LL.D., No. 18 Foley Place, Cavendish Square, Lon-
" don. He did not marry, and it is supposed he died
" in 1822. His letters evince the spirit of ambitious
" and persevering labor, of great affection for his
" brothers and sisters in America, and an abiding
" faith in the overruling Providence of God for all
" the issues of his life work.

"Joseph L. Biggs was appointed Midshipman in the
" Navy of the United States, and his commission is
" signed by Thomas Jefferson, President of the United
" States, the 16th of January, 1809. The following
" April he was stationed on the Frigate President;
" in the winter of 1810 and 1811, he was with his
" brother, James, in London, England, on a furlough;
" July 29, 1811, he was ordered to the ' Essex;' in
" October, 1812, he was Lieutenant on the Frigate
" Constellation. He was an efficient officer, and distin-
" guished himself in several naval engagements. On
" the 15th of April, 1813, off Norfolk, Virginia, he was
" sent from the Frigate Constellation, in command of
" a boat and its crew, to the relief of a vessel; 'his

                                        boat

" boat was struck by a flaw of wind and upset;' he
" and 'another officer were drowned.' His body was
" recovered on the 22nd, and on the 23rd of April,
" 1813, Joseph L. Biggs was interred in the Protestant
" Episcopal burial gound, at Norfolk, Virginia, 'with
" the honors due him as an officer.' He was not mar-
" ried. He was a conscientious Christian, patriot,
" and soldier. His loss was deeply lamented by his
" comrades.

"Phoebe Biggs married, in 1815, the Rev. H. R.
" Weed, D.D., of the Presbyterian Church. She was
" a woman of deep personal piety, and an earnest
" helper to her husband in all church work, and par-
" ticularly successful among the young people who
" came under her influence. Dr. Weed was for many
" years settled over the church at Wheeling, West
" Virginia. He died December 14, 1870. She died
" August 12, 1864.

"Sarah Biggs married Lund Washington, Jr., of
" Washington, D. C. She died at Marlin, Texas,
" 1866. Sarah wrote to Phoebe, October 28, 1837, some
" items about the old rumor of an inheritance lying
" in Virginia for them, stating that an advertisement
" had, within a few years, appeared in the Philadel-
" phia newspapers inquiring for the heirs of Benjamin
" Biggs; that this Benjamin Biggs was probably the
" same Biggs, who, in 1791 or 1792, came to Philadel-
" phia, Pa., and solicited their father, John Biggs, to
" join him in asserting legal claims for an estate in
" Virginia belonging to them. It has always been

                                         supposed

" supposed that this Benjamin Biggs died of yellow
" fever, in 1793, as nothing farther was heard from him
" after the death of John Biggs.   The children were
" all young.   She also wrote that the papers, vouchers,
" evidence, etc., pertaining to this inheritance, were
" in the possession of Alderman Baker, Esq., of Phil-
" adelphia, Pa., up to a recent date.

" Thomas J. Biggs was born 30th October, 1787, at
" Philadelphia, Pa.   After the death of his parents,
" he was taken by Joseph and Ann Jacobs, of Phila-
" delphia, to be brought up and educated.   They were
" Wesleyan Methodists.   The account of Rev. Thomas
" J. Biggs is previously given.   He married Rebecca
" Neff, the 7th September, 1820.

" Descendants of the Rev. Thomas J. Biggs, D.D.,
" and Rebecca Neff Biggs :

Children.

Sarah A. Biggs,	
Joseph A. Biggs,	Deceased,
John W. Biggs,	Deceased,
Rebecca N. Biggs,	Deceased,
Henry W. Biggs,	A.M., D.D.,
Maria Biggs,	Deceased,
Thomas J. Biggs.	

Grandchildren.

For children of Sarah A. Biggs, who married Peter
Neff, see page 253.

Cleveland Biggs,   Deceased,
Kate Biggs,   Deceased,
Frank D. Biggs,
Josephine A. Biggs,
Children of Joseph A. Biggs, who married Catherine
Vankirk.

———

Rebecca Andrews,
Jeanette Andrews,
Children of Maria Biggs, who married William H.
Andrews.

———

Nathan Hazen Biggs,
Thomas J. Biggs, Jr.,
Henry W. Biggs,
Josephine Hazen Biggs,
Children of Thomas J. Biggs, who married Josephine
Hazen.

———

Great-grandchildren.
Nathan Hazen,
Child of Nathan Hazen Biggs, who married Anna
Danforth Keys.

255 Thomas J. Biggs.
Born October 30, 1787.
Married September 7, 1820.
Died February 9, 1864.

AND

255 Rebecca Neff Biggs.
Born May1 , 1796.
Married September 7, 1820.
Died August 24, 1885.

1   Sarah A.,
Born June 15, 1821.
Married Peter Neff.*
Died.

2   Joseph A.,
Born November 12, 1822.
Married Catherine Vankirk.
Died January 14, 1868.

3   John N.,
Born July 20, 1824.
Married.
Died April 24, 1858.

4   Rebecca N.,
Born April 10, 1826.
Married.
Died August 31, 1865.

5   Henry W.,
Born March 15, 1828.
Married Cornelia S. Poinier.
Died.

6   Maria,
Born July 22, 1830.
Married Wm. H. Andrews.
Died October 20, 1879.

7   Thomas J.,
Born May 11, 1834.
Married Josephine Hazen.
Died.

Children of

* For children of this marriage, see
page 253.

2552 JOSEPH A. BIGGS.
Born November 12, 1822.
Married July 3, 1859.
Died January 14, 1868.

AND

2552 CATHERINE VANKIRK
BIGGS.
Born May 8, 1834.
Married July 3, 1859.
Died April 8, 1871.

1 Cleveland,
Born September 2, 1860.
Died July 24, 1861.

2 Francis Dane,
Born December 22, 1861.
Married.
Died.

3 Kate,
Born July 24, 1864.
Died December 10, 1865.

4 Josephine A.,
Born November 4, 1866.
Married.
Died.

Children of

2555 HENRY W. BIGGS.
Born March 15, 1828.
Married August 18, 1853.
Died.

AND

2555 CORNELIA S. POINIER
BIGGS.
Born June 3, 1834.
Married August 18, 1853.
Died.

Children of

No children.

(The above parties reside at Chillicothe, Ross Co., O.)

279

2556 WILLIAM H. ANDREWS.
Born April 3, 1833.
Married June 5, 1860.
Died May 14, 1866.

AND

2556 MARIA BIGGS ANDREWS.
Born July 22, 1830.
Married June 5, 1860.
Died October 20, 1879.

1 | Children of | Rebecca,
Born October 17, 1863.
Married.
Died.

2 | Jeannette,
Born August 16, 1866.
Married.
Died.

(The above parties reside at Chillicothe, Ross county, O.

2557 THOMAS J. BIGGS.
Born May 11, 1834.
Married November 14, 1860.
Died.

AND

**2557 JOSEPHINE HAZEN
BIGGS.**
Born August 19, 1835.
Married November 14, 1860.
Died.

(Residence, at present, of above parties, Glendale, O.)

Children of

1 Nathan Hazen,
Born November 22, 1861.
Married Anna Danforth
Keys.
Died.

2 Thomas J.,
Born June 17, 1865.
Married.
Died.

3 Henry W.,
Born July 19, 1867.
Married.
Died.

4 Josephine Hazen,
Born September 25, 1875.
Married.
Died.

25571 Nathan Hazen Biggs.
Born November 22, 1861.
Married March 20, 1884.
Died.

And

25571 Anna Danforth Keys
Biggs.
Born.
Married March 20, 1884.
Died.

1 Children of

Nathan Hazen,
Born April 16, 1885.
Married.
Died.

(Present residence of above parties,
Glendale, O.)

CHAPTER XIV.

The third son of Peter and Rebecca Neff, who was born on the 31st of March, 1798, in the old homestead, in Frankford, was a man of successful business attainments. The most of his life was spent in Cincinnati, Ohio, the details of which are contributed by his son, William Howard Neff, at the request of the compiler:

"Peter Neff, retired merchant, was born March 31, "1798, at Frankford, near Philadelphia, Pennsylva-"nia. The family emigrated to this country, from "Switzerland, before the American revolution. When "he was very young his father died, and the means "of the family being all required for the support of "his mother and sisters, he was early taught the ne-"cessity of making a living for himself. He received "careful instruction in the plain branches of an En-"glish education. At the age of fourteen he left "school and became a clerk, of Philadelphia. Dur-"ing this time, and, in fact, during life, he neglected "no opportunity for self improvement. His penman-"ship was remarkably clear and distinct, and in all "mercantile and arithmetical calculations he attained

" a marked prominence. The interruption of busi-
" ness, during the war of 1812–1815, threw him out
" of employment, but when peace was proclaimed, he
" again obtained a clerkship, and from that time was
" enabled to support himself without depending upon
" the family for assistance. His close attention to
" business induced a favorable proposition for co-
" partnership from Mr. Charles Bird, a prominent
" hardware merchant, of Philadelphia, who desired to
" establish a branch at Baltimore, and Mr. Neff, at
" the age of twenty, became a partner in that busi-
" ness, with which he was at that time unacquainted.
" He soon mastered this branch of mercantile busi-
" ness in all its details, while his sterling integrity of
" character soon obtained for him a credit, which he
" preserved untarnished during more than fifty years
" of active business life. In June, 1824, Mr. Neff,
" with his brother, William, visited Cincinnati. Al-
" though the city then numbered but a few thousand
" inhabitants, he proposed that if his brother would
" leave Savannah and reside in Cincinnati, he would
" join him in the wholesale hardware business, and
" would continue to reside in Baltimore and make all
" the purchases for the firm. The proposition was
" accepted, and the brothers, together with John and
" George, the only remaining male members of the
" family, united in forming the first importing hard-
" ware house west of the Alleghanies. Peter only
" was acquainted with the business, and he made all
" the purchases for the firm. He went to Cincinnati,

                                    marked

" marked the goods, and fixed the price, which was
" firmly adhered to. On his return trip Mr. Neff was
" twenty-three days reaching New York, by the most
" direct route. The facilities of the new firm, and
" their high commercial credit, soon led on to fortune.
" In 1827 Mr. Neff married Mrs. Isabella Lamson
" [Freeman], a lady as remarkable for her mental
" ability as for her personal graces, whose advice and
" assistance through life were of very great value to
" him. Her death occurred March 6, 1844, and was
" the severest trial he ever experienced. He never
" re-married.

" In 1828 Mr. Neff established a business house in
" Louisville, Kentucky, which was very successful,
" and in 1838 it was united with his Cincinnati house.
" In 1835 he removed from Baltimore to Cincinnati,
" where he resided the remainder of his life. At the
" death of his accomplished and lovely wife, his at-
" tention was directed to the necessity of a cemetery
" for the city, and by his exertions, and the assistance
" of his brothers, William and George, and other
" gentlemen, Spring Grove Cemetery was purchased
" by subscription. It is celebrated for the extent and
" beauty of the grounds and the costliness and variety
" of its monuments. Mr. Neff was always a liberal,
" public spirited, Christian citizen, ever ready to aid
" in promoting the welfare and prosperity of the city
" and the cause of good morals and religion. The
" temperance reform found in him one of its best
" friends and earliest advocates. Mr. Neff earnestly

                                    and

" and zealously advocated the establishment of the
" Chamber of Commerce, for the adjustment of diffi-
" culties among merchants. The enterprise was
" crowned with success, and he was appointed one of
" its first Vice-presidents. The improvement of the
" architecture of business houses received his atten-
" tion in 1850; and to his enterprise, sagacity, and
" example, the Queen City is indebted for many of its
" beautiful buildings. He always manifested a deep
" interest in the education of the young, especially in
" their religious training, and the Sabbath-school
" found in him a liberal benefactor and wise coun-
" selor. The organization and establishment of the
" Poplar Street Presbyterian Church was due to him,
" and credit is given him for personal supervision and
" liberal contributions to the same.

" For more than forty years he was a member of
" the Second Presbyterian Church, and for many
" years was President of the Board of Trustees.

" During the war of the rebellion he took very de-
" cided ground in favor of the United States govern-
" ment. As Chairman of the Finance Committee of
" Hamilton County, he directed the movement and
" took a very active part in raising the amount, $250,-
" 000, which prevented a draft in the county.

" During the Kirby Smith raid, 'a siege of Cincin-
" nati,' he was untiring in his efforts, and the first re-
" serve regiment will bear witness to his zeal and de-
" votion. But his patriotic efforts during the war de-
" serve still higher commendation.

                                    From

"From an examination of his papers after his
" death, it was ascertained that he suggested to Mr.
" Chase the issuing of government bonds as a means
" of obtaining the money necessary for carrying on
" the war. His language was remarkable—'The
" banks can not give you the money you want. They
" have not got it to give. Issue the bonds and obli-
" gations of the government. The people will take
" them, and they will give you all the money you
" want.'

"The later years of his life were spent in the devel-
" opment of his property in the western part of the
" city, where he often received visits from many whom
" he had aided with loans of money and advice, and
" thus saved from financial ruin. He was one of the
" earliest and most steadfast friends of the Cincin-
" nati Southern Railroad, and constantly predicted its
" success and great benefit to the city. He died on
" the 20th of July, 1879, in the 82nd year of his age,
" and is buried in Spring Grove Cemetery, beside his
" wife. He left two sons, William Howard and Peter
" Rudolph Neff."

Descendants of Peter and Isabella Neff:

Children.

William Howard,
John R.,   Died in infancy,
Peter Rudolph.

        Grandchildren.

Grandchildren.

Wallace Neff,	A. M., M. D.,
Helen Neff,	Deceased,
Lucy W. Neff,	
Howard Neff,	Deceased,
Isabel Howard Neff,	
Mary Shillito Neff,	
Edith Sterrett Neff,	

Children of William Howard Neff, who married Lucy
Wallace.

Isabella Neff,	
Margaret Currie Neff,	
Caroline Burnet Neff,	
Frederick Rudolph Neff,	Deceased,
Alice Gray Neff,	

Children of Peter Rudolph Neff, who married Caroline Burnet.

Peter Rudolph Neff, Jr.,	Deceased,
Josephine Clark Neff,	Deceased,
Hope Neff,	Deceased,
Rudolph Neff,	
Susan Clark Neff,	
Robert Burnet Neff,	
Rebecca Neff,	

Children of Peter Rudolph Neff, who married Josephine Clark Burnet, a second wife.

 Great-grandchildren.

Great-grandchildren.
Caroline Neff Maxwell,
Nathaniel Hamilton Maxwell,
Rudolph Neff Maxwell,
Children of Isabella Neff, who married Colonel Sidney
D. Maxwell.

———

Hugh Gordon Burnet,
Child of Alice Gray Neff, who married Arthur G.
Burnet.

256 PETER NEFF.
Born March 31, 1798.
Married July 10, 1827.
Died July 20, 1879.

AND

256 ISABELLA LAMSON NEFF.
Born.
Married July 10, 1827.
Died March 6, 1844.

1 William Howard,
Born March 29, 1828.
Married Lucy Wallace.
Died.

2 John R.,
Born August 25, 1829.
Died September 2, 1829.

3 Peter Rudolph,
Born June 19, 1832.
Married 1st Caroline Burnet
2d Josephine Burnet
Died.

Children of

2561 WILLIAM HOWARD NEFF.
Born March 29, 1828.
Married.
Died.

AND

2561 LUCY WALLACE NEFF.
Born.
Married.
Died.

(Residence of above parties, Cincinnati, O.

Children of

1. Wallace,
Born.
Married.
Died.

2. Helen
Born.
Married.
Died.

3. Lucy W.
Born.
Married.
Died.

4. Howard,
Born.
Married.
Died.

5. Isabel Howard,
Born.
Married.
Died.

6. Mary Shillito,
Born.
Married.
Died.

7. Edith Sterrett,
Born.
Married.
Died.

	1	Isabella, Born April 15, 1854. Married Sidney D. Maxwell. Died.
2563 PETER RUDOLPH NEFF. Born June 19, 1832. Married June 30, 1853. Died.	**2**	Margaret Currie, Born June 22, 1857. Married Lawrence Mendenhall. Died.
	3	Caroline Burnet, Born June 13, 1859. Married William B. Burnet. Died.
AND		
2563 CAROLINE MARGA-RETTE BURNET NEFF. Born December 6, 1833. Married June 30, 1853. Died August 6, 1864.	**4**	Frederick Rudolph, Born June 15, 1861. Died March 7, 1874.
	5	Alice Gray, Born January 11, 1863. Married Arthur G. Burnet. Died.

Children of

	6	Peter Rudolph, Born April 17, 1868. Died July 21, 1868.
	7	Josephine Clark, Born February 7, 1870. Died March 8, 1874.
2563 PETER RUDOLPH NEFF. Married June 19, 1867.	**8**	Hope, Born August 30, 1872. Died June 22, 1873.
	9	Rudolph, Born January 25, 1876. Married. Died.
AND	**0**	Susan Clark, Born April 11, 1877. Married. Died.
2563 JOSEPHINE CLARK BURNET NEFF. Born December 3, 1848. Married June 19, 1867. Died.	**1'**	Robert Burnet, Born May 20, 1878. Married. Died.
(Residence of above parties, Cincinnati, O.)	**2'**	Rebecca, Born September 5, 1884. Married. Died.

Children of

25631 SIDNEY DENISE
    MAXWELL.
    Born December 23, 1831.
    Married June 30, 1875.
    Died.

AND

25631 ISABELLA NEFF
    MAXWELL.
    Born April 15, 1854.
    Married June 30, 1875.
    Died.

1   Caroline Neff,
    Born September 25, 1877.
    Married.
    Died.

2   Nathaniel Hamilton,
    Born January 28, 1879. *80*
    Married.
    Died.

3   Rudolph Neff,
    Born February 7, 1882.
    Married.
    Died.

Children of

(Present residence of above parties,
Cincinnati, O.)

25632 LAWRENCE MENDEN-
HALL.
Born.
Married September 21, 1880.
Died.

AND

25632 MARGARET CURRY
MENDENHALL.
Born June 22, 1857.
Married September 21, 1880.
Died.

(Present residence of above parties,
Cincinnati, O.)

Children of

25633 WILLIAM B. BURNET.
Born.
Married September 19, 1882.
Died.

AND

25633 CAROLINE BURNET
NEFF BURNET,
Born June 13, 1859.
Married September 19, 1882.
Died.

(Present residence of above parties,
Cincinnati, O.)

25635 ARTHUR G. BURNET.
Born July 25, 1856.
Married September 19, 1882.
Died.

AND

25635 ALICE GRAY NEFF
BURNET.
Born January 11, 1863.
Married September 19, 1882.
Died.

1   Children of

Hugh Gordon,
Born September 17, 1883
Married.
Died.

(Present residence of above parties,
Cincinnati, O.)

CHAPTER XV.

The following pages, regarding George Washington Neff, the fourth son of Peter and Rebecca Neff, of Frankford, Pennsylvania, are kindly contributed by his granddaughter, Laura S. Neff, in response to a request from the compiler:

"George W. Neff was born May 19, 1800, at Phil-
" adelphia, Pennsylvania, and died August 9, 1850, at
" Yellow Springs, Ohio.

" He received a good practical education, and grad-
" uated at Princeton College, with highest honors, in
" 1818, when only eighteen years of age, and after-
" wards received a thorough business training.

" He studied law with Hon. Horace Binney, the
" Nestor of Philadelphia bar at that period, in his
" first case having as an opposing counsel his old pre-
" ceptor, over whom he gained a victory. Young
" Neff, appreciating the grand chances for success
" in the then far west, came to Cincinnati, in 1824,
" and commenced a mercantile career which soon
" ranked him among our ablest and most discreet fi-
" nanciers, which is saying much, when we remember
" that Josiah Lawrence, Griffin Taylor, John Kilgour,

 John

" John C. Culbertson, R. R. Springer, William Barr,
" and others of the same class of old-school mer-
" chants, were then in their prime.

" George W. Neff was active and far-seeing. His
" business shrewdness intuitively taught him that
" Cincinnati was admirably located to become a vast
" metropolis; but, to give it a fair chance to outstrip
" its would-be rivals, it must have canals, turnpikes,
" railroads, and other means of transportation, and
" at once Mr. Neff successfully put into operation our
" system of turnpikes, and became one of the most
" zealous advocates of our canal and railroad systems,
" being one of the foremost in advocating the con-
" struction of a great railroad to the south. He was
" one of the first presidents of the Little Miami Rail-
" road, and as President of Council, secured the credit
" of the city in aiding that road.

" In those days we had no paid fire department, and
" the very best citizens were volunteers to fight the
" fiery elements, and of all these brave men, none
" was more gallant than George W. Neff, the Presi-
" dent of the famous 'Independent Red Rovers.'

" George W. Neff married, October 1, 1827, Miss
" Maria White, daughter of Ambrose White, Esq.,
" of Philadelphia, Pennsylvania.

" In business Mr. Neff was quick and positive, but,
" withal, extremely conservative; and it was this care-
" ful weighing of cause and effect which caused him
" to be selected as the President of the Firemen's In-
" surance Company, as its first president, and as Pres-

                                    ident

" ident of the Lafayette Bank; the former a corpora-
" tion which, from its foundation, has always been
" noted for its solidity. Mr. Neff was a member of
" the Presbyterian Church.

"George W. Neff left three children—Ambrose W.,
" George W., late federal officer in the great rebel-
" lion, and Caroline. Of these children Ambrose is
" deceased; he died December 12, 1862. Ambrose
" married Miss Rebecca Smith. George W. Neff mar-
" ried Miss Clara Stanbery, of Columbus, Ohio, daugh-
" ter of Charles Stanbery, Esq., and niece of Hon.
" Henry Stanbery, of Kentucky, and Attorney-Gen-
" eral under the administration of Andrew Johnson,
" President of the United States. Caroline Neff mar-
" ried Mr. Samuel C. Humes, who died June 18,
" 1879."

The descendants of George W. and Maria W. Neff:

Children.

Ambrose W., Deceased,
George W.,
Caroline.

Grandchildren.

George W., Deceased,
Stewart,
Clarence,
Children of Ambrose W. Neff, who married Rebecca
Smith.

Laura S.,

Laura S.,
Ambrose W.,
Stanbery,   Deceased,
George W.,
Mary S.,
Bond,
Children of George W. Neff, who married Clara
Stanbery.

———

James,
Maria N.,
Clara N., Deceased,
Children of Caroline Neff, who married Samuel C.
Humes.

257 GEORGE WASHINGTON NEFF.
Born May 19, 1800.
Married October 1, 1827.
Died August 9, 1850.

AND

257 MARIA WHITE NEFF.
Born.
Married October 1, 1827.
Died.

1 Ambrose W.,
Born August 28, 1830.
Married Rebecca Smith.
Died December 12, 1862.

2 George W.,
Born.
Married Clara Stanbery.
Died.

3 Caroline,
Born.
Married Samuel C. Humes.
Died.

Children of

2571 AMBROSE W. NEFF.
  Born August 28, 1830.
  Married.
  Died December 12, 1862.

AND

2571 REBECCA SMITH NEFF.
  Born.
  Married.
  Died.

1   George W.,
  Born.
  Married.
  Died.

2   Stewart,
  Born.
  Married.
  Died.

Children of

3   Clarence,
  Born.
  Married.
  Died.

2572 GEORGE W. NEFF.
Born.
Married.
Died.

AND

2572 CLARA STANBERY NEFF.
Born.
Married.
Died.

(Present residence of above parties, Newport, Ky.)

Children of

1 | Laura S.,
Born.
Married.
Died.

2 | Ambrose W.,
Born.
Married.
Died.

3 | Stanbery,
Born.
Married.
Died.

4 | George W.,
Born.
Married.
Died.

5 | Mary S.,
Born.
Married.
Died.

6 | Bond,
Born.
Married.
Died.

303

2573 Samuel C. Humes.
Born.
Married.
Died.

AND

2573 Caroline Neff Humes.
Born.
Married.
Died.

Children of

1 | James,
Born.
Married.
Died.

2 | Maria N.,
Born.
Married.
Died.

3 | Clara N.,
Born.
Married.
Died.

(Present residence of above parties,
Cincinnati, O.)

CHAPTER XVI.

Mary Amanda Neff was born on the 16th of December, 1802, at Frankford, Pennsylvania; was educated in Philadelphia, at Mrs. Baisley's school, and grew up a young woman of lovely character and engaging manners. Upon the marriage of her brother, William, she arranged to accompany him, with his wife, Clifford, to their western home, in Cincinnati, Ohio. As a result of this, Clifford and Mary became life-long and endeared friends, as well as sisters. While visiting, with her brother, in Cincinnati, Mary met Kirkbride Yardley, a young man from Pennsylvania, and who was associated with the firm of Neff and Brothers. An attachment grew out of the acquaintance, which resulted in an engagement. Mary, however, returned to her mother in Frankford. Mr. Yardley soon followed, and they were married, leaving immediately for Cincinnati, where they made for themselves a home. Of their children, two in number, William and Thomas, both died in their youth. The younger, Thomas, died when but five years old, after a long and painful illness. William, whose attachment to his mother had been peculiarly strong,

seemed

seemed reckless of life after his mother's death, which occurred in July, 1849, of cholera. He was seized with the enthusiasm for western adventure, and, in 1851, went to California. Returning shortly, by way of Panama, he was taken with the Panama fever, of which he died, in New York City.

Later, and in the year 1860 or 1861, Kirkbride Yardley also died; so, briefly, and with feelings of grief, the curtain must fall upon this branch of the family, leaving no descendants to continue the line.

258 KIRKBRIDE YARDLEY.
Born.
Married September 22, 1828.
Died.

AND

**258 MARY AMANDA NEFF
YARDLEY.**
Born December 16, 1802.
Married September 22, 1828.
Died July 11, 1849.

1   William,
Born August 2, 1830.
Married.
Died December 2, 1852.

2   Thomas,
Born.
Married.
Died.

Children of

CHAPTER XVII.

The Following Tables of Descent

are of

Samuel Neff

and his

Descendants.

308

27 Samuel Neff.
Born June 27, 1768.
Married February 3, 1787.
Died July 4, 1839.

AND

27 Eleanor Helveston Neff.
Born January 16, 1763.
Married February 3, 1787.
Died May 31, 1829.

Children of

1 Elizabeth,
Born November 25, 1787.
Married William Bruner.
Died September 7, 1864.

2 Jacob,
Born December 2, 1788.
Married Mary Jones.
Died April 15, 1845.

3 Mary,
Born December 25, 1790.
Married Gardener Fulton.
Died February 18, 1872.

4 Robert,
Born April 2, 1792.
Married Harriet Hilt.
Died April 9, 1835.

5 Benjamin,
Born June 10, 1795.
Married.
Died August 9, 1860.

6 Hester,
Born January 29, 1799.
Married John C. Jennings.
Died February 5, 1878.

7 Hannah,
Born January 29, 1799.
Married Amos Corson.
Died July 8, 1879.

} Twins.

8 Eleanor,
Born June 10, 1802.
Married Jonathan T. Hough.
Died December 24, 1878.

9 Sarah,
Born December 11, 1806.
Married.
Died August 25, 1872.

271 WILLIAM BRUNER,
Born September 10, 1779.
Married July 21, 1810.
Died May 14, 1863.

AND

271 ELIZABETH BAKER
NEFF BRUNER,
Born November 25, 1787.
Married July 21, 1810.
Died September 7, 1864.

1 | Mary Ann,
Born August 28, 1811.
Married March 14, 1833.
Died July, 1873.

2 | William Martin,
Born June 7, 1813.
Married September 6, 1835.
Died December 4, 1853.

3 | James Patterson,
Born September 28, 1815.
Married July 25, 1839, and May 20, 1868.
Died.

4 | Elizabeth Neff,
Born September 2, 1817.
Married November 22, 1840.
Died.

5 | Adam,
Born August 15, 1819.
Died April 30, 1823.

6 | Henry,
Born May 13, 1821.
Married January 9, 1844.
Died November 29, 1883.

7 | Sarah Jane,
Born January 11, 1823.
Married June 12, 1855.
Died.

8 | John Adam,
Born November 20, 1824.
Married May 5, 1846.
Died.

9 | Thomas Jefferson,
Born July 21, 1826.
Died July 20, 1827.

0 | Charles Edward,
Born April 27, 1828.
Married December 4, 1846.
Died.

1' | Ellen Matilda,
Born June 10, 1832.
Married June 16, 1858.
Died.

Children of

272 JACOB NEFF,
Born December 2, 1788.
Married.
Died April 15, 1845.

AND

272 MARY JONES NEFF,
Born May 8, 1789.
Married.
Died October 12, 1876.

Three sons and four daughters.

311

1 ———
Born.
Married.
Died.

2 ———
Born.
Married.
Died.

3 ———
Born.
Married.
Died.

4 ———
Born.
Married.
Died.

5 ———
Born.
Married.
Died.

6 ———
Born.
Married.
Died.

7 ———
Born.
Married.
Died.

Children of

273 GARDENER FULTON,
Born December 25, 1783.
Married December 25, 1811.
Died February 5, 1861.

AND

273 MARY NEFF FULTON,
Born December 25, 1790.
Married December 25. 1811.
Died February 18, 1872.

1 Children of

James R.,
Born , 1814.
Married , 1834.
Died , 1856.

274 ROBERT NEFF,
Born April 2, 1792.
Married.
Died April 9, 1835.

AND

274 HARRIET HILT NEFF,
Born.
Married.
· Died.

1

2

Children of

Born.
Married.
Died.

Born.
Married.
Died.

Two sons, deceased.

275 Benjamin Neff,
Born June 10, 1795.
Married.
Died August 9, 1860.

AND

275 ————
Born.
Married.
Died.

Children of

276 JOHN C. JENNINGS,
   Born September 18, 1792.
   Married June 28, 1821.
   Died May 1, 1825.

AND

276 HESTER NEFF JENNINGS,
   Born January 29, 1799.
   Married June 28, 1821.
   Died February 5, 1878.

1 John C.,
   Born.
   Married.
   Died.

2 Eleanor Neff,
   Born.
   Married.
   Died.

Children of

277 Amos Corson,
Born.
Married March 30, 1820.
Died.

AND

277 Hannah Wilmerton Neff,
Born January 29, 1799.
Married March 30, 1820.
Died July 8, 1879.

Children of

1 Hester Neff,
Born February 10, 1821.
Married.
Died February 27, 1825.

2 John G.,
Born October 5, 1822.
Married.
Died February 8, 1871.

3 Eleanor Neff,
Born January 21, 1825.
Married —— Kemp.
Died.

4 Rufus L. T.
Born December 17, 1826.
Married.
Died August 17, 1884.

5 Henry B.,
Born November 30, 1828.
Married.
Died.

6 William A.,
Born November 11, 1830.
Married.
Died.

7 Rachel A.,
Born August 17, 1832.
Married.
Died.

8 Benjamin F.,
Born July 3, 1834.
Married.
Died.

278 Jonathan T. Hough,
Born.
Married.
Died.

AND

278 Eleanor Neff
Hough,
Born June 10, 1802.
Married.
Died December 24, 1878.

Four sons and three daughters.

1
Born.
Married.
Died.

2
Born.
Married.
Died.

3
Born.
Married.
Died.

4
Born.
Married.
Died.

5
Born.
Married.
Died.

6
Born.
Married.
Died.

7
Born.
Married.
Died.

Children of

317

CHAPTER XVIII.

In concluding this chronicle, which has been a work purely of love—one that has cost very many days of tedious labor, several years of research, and some travel—the compiler is aware that much might be said apologetically. Many imperfections necessarily appear. The materials from which information has been gathered have been meagre, and, for the comparatively limited work of this volume, rather widely scattered. The records of families, except of recent date, have been but imperfectly preserved, compelling, in some instances, a resort to public documents that were difficult of access. For these reasons, omissions and shortcomings will, it is hoped, be dealt with generously. Many kindnesses have been extended by those appealed to, in contributing all the information within their power, which should be and is gratefully acknowledged.

It is not unlikely that this volume contains little to interest those who do not find in it the names of their ancestors. But to those who claim, through the family of Neff, an unbroken line to their ancestral home in Switzerland, an interest and enthusiasm, it is

trusted,

trusted, have been awakened—an enthusiasm that will lead to the making of further records, records more full, and of such facts, as will be conducive of comfort, and pleasure, and instruction to succeeding generations.

Should this work accomplish as a result a further and more searching inquiry into the history of the family, the compiler will have reason to be gratified that her work was undertaken.

To many of the readers, it is the hope that this history of relationship may recall many pleasant memories of the past; to all, that it will inspire them to nobler efforts; and to the few whose births date far back in time, the wishes of the author will be fulfilled, if the incidents here related will carry them back to days of early and delightful associations, and be a means of linking their youthful and declining days.

Before closing, a desire might, with propriety, be expressed, that succeeding generations venerate and esteem their ancestors, and emulate their good deeds, verifying the prayers and wishes expressed at the 350th anniversary, at Cappel.

Index
of
Names on Tables of Descent.

LANCASTER COUNTY, PENN.

Index

of

Names on Tables of Descent.

JACOB NÄF.

327

Index.

341

Data for a chronological table of Dr. John Henry Neiff and his descendants, brother of Francis Neiff (see page 93), has been obtained in a large degree from the work of " Milton B. Eshleman, of Paradise, Lancaster County, Pa., completed July 4, 1867," being a blank book, systematized by headings of his own, in print, and filled out by pen, of which he writes he thinks he made five or six copies, entitled " Register of Consanguinity, containing a Record of Seventy-five Families and the Names of Three Hundred and Twenty Descendants of Rev. Jacob Neff, who resides at Strasburg, Lancaster County, Pennsylvania." This Rev. Jacob Neff was a son of Dr. John Henry Neff. Information on this line of descent, as well as that of others bearing the name of Neff, who are not mentioned in this volume, can in many instances be obtained by communicating with the compiler, as the data was not furnished until after this edition had gone to press.

Addenda.

Näf = Neff History

Regarding the Origin and
Meaning of the Name of Neff.

Together with the Revolutionary
Records of

Captain Rudolph Neff
Ensign Aaron Scout
Major Thomas Smyth, Jr.

By
Elizabeth Clifford Neff, Geneaologist,
Compiler of the Näf=Neff History.

Published and For Sale by the Author

Cleveland, Ohio
1899

Addenda.

Näf = Neff History

Regarding the Origin and Meaning of the Name of Neff.

Together with the Revolutionary
Records of

Captain Rudolph Neff
Ensign Aaron Scout
Major Thomas Smyth, Jr.

By
Elizabeth Clifford Neff, Geneaologist,
Compiler of the Näf=Neff History.

Published and For Sale by the Author

Cleveland, Ohio
1899

PLAIN DEALER PUBLISHING CO.
PRINTERS
CLEVELAND, OHIO

Rudolph Neff

Origin and Meaning of the Name.

"Rodulph   { Old High German.
Rodolphus   { Famous Wolf or Hero."

" Neff (German): Nephew."

Rudolph Neff.

The publication and examination of old records in America, particularly those referring to the Revolution·ary period, to meet the demand for information occasioned by the many patriotic societies, has brought within the reach of many a hungry genealogist, facts long buried from sight. It is to such investigation and examination made subsequent to the publishing of the Näf-Neff History in 1886, that the compiler of that volume is indebted for information here given, which calls attention to a fact that will surely interest the descendants of RUDOLPH NEFF.

On page 65 of the Näf-Neff History, being "A chronicle together with a little romance, regarding Rudolf and Jacob Näf, of Frankford, Pennsylvania, and their descendants, including an account of the Neffs in Switzerland and America." (Rudolf and Jacob Näf, becoming on naturalization, Rudolph and Jacob Neff,) find the statement that Rudolph was too old for active service in the Revolutionary war, and Peter too young in 1776 True, Rudolph was 49 years old, but many men fought bravely in the Revolution older than that.

In

In 1833, one Jacob Foulkrod, "who was then 73 years old, in a petition for a pension, made affidavit that he had been a soldier in the Revolutionary war. That in August, 1776, he joined the militia of the state of Pennsylvania, in the company commanded by CAPTAIN RUDOLPH NEFF, and was in the regiment commanded by Colonel Robert Lewis and continued two months in that command. That Generals Roberdeau and Mercer were in command as Continental officers at that time."

(LETTER FROM W. W. FOULKROD, 16 MAR. '98.)

The portion of the affidavit of Jacob Foulkrod for application for pension, that refers to RUDOLPH NEFF, reads as follows; "He was drafted in the month of August, in the year 1776, and marched to Amboy in the state of New Jersey under the command of Capt. RUDOLPH NEFF, and in the regiment commanded by Colonel Robert Lewis, and continued two months Generals Roberdeau and Mercer were in command as Continental officers at that time."

(LETTER FROM W. W. FOULKROD, 22D APRIL, '98)

This Jacob Foulkrod was but 16 years old when he entered the service as a fifer. He cites in his affidavit his various services, at times enlisting, at others being drafted.

That there was a Rudolph Neff a captain of militia in Philadelphia in 1776, there can be no doubt. What do the records of Washington, D. C., say? The following from Colonel Ainsworth, 14th April, 1898, tells of the investigation for records there.

                                         "The

"The name Rudolph Neff has not been found on the rolls on file in this office of any Pennsylvania military organization, or on the rolls of any organization of Continental troops in service during the war of the Revolution.

It is proper to add, however, that the collection of Revolutionary war records in this office is far from complete, and that the absence there-from, of any name is by no means conclusive evidence that the person who bore the name did not serve in the Revolutionary war."

The following affidavit is from the state librarian of Pennsylvania, Harrisburg, Pa., dated 19th April, 1898:

"To Whom It May Concern:

I hereby certify to the Revolutionary services of Captain RUDOLPH NEFF as follows:

RUDOLPH NEFF was a captain in Col. Robert Lewis' Philadelphia Battalion of the 'Flying Camp,' in active service in 1776 on Long Island and at Fort Washington. Reference as to Pennsylvania Archives, Second Series, volume xiii, page 558.

Yours with respect,

WILLIAM H. EGLE, M. D.
State Librarian and Editor Pennsylvania Archives."

Referring to Pennsylvania Archives, Second Series, volume xiii, pages 553 and 558, find as follows:

Page 553. "Muster rolls and papers relating to the associators and militia of the city and county of Philadelphia." For the same city and county find on page 558

"OFFICERS

COLONEL—Robert Lewis.
LIEUT. COL.—Isaac Hughes.
MAJOR—John Moore.
SECOND MAJOR—Marshall Edwards.
ENSIGN—Dr. Enoch Edwards.
ADJUTANT—Solomon Bush.
CAPTAINS—* * * * Rudolph Neff, * * * *

See also "American Archives 5th series, by Peter Force, volume I, published Washington, April, 1848," page 349.   "PHILADELPHIA COMMITTEE.

Philadelphia County Committee, 15 July, 1776.

Resolved, that this committee, in consequence of a letter from the honourable Continental Congress, as well as from a recommendation of the Provincial Conference, do proceed to raise our part of the Flying Camp, and that the following gentlemen be appointed officers:

COLONEL—Robert Lewis
LIEUT. COL.—Isaac Hughes.
MAJOR—John Moore, Esq.
SURGEON—Enoch Edwards
QUARTERMASTER—Marshall Edwards.
ADJUTANT—Solomon Bush.
CAPTAINS—* * * * Rudolph Neff, * * * *
FIRST LIEUTENANTS—* * * * * * * * * * *
SECOND LIEUTENANTS—* * * * * * * *
ENSIGNS—* * * * * * * *

Extracts from the minutes.

ENOCH EDWARDS."

                                        Also

Also "History of Philadelphia," volume 1, page 331, by Scharf and Westcott.

"The officers of the Flying Camp for Philadelphia were: Robert Lewis, Colonel.

Isaac Hughes, Lieutenant Colonel.

John Moore, Major.

Enoch Edwards, Surgeon.

Marshall Edwards, Second Major.

Solomon Bush, Adjutant.

* * * * Rudolph Neff, * * * * Captains."

The following is a copy of a portion of a letter from the office of the adjutant general of the state of New Jersey, Trenton, to Mr. Peter Neff, Western Reserve Historical Society, Cleveland, O.

"I am quite familiar with the part taken by the 'Flying Camp' of Pennsylvania, in December, 1776. It was sent to Perth Amboy for the purpose of protecting that part of the coast, and the Raritan River from the incursions of the British naval vessels at the time Washington was making his retreat through the Jerseys. I know that the distinguished statesman, John Dickinson, was a volunteer in that expedition and that is all the military service he did, but in New Jersey we have no records whatever, which give an account of this movement, either in the New Jersey Historical Society Library, or in this office, where the military Revolutionary records are kept. I can give you no facts concerning Colonel Robert Lewis' Philadelphia regiment. I regret that this is so.   Yours truly,   WILLIAM S. STRYKER,

Adjutant General."

In

In the volume entitled "Life and Times of Jno. Dick·inson," by Chas. J. Stille, LL. D. J. B. Lippincott & Co., 1891, on page 155 is found the following regarding Pennsylvania troops, including those from Philadelphia, 1776, he says: "In addition to these two brigades, 'Flying Camps,' as they were called, were established during the summer of 1776 in various parts of New Jersey, composed chiefly of Pennsylvania troops and designed as advance posts to defend the Province from invasion by the British army then encamped on Staten Island."

To all this may be added the question, how can it be proved that Captain Rudolph Neff was Rudolph Neff, one of the two brothers who came to Frankford, now a part of Philadelphia, in 1749?

The following is a copy of a letter from the Historical Society of Pennsylvania, dated 1st April, 1898, addressed to Mr. Peter Neff, Librarian, Cleveland, O.

"Colonel Robert Lewis in the Flying Camp, 1776, Pennsylvania Archives, 2 series, volume xiii, page 558.

The records and probably half of the rolls of the Flying Camp, are lost or destroyed, and it is mainly through the correspondence of officers and men, were we indebted for the details we have. I am of the opinion that the regiment of Colonel Lewis for a time was stationed in New Jersey, but whether it was in any engagement I cannot say.

I cannot find any will of a Rudolph Neff in this county (Philadelphia) but letters of administration were taken out in 1809, on the estate of a man of that name.

I may add that his name does not appear in the list of Pennsylvania soldiers entitled to 'Depreciated Pay,' from which I infer that he did not enter the service again after his regiment was mustered out. The term of service was probably six months.

Truly yours,

Jno. W. Jordan."

Turn now if you will to page 169 of Näf-Neff History, find there copy of the grave stone inscription from the old grave yard back of the Frankford Presbyterian church, which reads:

"In Memory of
RUDOLPH NEFF,
Who departed this life
February 14. 1809,
Aged 82 years."

On page 170 of the same history is given a copy of a paper signed by Rudolph Neff in 1804, revoking all previous wills and ordering distribution of his estate to be according to the laws of Pennsylvania, which paper was filed with the administration papers of Rudolph Neff, deceased 1809, certified to by Charles Irwin, clerk in the office of Register of Wills, before a notary public

There seem to be two ways of establishing the identity of Captain Rudolph Neff, with the man of the same name who died in 1809, viz.:

1st. If the said captain was a man possessed of an estate he would have made a will, or his estate would have been administered on according to the laws of the state.

11
2d.

2d. If the said Captain Rudolph Neff of the "Flying Camp" in 1776, had been a poor man, surely he or some one for him, would have obtained a pension. Also if not possessed of an estate, he would probably have enlisted again and so have been entitled to the "Depreciated Pay."

The first point seems answered by the examination of wills and papers of administration before quoted, which show reference to but one man of the name Rudolph Neff, and he died in 1809.

As to the second point, the letter from the Bureau of Pensions shows that no man of that name received a pension.

The department of the Interior Bureau of Pensions on the 31st August, 1898, in reply to an inquiry for Peter Neff of Cleveland, O., returned the statement that "a careful search has been made, but from the data given no record of a claim filed in the name of Rudolph Neff can be found."

It has been shown that no one of the name received "Depreciated Pay."

The facts therefore justify the conclusion that Rudolph Neff, who died in 1809, was the Captain Rudolph Neff of 1776.

Family tradition comes in just here to help strengthen the evidence. A grandson of Rudolph Neff, William, was wont to tell his son Peter (the writer's father) that his grandfather (Rudolph Neff) had something to do with taking Washington across the Delaware River. This story was often repeated, yet did not seem of special

interest,

interest, and never suggested any Revolutionary connection, until the finding of this record of Captain Rudolph Neff as a member of the "Flying Camp," together with the dates given in the affidavit of Jacob Foulkrod.

Esther Neff, the niece of Rudolph Neff, who died in 1809, married a man by the name of Jacob Foulkrod (see Näf-Neff, page 129) and the writer hopes to prove that it is the same Jacob Foulkrod whose affidavit has been quoted in this article. If such is the case, the relationship would confirm the evidence regarding the identity of Captain Rudolph Neff.

As a summary of the above statements, find that Rudolph Neff was captain in the Pennsylvania "Flying Camp" militia, in August, 1776.

The term of service was probably six months, and the "Flying Camps" in New Jersey were largely made of Pennsylvania troops.

Washington crossed the Delaware on the 25th of December, 1776.

Family tradition says Rudolph Neff, who died in 1809, had something to do with Washington crossing the Delaware, and the evidence is conclusive that Captain Rudolph Neff of the Pennsylvania "Flying Camp" was the Rudolph Neff who came to America in 1749 and died in 1809.

Having proved that Rudolph Neff was a defender of his country, serving as Captain in the Revolutionary war, it is of interest to turn to the records regarding Aaron Scout, who was the father of Rebecca Scout, the wife of Peter Neff, the son of Rudolph Neff. See Näf-Neff History, page 155. In that valuable addition to the Pennsylvania Archives, for all searchers for Revolutionary records in Pennsylvania, known as "Pennsylvania in the War of the Revolution, Associated Battalions and Militia, 1775-1783, Volume I, edited by William H. Egle, M. D.," published "1887," being otherwise entitled "Pennsylvania Archives, Second Series, published under the direction of W. S. Stenger, Secretary of the Commonwealth, edited by William H. Egle, M. D., Volume xiii, 1887," references are found as follows:

Under "alphabetical list of Revolutionary Soldiers, 1775-1783" on page 201, find "Aaron Scoutt." Of this list it is stated on page 2, "the following alphabetical list of Soldiers of the War for Independence has been compiled chiefly from the Depreciation Account books in the office of the Auditor General of Pennsylvania." (It is

14   but

but just to notice that this publication was not made until
1887, one year after the publication of Näf-Neff History.)
Same volume, page 553, "Muster Rolls and papers relating to the Associators and Militia of the city and county
of Philadelphia."

Page 588, "Philadelphia County Associators—1777."
* * *

Page 589, "Fourth Battalion."
* * *

"COLONEL—William Dean, Esq.
LIEUT. COLONEL—Robert Soller, Esq.
MAJOR—George Right, Esq.

Page 591, *"Fourth Battalion Philadelphia County.
A return of the names of officers and their rank of the
Fourth Battalion, Philadelphia County Militia 1777."*
* * * * * *

"Seventh Company
CAPTAIN—John Mann.
FIRST LIEUT.—James Crevens, Jr.
SECOND LIEUT.—Rudolph Bartle.
ENSIGN— Aaron Scout."

Also same volume, page 752.

"Officers County Militia—1780.

*Return of the officers elected for the several battalions
of the Militia for the County of Philadelphia.*
First Battalion
LIEUT. COLONEL—George Smith, Esq.
MAJOR—Josiah Hart, Esq."
* * * * *

Page 753. *"Sixth Company*
CAPTAIN—John Shelmire.
LIEUTENANT—Henry Puff.
ENSIGN—Aaron Scout."

                                        Also

Also "Pennsylvania in the War of the Revolution, Associated Battalions and Militia—1775-1783, Volume II, edited by William H. Egle, M. D., 1888," being "Pennsylvania Archives, Second Series, published under direction of C. W. Stone, Secretary of the Commonwealth, edited by William H Egle, M. D., volume xiv, 1888."

Page 10, "Militia in the United States Service."

* * * *

"Aaron Scout, May 19th, 1777."

The following certificate from Dr. Egle, of Harrisburg, Penn., confirms the references given above

"State Library of Pennsylvania.

Harrisburg, Pa., August 21st, 1896.

To whom it may concern :

I hereby certify that Aaron Scout was an Ensign of the Seventh Company, Fourth Battalion, Philadelphia County Militia, in service in 1777. For reference see Pennsylvania Archives, Second Series, volume xiii, page 591.

Aaron Scout was an Ensign in the Sixth Company of the First Battalion, Philadelphia County Militia, commanded by Lieutenant Colonel George Smith, and in actual service in 1780. For reference see the same volume of Archives, page 753.

Yours with respect,

WILLIAM H. EGLE, M. D.

State Librarian and Editor Pennsylvania Archives."

In the August number, 1893, of the "American Monthly Magazine," occurs this paragraph in an article entitled, "Maryland and her Governor in 1776." "Maryland was with Massachusetts and Virginia in their indignant protests from the first, and as soon as the prorogued assembly met, made forcible appeals through her legislative bodies. It is a proud boast of this State that her soil was never contaminated by the obnoxious stamps, and Frederick County Court had the high honor of first deciding in a legal manner the unconstitutionality of the Stamp Act."

"McMahon 359."

By a descendant of one of the men who helped to make memorable the history of Maryland, as referred to above, the following genealogical record is given to show the part one hero played in that crisis of American History.

Kent County, Maryland, stands as an old land mark of history, whose annals have been preserved in a publication called "Old Kent," and by records of Parishes formed in the 17th Century, whose ritual, that of the

Church

Church of England is today the same as when the Parishes were created two centuries ago.

Two names were conspicious in England in the time of Elizabeth, viz: Smythe and Gresham, and both of these names are found in the early history of Maryland

The famous Sir Thomas Gresham who built and established the Royal Exchange in London, in the time of Elizabeth, and gave largely to advance educational projects, endowing Gresham College, was born in 1519, died 1579. It is well known that his only child, a son, died when young, and unmarried. The Greshams of America, therefore, are not *lineal* decendants of Sir Thomas Gresham. The history of the family of Sir Thomas Gresham is interesting, and from a branch of the same family the Greshams of America are undoubtedly descended.

It is stated that ''early in the reign of King Henry the Eighth, a wealthy Norfolk gentleman by the name of Gresham established his four sons'' as merchants in London, dealers in silks and woolen cloths. One of the four brothers became a minister, the remaining three continued the business established for them by their father. Of the three brothers in partnership, one was more successful than the others, he having other interests; his name was Richard Gresham. He was said to be ''a sort of banker to King Henry the Eighth and Edward the Sixth.'' He was eminent for his goodness and philanthropic character. To illustrate his character may be cited the fact that he induced King Henry the Eighth to allow certain Monasteries, three in number, to

be

be given to the City of London for Hospitals. This Richard Gresham was the father of the before mentioned Sir Thomas Gresham who died in 1579.

John Gresham, Sr., gent., came to America in 1670, and died about 1712. "This John Gresham settled on the Western shore of the Chesapeake, and named his home place 'Fortune' and once I believe 'Fortuna,' which is on the seal of Sir Thomas."

In 1684, John Gresham "entered 500 acres near the head of the bay close to Abingdon and Belair in Harford county, (then Baltimore county)" which he named "The Gresham College Tract." He purchased also many more acres on both shores. This John Gresham, Sr. gent., who came to America in 1670, was the grandfather of Richard Gresham, whose daughter Sarah became the wife of Thomas Smyth (spelled first in this country Smythe) who was a member of the Maryland Council of Safety, of whom this article treats Contemporary with Sir Thomas Gresham 1519 to 1579, was Thomas Smythe, a "prosperous trader" of London. He was also "customer to the Queen." In 1560 his son Thomas was born, who became the famous Sir Thomas Smythe, first governor of the East India Company. He died in 1625. It is stated that "during his life time, indeed, and whether in actual office or not, Sir Thomas Smythe was the real master of the East India Company. All its members regarded him as their head and champion; all its enemies considered him their great opponent ; and all its successes were mainly attributed to his wisdom and energy." He was also the treasurer and governor of the "Virginia

Company"

Company" and president of the council during the first twelve years of its existence, which ended 18th November, 1618.

He was one of the parents of the New England colony in 1620.

Lieut. Peary's expedition to North Greenland, as described in the volume entitled "In Arctic Seas; the Voyage of the 'Kite' 1892," on page 493, has this paragraph: Wm. Baffin, navigator, 1616, in the Discovery, sailed round Baffin's Bay and "Baffin named the most northern opening Smythe (Smith) Sound, after the first governor of the East India Company, and munificent promotor of the expedition, Sir Thomas Smythe."

For fuller details regarding Sir Thomas Smythe and his connection with explorations and remote places named for him, see "The Genesis of the United States," by Alexander Brown. Vol. ii, page 1013.

In 1635 mention is made of Thomas Smythe, gent., who was associated with William Claiborne, Kent Island and in Virginia. He was captured and killed 1635, and his property in Kent Island was seized and confiscated.

In 1666 William Smyth took out a patent for "Staunaway" in Langford Bay. Colonel Thomas Smythe (or Smyth) in this country from 1682 till his death in 1719, is the first of the name from whom the writer of this article can *prove* lineal descent.

The links can undoubtedly be found to unite this family with the Sir Thomas Smythe of London, as the circumstantial evidence quoted, regarding the continued

interest

interest in, and association with America of those bearing the name goes to prove.

See "The Genesis of the United States" by Alexander Brown. Vol. ii, page 1011, etc.

The foregoing facts regarding the Greshams and Smythes of England, may enable the genealogist to trace the connection accurately with the American descendants, but to a daughter of the American Revolution, the records in America are of the greater importance.

Colonel Thomas Smyth, 1682-1719.

There is much of interest attached to the history of this Thomas Smyth, both as associated with public affairs and with the church in Kent County Province of Maryland.

He is found to have been appointed judge of the County Court of *the Quorum*, in October, 1694. Reappointed in 1696. Member of the Maryland Assembly in 1694-5-6-7, and again in 1704-5-6-7. He was Deputy Commissary General from July 16, 1707 to 1718. From 1715 to 1718, member of the Provincial council and continued as a member till his death in 1719 and judge of the Provincial Court.

Colonel Thomas Smyth, it would seem, was twice married. The name of his first wife was Eliner, by whom it would appear from his will probated 4th August, 1719, that he had no children. Her name is associated with his in relation to the interests of the church.

On the 9th of April, 1699, he presented to the Parish of St. Paul's on the North side of Chester River, the gift of one chalice and paton of silver, engraved thus: "The gift of T. S. to the Parish of St. Paul's on the North side

                    Chester."

Chester." In the present year, (1893), the Bi-Centennial of Old St. Paul's was celebrated.

The following is quoted from the account published of the celebration: "On Wednesday and Thursday of last week, May 24th and 25th, Old St. Paul's vigorous in its hoary age and beautiful in its consecrated mission, celebrated its two hundredth anniversary. The Bi-Centennial exercises commenced at six o'clock on Wednesday morning, when the Holy Communion was administered by the Rector, Rev. C. T. Denroche. This was one of the most impressive services of the Bi-Centennial ceremonies. In the dewy freshness of a beautiful morning, the brilliant colors sifted through the stained glass windows and fell upon the consecrated vessels which were presented to St. Paul's by Thomas Smyth in 1699, and which through the sunshine and shadows of the past, have reechoed to troubled hearts." For this celebration a pamphlet was published, bearing the following title:

"A Souvenir History
of the
Parish of St. Paul's,
Kent County, Maryland,
Compiled for the
Bi-Centennial Celebration
of its
Foundation in 1693,
by
The Rev. Chris. T. Denroche,
Rector of
St. Paul's Church and of Christ Church, I. U. District,
Kent County, Maryland,
in 1893."

To

To this same church the wife of Thomas Smyth, Eliner, presented a pulpit cloth. It is thus described in the Souvenir Pamphlet, on page 7: "Eliner Smyth's presentaton, August the 3d, 1703, Eliner Smyth, wife of Thomas Smyth, this day was pleased to present the church with a pulpit cloth and a cushion, with this motto or inscription in the pulpit cloth:

"I. ^{S} H.
The Gift of E S.
To St. Paul's Church,
North Side Chester River, 1703."
Colonel Thomas Smyth's wife, by whom he had two
children, was Martha, they were:
Thomas Smyth, born 21st February, 1710.
Martha Smyth, born 2d December, 1712.

Of Colonel Thomas Smyth, the Parish Register of St. Paul's Parish states that he was buried on the 21st May, 1719.

Thomas Smyth born 21st February, 1710, married on the 14th February, 1728, Mary Ann Ringgold. His sister, Martha Smyth, married Richard Gresham. It is probable that it was her daughter Sarah who married her cousin, Thomas Smyth, as note continued records.

Mary Ann Ringgold, who married Thomas Smyth, and who was his first wife, was the daughter of Thomas Ringgold and Francis, his third wife. Thomas Ringgold, her father, was buried October the 10th, 1711. He was the son of Major James Ringgold, of Huntingfield, spoken of as "the Lord of the Manor on Eastern Neck." The

23   second

second wife of Thomas Smyth, was Mary Frisby, whom he married the 20th June, 1734. He had four children. Thomas, William, Martha and Mary. He was member of the Maryland Assembly in 1738, died in 1741, 31 years old. He states in his will that he was in poor health. In examining the old wills it is interesting to note the entailing of the same property, which assists greatly in determining the lines of descent.

The will of Thomas Smyth (1741) is otherwise interesting, as bearing upon an early custom in this country; when parents seem to have bound their sons out to sea, not, however, as is generally understood, but to learn a system of seamanship which was to render them more successful merchants. Undoubtedly this is the service to which Thomas Smyth refers in his will, wherein he appoints James Ringgold to be the trustee for his two sons, and directs that Thomas shall be bound to James Calder, practitioner of the law (whom it is said, was one of the most distinguished lawyers on the Eastern Shore) to learn the law; and William was to be bound to Captain William Hopkins, mariner, to learn the art of sailing the seas. The reference made to the early custom of instruction or apprenticeship to the sea as adopted in this country, can be more fully appreciated by reading the article entitled "The Life of the Merchant Sailor," that appeared in Scribner's Monthly for July, 1893. In the genealogical sequence, the character of special interest for this paper is now reached, viz.: Thomas Smyth, the son of Thomas Smyth and his wife, Mary Ann Ringgold Smyth, born 12th April, 1730 at "Trumpington" at the

lower

lower end of Kent County, Maryland. This tract of land
was patented in 1658 to Thomas South, came into the
possession of Colonel Thomas Smyth about 1680

It was the residence of Colonel Thomas Smyth, then
of his son, and later of his grandson, all bearing the same
name, and "all of whom were buried there." Tradition
has it "that this was the first land on the Eastern Shore
upon which the white settlers landed after leaving Kent
Island, or the Isle of Kent, as it was then named."
There are numberless references to this Thomas Smyth
born in 1730, to be found in "Force's American Archives," also in a publication "published by authority of
the state, under the direction of the Maryland Historical
Society;" volume published in 1892 edited by William
Hand Browne, called "Archives of Maryland." Thomas
Smyth (b 1730) certainly made good use of the apprenticeship his father named for him in his will, for he is
found to have been Judge of the County Court of Kent of
the *quorum*, November the 16th, 1757, retained that position until 1759. Judge of the Court of Oyer and Termi-
ner, May 4th, 1761, and continued in that office until 1765.

Judge of the County Court of Kent from 1762 to
1769 of the *quorum*. On July 26th, 1775, he was one of
the signers of the Association of Freemen. Just what
such signing meant can be appreciated only by knowing
what the resolution was to which the Colonists subscribed.
A full copy of the Articles of the Association of Freemen
as signed by Thomas Smyth and others the 26th July,
1775, is found on pages 66 and 67 of the before mentioned
volume published in 1892 of the "Archives of Maryland."

From

From which the following will be sufficient to quote, to show how surely Maryland was entitled to the honor ascribed to her in the paragraph, that heads this paper, and how truly Thomas Smyth may be adjudged one of the heroes who helped to make memorable that period

After reciting the grievances against Great Britain, it is "Resolved, that the said Colonies be immediately put into a state of defence, and now supports at the joint expense an army to restrain the further violence, and repel the future attacks of a disappointed and exasperated enemy.

We, therefore, inhabitants of the Province of Maryland, firmly persuaded that it is necessary and justifiable to repel force by force, do approve of the opposition by arms to the British troops employed to enforce obedience to the late acts and statutes of the British Parliament for raising a revenue in America, and altering and changing the Charter and Constitution of the Massachusetts Bay, and for destroying the essential securities for the lives, liberties and properties of the subjects of the united Colonies. And we do unite and associate as one band, and firmly and solomenly engage and pledge ourselves to each other, and to America, that we will to the utmost of our power, promote and support the present opposition, carrying on, as well by arms, as by the Continental Association restraining our commerce."

This act of Thomas Smyth left no question as to where and how he stood. In 1774-5-6 he was a member of the Maryland Convention. Member of Maryland Council of Safety in 1775-6.

In

In 1776 he was also member of the Committee of
Safety of Kent County. On the 12th March, 1752, he
married Sarah Gresham, the daughter of Richard
Gresham, as appears by the will of Richard Gresham,
wherein he speaks of his two grandchildren, the children
of Thomas Smyth, of Chestertown, Maryland.

By his marriage to Sarah Gresham, he had five children, viz: Thomas Smyth, born 29th January, 1753, died
12th March, 1757 ; Richard Gresham Smyth, born 31st
May, 1755 ; Thomas Smyth, born 30th April, 1757 ;
William Smyth, born 22d June, 1759, died 28th June,
1759 ; William Smyth, born 20th September, 1760, died
26th September 1760 ; of these five children, only Richard
Gresham Smyth and Thomas Smyth, born 30th April,
1757, attained manhood.

Richard Gresham Smyth died in Wilmington, Del.,
in 1791, when about 36 years old. There is no record of
his having married. The decendants, therefore, of
Thomas Smyth and his wife Sarah Gresham Smyth, are
to be traced through the children of Thomas Smyth, Jr.
Major Thomas Smyth, Jr., born 30th April, 1757, married his cousin, Mary Sudler, and had two children,
Thomas Gresham Smyth and Julianna Smyth. The son
Thomas Gresham Smyth, married, but died without children. The daughter, Julianna Smyth married Richard
Wayne, Jr., of Augusta, Ga.; she died early, leaving a
family of four children, viz : Richard Wayne, who married Henrietta Harden. Thomas Smyth Wayne, who
married Eliza Caldwell Roe, Mary Eliza Wayne, who

                                    married

married Robert Pooler, Elizabeth Clifford Wayne, who married William Neff.

See Näf-Neff History, page 250, compiled by Elizabeth Clifford Neff, published in 1886.

The children of Richard and Thomas Smyth Wayne all settled in southern states. Mary Eliza Wayne, who married Robert Pooler, had only one child, a son, who died, leaving one child, a daughter. Elizabeth Clifford Wayne, who married William Neff, had nine children, of whom six sons attained manhood, all married and had a child or children, save Richard Wayne Neff, who was a brave and gallant soldier in the Civil War, and met his death with unflinching bravery, as captain in the 4th Ohio Cavalry, while acting as major at the battle of Chickamauga. For six months his body lay unburied on the field, when Prof. M. C. Read of Hudson, O., found it while engaged in the sanitary commission service. When the rude grave his body later occupied was opened, there was little left to tell the searchers who it was; however, the remains were identified and brought home to rest quietly beside the other loved ones in Spring Grove cemetery, Cincinnati, O. A mother's anxious love survived this shock, only to follow in a short time, the loved and brave son.

The oldest of the nine children of Elizabeth Clifford Wayne, who married William Neff, was Peter Neff, who married and had children; for details see Näf-Neff History. His oldest child, the compiler of this article, and Daughter of the American Revolution National No. 2614, thus proves her lineal descent from Thomas Smyth,

                                    member

member of the Maryland Council of Safety, and his son, Major Thomas Smyth, Jr.

Having shown the descent of Major Thomas Smyth, Jr., by his marriage with Mary Sudler, and through the children of his daughter Julianna, a return is made to note his subsequent career.

It is not stated when his first wife died ; it is known to have been when the two children were very young, and they were placed in the care of a relative and educated in England.

In December, 1793, Major Thomas Smyth, Jr., married his second wife, Anna Maria Garnett. There were no children by this marriage; she long survived him. In "Force's American Archives" many letters to and from the Council of Safety of Maryland, to Thomas Smyth, his father, mention the son, Major Thomas Smyth, Jr. From the same "American Archives" the following facts regarding Major Thomas Smyth, Jr., have been extracted. The references have been duly cited with page and volume given, in the application for membership by the compiler of this article, when admitted to the Daughters of the American Revolution, hence that technicality is omitted here.

On the 14th January, 1776, Thomas Smyth, Jr., was appointed by the Maryland convention, first lieutenant in a company of light infantry. Then follows a notice of Richard Gresham as third lieutenant of Captain Smyth's company of light infantry in Kent County, Maryland, belonging to the 13th Battalion.

In

In a letter from the Council of Safety to Thomas Smyth, August 3, 1776, is found the statement that the Battalion of the Eastern Shore is called "The Flying Camp Militia," to this Thomas Smyth, Jr., (captain) was to apply for orders. From the records of the Council of Safety, 2d August, 1776, the date of his commission as captain of the "Flying Camp" was 9th July, 1776.

In the index of vol. ii, of the fifth series of "Force's American Archives," it reads "Smyth, Thomas, Jr., recommended to the favor of General Washington, page 1021;" turning to the page indicated in the volume, a letter from William Fitzhugh to General Washington is found, dated "Annapolis, Md., Oct. 13, 1776," from which letter the following postscript is taken, the letter being too long to copy entire.

"P. S. Permit me to recommend to your countenance and favor Captain Thomas Smyth, Jr. of Colonel Richardson's Battalion, Flying Camp, formerly a Lieutenant in Colonel Smallwood's regiment. He is a son of my particular friend, Thomas Smyth, Esq., of Chestertown, who is now a member of our Council of Safety and Convention, and is a brave and worthy young gentleman. This will be delivered to you by Thomas Contee, Esq., who goes to the camp as one of our commissioners. I beg leave to introduce him to your usual civility. The enclosed is a part of our commissioner's instructions, referred to in this letter.

Dear Sir, Yours affectionately,

WILLIAM FITZHUGH."

                                    Following

Following this letter in the "American Archives" by Force, is this note, which evidently was made by Gen. Washington's Aid de Camp, to call attention to the matter contained in the letter, "That the commissioners be instructed to consult with, and take advise from his Excellency (General Washington) respecting the promotion or appointment of officers in Colonel Smallwood's regiment, and appointments to be made in the Battalions, to be formed of the Independent Companies and Flying Camp of this state."

The following letter explains itself:

"Land Office of Maryland

     Annapolis, Md., April 23d, 1892.
Miss Elizabeth Clifford Neff,

     Cleveland, Ohio.
The Honorable Secretary of State has referred your letter to this department. 'Major Thomas Smyth, 5th Maryland Regiment enlisted 10th December, 1776.'

     Very respectfully,

      GEO. H. SHAFER."

It will be observed that the letter from William Fitzhugh to General Washington was dated 13th October, 1776, and Captain Thomas Smyth, Jr., received his appointment as Major the 10th of December following.

From the Pension Department, Washington, D. C., it is learned that the widow of Major Thomas Smyth, Jr., Anna Maria Garnett Smyth, applied for and was granted a pension in 1838. Major Thomas Smyth, Jr., died in 1807. Thus is completed the line of descent from Thomas

          Smyth

Smyth, member of the Maryland Council of Safety by his marriage with Sarah Gresham.

On the 11th October, 1764, Thomas Smyth (born 1730) married as his second wife, Margaret Hands, the daughter of Hon. Thomas Bedingfield Hands. The children of this second marriage were: William Bedingfield Smyth, born 14th June, 1771. Married twice, first wife Mary Perry (no children); second wife, Isabel Thornburg, had two sons, William Bedingfield Smyth and James Hindman Smyth. In an old letter written in 1856, relating to family affairs, is given a copy of the records from the family Bible of Thomas Smyth (born 1730) from which these facts are taken. The letter also states that the Bible was given to William Bedingfield Smyth by his father in 1819, and that it was to be sent (in 1856) to *his* son William Bedingfield Smyth, who had eight children and was living in New Britain, Conn.

In November, 1894, the editor of the ''American Historical Register'' having accepted this manuscript for publication, without consent published a series of clippings from this paper, which omitted the interesting details, and was unsatisfactory to the writer.

The same publication, however, was the means of opening up a correspondence that succeeded in locating the Bible referred to in the letter just quoted.

Through the courtesy of Mr. Edmund Tilghman Smythe, of New York City, the compiler received a full copy from the old family Bible of the records, on the 8th of November, 1896. This Bible that belonged to Thomas

Smyth,

Smyth, born in 1730, and which he left to his son, William Bedingfield Smyth, is now in the possession of a brother of Mr. Edmund Tilghman Smythe, a grandson of William Bedingfield Smyth.

Margaret Smyth married George Hayward; no children.

Observe that a sister of Sir Thomas Smythe, first Governor of the East India Company married Sir Rowland Hayward, which is additional proof of the descent from Sir Thomas Smythe. The continued inter-marriage between families goes far to prove lines of descent. See "The Genesis of the United States" by A. Brown. Vol. ii, page 1012.

Henry Smyth died unmarried.

Dr. James Smyth died unmarried. He "practiced medicine in Baltimore in partnership with Dr. Colin Mackenzie, at the Maryland Hospital, on the site of the present Johns Hopkins Hospital."

Robert Smyth died young.

Theodore Smyth died young.

Elizabeth Smyth married Samuel Nicols ; had seven children.

Mary Smyth married Thomas Hayward; had son William Hayward.

Maria Smyth married Dr. Thomas Willson; had seven children.

Two grandchildren of Thomas Smyth, (born 1730) are now living, (1893), viz : Mary Elizabeth Browne, of Baltimore, and Richard Bennet Willson, of Trumpington, both children of Maria Smyth, who married Dr. Thomas Willson. Further details regarding the decendants can be obtained from an article that appeared in the Chestertown, (Md.,) "Transcript," of July 20th, 1893, entitled, "Biographical Sketch of Colonel Thomas Smyth," pre-

pared

pared for publication by Dr. Bennet Bernard Brown, of Baltimore, the great grandson of the Thomas Smyth who was member of the Maryland Council of Safety.

Sarah Smyth married "Mathew Tilghman, of Chestertown, Maryland, son of Colonel Edward Tilghman, of Wye, and his third wife, Julianna Carroll, and had children."

Edward "married Anna Maria Tilghman of the White House, Queen Annie's County, and had one daughter, Elanor, who married Mathew Tilghman Goldsborough of Talbot Co."

Horatio Smyth died young.

William Smyth and Elizabeth Smyth died in infancy.

There were five children by the first marriage of Thomas Smyth (1730) with Sarah Gresham, and thirteen by the second marriage, making a total of eighteen children.

The late George Lynn Lackland Davis prepared in part a history of Maryland that was never completed, one volume was published, called "The Day Star of Maryland," but is now out of print. He wrote from Chestertown, Maryland, to Captain George Hayward Willson, a grandson of Thomas Smyth, (b. 1730), in October, 1852, as follows: "Your grandfather, your great grandfather, and your great-great grandfather, (all of whom were named Thomas) resided at Trumpington, a spot consecrated in the affection of your family, and dwelling place of so many generations, and which I hope will continue in your possession during many more yet unborn. My history, (the second or third part) will

                                         contain

contain a sketch of your grandfather's grandfather, the Honorable Thomas Smyth.

He was a member of the first vestry of St Paul's (then St. Peter's) elected under the law of 1692. A judge also of the County Court at a subsequent period, a Deputy Commissary General, a Councillor of State (an office next in rank to that of Governor) and also a judge of the Provincial Court of Maryland, a court which formed the original of the present Court of Appeals. He owned also a lot in New Yarmouth, and gave a tract in trust for a free school, the first I have yet met with in St. Paul's parish. Your grandfather built the house in which I now address you this letter.

While you cannot but feel a just pride in your descent from those whose name is connected with the early history, indeed with the honor of the country, my main object is not to flatter the vanity of the living, but to do justice to the memory of the dead. In doing so I have rescued already from oblivion, the name and mentioned deeds of many a worthy sire."

A miniature, by Peale, of Major Thomas Smyth, Jr., together with copies of a miniature, also by Peale, and portrait done in pen and ink of Thomas Smyth, born (1730), are in the possession of the writer of this article, who is the great-great-grand-daughter of Major Thomas Smyth, Jr., whose further genealogy is to be found in the Näf-Neff history, which was compiled by the writer of this article in 1886.

MISS ELIZABETH CLIFFORD NEFF,
Cleveland, O., 1899.   GENEALOGIST.

9 783337 196950